J.M. COETZEE

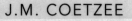

J.M. Coetzee's work includes *Waiting for the Barbarians*, *Life & Times of Michael K*, *Boyhood*, *Youth*, *Disgrace*, *Summertime* and *The Childhood of Jesus*. He was the first author to win the Booker Prize twice and was awarded the Nobel Prize in Literature in 2003. *The Schooldays of Jesus* was longlisted for the Booker Prize 2016.

ALSO BY J.M. COETZEE

J.M. COETZEE

The Schooldays of Jesus

VINTAGE

1 3 5 7 9 10 8 6 4 2

Vintage
20 Vauxhall Bridge Road,
London SW1V 2SA

Vintage is part of the Penguin Random House group of companies
whose addresses can be found at global.penguinrandomhouse.com.

Penguin
Random House
UK

First published in Vintage in 2017
First published in hardback by Harvill Secker in 2016

penguin.co.uk/vintage

A CIP catalogue record for this book is
available from the British Library

ISBN 9781784705336

Printed and bound by Clays Ltd, St Ives plc

Penguin Random House is committed to a sustainable future
for our business, our readers and our planet. This book is made
from Forest Stewardship Council® certified paper.

MIX
Paper from
responsible sources
FSC® C018179

Algunos dicen: Nunca segundas partes fueron buenas.

Don Quixote II.4

Chapter 1

He was expecting Estrella to be bigger. On the map it shows up as a dot of the same size as Novilla. But whereas Novilla was a city, Estrella is no more than a sprawling provincial town set in a countryside of hills and fields and orchards, with a sluggish river meandering through it.

Will a new life be possible in Estrella? In Novilla he had been able to rely on the Office of Relocations to arrange accommodation. Will he and Inés and the boy be able to find a home here? The Office of Relocations is beneficent, it is the very embodiment of beneficence of an impersonal variety; but will its beneficence extend to fugitives from the law?

Juan, the hitchhiker who joined them on the road to Estrella, has suggested that they find work on one of the farms. Farmers always need farmhands, he says. The larger farms even have dormitories for seasonal workers. If it isn't orange season it is apple season; if it isn't apple season it is grape season. Estrella and its surrounds are a veritable cornucopia. He can direct them, if they wish, to a farm where friends of his once worked.

He exchanges looks with Inés. Should they follow Juan's advice? Money is not a consideration, he has plenty of money in his pocket, they could easily stay at a hotel. But if the authorities from Novilla are really pursuing them, then perhaps they would be better off among the nameless transients.

'Yes,' says Inés. 'Let us go to this farm. We have been cooped up in the car long enough. Bolívar needs a run.'

'I feel the same way,' says he, Simón. 'However, a farm is not a holiday camp. Are you ready, Inés, to spend all day picking fruit under a hot sun?'

'I will do my share,' says Inés. 'Neither less nor more.'

'Can I pick fruit too?' asks the boy.

'Unfortunately no, not you,' says Juan. 'That would be against the law. That would be child labour.'

'I don't mind being child labour,' says the boy.

'I am sure the farmer will let you pick fruit,' says he, Simón. 'But not too much. Not enough to turn it into labour.'

They drive through Estrella, following the main street. Juan points out the marketplace, the administrative buildings, the modest museum and art gallery. They cross a bridge, leave the town behind, and follow the course of the river until they come in sight of an imposing house on the hillside. 'That is the farm I had in mind,' says Juan. 'That is where my friends found work. The *refugio* is at the back. It looks dreary, but it's actually quite comfortable.'

The *refugio* is made up of two long galvanized-iron sheds linked by a covered passage; to one side is an ablution block. He parks the car. No one emerges to greet them save a grizzled, stiff-legged dog who, from the limit of his chain, growls at them, baring yellowed fangs.

Bolívar unfolds himself and slides out of the car. From a distance he inspects the foreign dog, then decides to ignore him.

The boy dashes into the sheds, re-emerges. 'They've got double bunks!' he shouts. 'Can I have a top bunk? Please!'

Now a large woman wearing a red apron over a loose cotton frock appears from the rear of the farmhouse and waddles down the path toward them. 'Good day, good day!' she calls out. She examines the laden car. 'Have you come a long way?'

'Yes, a long way. We wondered if you can do with some extra hands.'

'We can always do with more hands. Many hands make light work – isn't that what the books say?'

'It will be just two of us, my wife and I. Our friend here has commitments of his own. This is our boy, his name is David. And this is Bolívar. Will there be a place for Bolívar? He is part of the family. We go nowhere without him.'

'Bolívar is his real name,' says the boy. 'He is an Alsatian.'

'Bolívar. That's a nice name,' says the woman. 'Unusual. I am sure there will be a place for him as long he behaves himself and is content to eat scraps and doesn't get into fights or chase the chickens. The workers are out in the orchards right now, but let me show you the sleeping quarters. On the left side the gentlemen, on the right side the ladies. No family rooms, I'm afraid.'

'I am going to be on the gentlemen's side,' says the boy. 'Simón says I can have a top bunk. Simón is not my father.'

'Do as you please, young man. There is plenty of space. The others will be back –'

'Simón is not my real father and David is not my real name. Do you want to know my real name?'

The woman casts Inés a puzzled look, which Inés pretends not to notice.

'We were playing a game in the car,' he, Simón, intervenes. 'To pass the time. We were trying out new names for ourselves.'

The woman shrugs. 'The others will be back for lunch soon, then you can introduce yourselves. The pay is twenty *reales* a day, the same for men and for women. The day is from sunup until sundown, with a two-hour break at midday. On the seventh day we rest. That is the natural order, that is the order we follow. As for meals, we supply the foodstuffs and you do the cooking. Are you happy with the terms? Do you think you can manage? Have you done picking before? No? You will soon learn, it is not a high art. Do you have hats? You will need hats, the sun can be quite fierce. What else can I tell you? You can always find me in the big house. Roberta is my name.'

'Roberta, pleased to meet you. I am Simón and this is Inés and this is Juan, our guide, whom I am going to drive back to town.'

'Welcome to the farm. I am sure we will get on well. It's good that you have a car of your own.'

'It has brought us a long way. It is a faithful car. You can't ask for more than that in a car, fidelity.'

By the time they have unloaded the car, workers have begun straggling back from the orchards. There are introductions all round, they are offered lunch, Juan included: home-baked bread, cheese and olives, great bowls of fruit. Their fellows are some twenty in number, including a family with five children whom David guardedly inspects from his side of the table.

Before he takes Juan back to Estrella, he has a moment alone with Inés. 'What do you think?' he murmurs. 'Shall we stay?'

'It seems a good place. I am prepared to stay here while we look around. But we must have a plan. I haven't come all this distance to settle into the life of a common labourer.'

He and Inés have been over the ground before. If they are being pursued by the law, then they ought to be prudent. But are they being pursued? Do they have reason to fear pursuit? Does the law have such ample resources that it can dispatch officers to the farthest corners of the land to hunt down a six-year-old truant? Is it of veritable concern to the authorities in Novilla whether a child does or does not go to school, so long as he does not grow up analphabete? He, Simón, doubts it. On the other hand, what if it is not the truant child who is being hunted but the couple who, perjuriously claiming to be his parents, have kept him out of school? If it is he and Inés who are being sought, rather than the child, then should they not lie low until their pursuers, exhausted, abandon the chase?

'A week,' he proposes. 'Let us be common labourers for a week. Then we can reassess.'

He drives to Estrella and drops Juan off at the home of friends of his who run a printing shop. Back at the farm, he joins Inés and the boy in exploring their new surroundings. They visit the orchards and are initiated into the mysteries of the shears and the pruning knife. David is wooed away from their side and disappears, who knows where, with the other children. He returns at supper time with scratches on his arms and legs. They have been climbing trees, he says. Inés wants to put iodine on the scratches but he will not let her. They retire early, like everyone else, David to his desired upper bunk.

By the time the truck arrives the next morning, he and Inés have had a hurried breakfast. David, still rubbing the sleep from his eyes, does not join them. Along with their new comrades they climb aboard and are delivered to the vineyards; following the example of their comrades, he and Inés hitch baskets on their backs and set to work.

While they labour the children are free to do as they please. Led by the eldest of the tribe of five, a tall, skinny boy named Bengi, with a mass of curly black hair, they race uphill to the earthen dam that waters the vineyards. The ducks that had been paddling there take off in alarm, all save a pair with young too immature to fly, who in an effort to escape urge their brood toward the far bank. They are too slow: the whooping children head them off, forcing them back to the middle of the dam. Bengi begins hurling stones; the younger ones imitate him. Unable to flee, the birds paddle around in circles, quacking loudly. A stone strikes the more gorgeously coloured male. He rises half out of the water, falls back, and splashes around trailing a shattered wing. Bengi gives a cry of triumph. The torrent of stones and clods of earth redoubles.

He and Inés harken uncertainly to the clamour; the other pickers pay no attention. 'What do you think is going on?' says Inés. 'Do you think David is safe?'

He drops his basket, clambers up the hillside, arrives at the dam in time to see David give the older boy so furious a shove that he staggers and nearly falls. 'Stop it!' he hears him shout.

The boy stares in astonishment at his assailant, then turns and hurls another stone at the ducks.

Now David plunges into the water, shoes and all, and begins splashing in the direction of the birds.

'David!' he, Simón, calls. The child ignores him.

Inés, in the vineyard below, drops her basket and begins running. Not since he watched her playing tennis a year ago has he seen her exert herself. She is slow; she has put on weight.

Out of nowhere the great dog appears and races past her, straight as an arrow. In a matter of moments he has leapt into the dam and is at David's side. Gripping his shirt in his teeth, he hauls the thrashing, protesting child to the bank.

Inés arrives. The dog slumps down, his ears cocked, his eyes on her, waiting for a sign, while David, in his sodden clothes, wails and beats him with his fists. 'I hate you, Bolívar!' he cries. 'That boy was throwing stones, Inés! He wanted to kill the duck!'

He, Simón, lifts the struggling child into his arms. 'Calm down, calm down,' he says. 'The duck isn't dead — see! — he just had a bump. He will soon get better. Now I think all you children should come away and let the ducks calm down and get on with their lives. And you must not say you hate Bolívar. You love Bolívar, we all know that, and Bolívar loves you. He thought you were drowning. He was trying to save you.'

Angrily David wriggles out of his arms. 'I was going to save the duck,' he says. 'I didn't ask Bolívar to come. Bolívar is stupid. He is a stupid dog. Now *you* have got to save him, Simón. Go on, save him!'

He, Simón, takes off his shoes and shirt. 'Since you insist, I will try. However, let me point out that a duck's idea of being saved may be different from your idea of being saved. It may include being left in peace by human beings.'

Other of the grape-pickers have by now arrived. 'Stay — I will go,' a younger man offers.

'No. It's kind of you, but this is my child's business.' He takes off his trousers and in his underpants wades into the brown water. With barely a splash the dog appears at his side. 'Go away, Bolívar,' he murmurs. 'I don't need to be saved.'

Clustered on the bank, the grape-pickers watch as the no-longer-young gentleman with the physique not quite as firm as it used to be in his stevedoring days sets about doing his child's bidding.

The water is not deep. Even at its deepest it does not rise to above his chest. But he can barely move his feet in the soft ooze of the floor. There is no chance at all that he can catch the duck with the broken wing, who splashes about on the surface in ragged circles, to say nothing of the mother duck, who has by now attained the farther bank and scuttled away into the undergrowth followed by her brood.

It is Bolívar who does the job for him. Sailing past like a ghost, with only his head showing above the water, he tracks the wounded bird, closes his jaws like a vice on the trailing wing, and hauls him toward the bank. At first there is a flurry of resistance, of beating and splashing; then all at once the bird seems to give up and accept its fate. By the time he, Simón, has emerged from the water the duck is in the arms of the young man who had offered to go in his place and is being inspected curiously by the children.

Though well above the horizon, the sun barely warms him. Shivering, he puts on his clothes.

Bengi, the one who cast the stone that caused all the trouble, strokes the head of the entirely passive bird.

'Tell him you are sorry for what you did,' says the young man.

'I'm sorry,' mutters Bengi. 'Can we fix his wing? Can we tie a splint on it?'

The young man shakes his head. 'He is a wild creature,' he says. 'He will not submit to wearing a splint. It is all right. He is ready to die. He has accepted it. Look. Look at his eyes. He is already dead.'

'He can stay in my bunk,' says Bengi. 'I can feed him till he gets better.'

'Turn your back,' says the young man.

Bengi does not understand.

'Turn your back,' says the young man.

To Inés, who is meanwhile drying off the boy, he, Simón, whispers: 'Don't let him look.'

She presses the boy's head into her skirts. He resists, but she is firm.

The young man grips the bird between his knees. A swift motion, and it is done. The head lolls awkwardly; a film comes over the eyes. He hands the feathered carcass to Bengi. 'Go and bury him,' he orders. 'Go on.'

Inés releases the boy. 'Go with your friend,' he, Simón, tells him. 'Help him bury the bird. Make sure he does it properly.'

Later the boy seeks him and Inés out where they are working among the vines.

'So: have you buried the poor duck?' he asks.

The boy shakes his head. 'We couldn't dig a hole for him. We didn't have a spade. Bengi hid him in the bushes.'

'That's not nice. When I have finished for the day I will go and bury him. You can show me where.'

'Why did he do it?'

'Why did that young man put him out of his misery? I told you. Because he would have been helpless with a broken wing. He would have refused to eat. He would have pined away.'

'No, I mean why did Bengi do it?'

'I'm sure he didn't mean any harm. He was just throwing stones, and one thing led to another.'

'Will the babies die too?'

'Of course not. They have a mother to take care of them.'

'But who is going to give them milk?'

'Birds are not like us. They don't drink milk. Anyhow, it is mothers who give milk, not fathers.'

'Will they find a *padrino*?'

'I don't think so. I don't think there are *padrinos* among birds, just as there is no milk. *Padrinos* are a human institution.'

'He is not sorry. Bengi. He says he is sorry but he isn't really sorry.'

'Why do you think so?'

'Because he wanted to kill the duck.'

'I don't agree, my boy. I don't believe he knew what he was doing, not fully. He was just throwing stones the way boys throw stones. He didn't in his heart intend to kill anyone. Then afterwards, when he saw what a beautiful creature the bird was, when he saw what a terrible thing he had done, he repented and was sorry.'

'He wasn't really sorry. He told me.'

'If he is not sorry now, he will be sorry soon. His conscience will not let him rest. That is how we human beings are. If we do a bad deed, we get no joy out of it. Our conscience sees to that.'

'But he was shining! I saw it! He was shining and throwing stones as hard as he could! He wanted to kill them all!'

'I don't know what you mean by shining, but even if he was shining, even if he was throwing stones, that doesn't prove that in his heart he was trying to kill them. We can't always foresee the consequences of our actions – particularly when we are young. Don't forget that he offered to nurse the bird with the broken wing, to shelter him in his bunk. What more could he do? Un-throw the stone he had thrown? You can't do that. You can't unmake the past. What is done is done.'

'He didn't bury him. He just threw him in the bushes.'

'I'm sorry about that, but the duck is dead. We can't bring him back. You and I will go and bury him as soon as the day's work is over.'

'I wanted to kiss him but Bengi wouldn't let me. He said he was dirty. But I kissed him anyway. I went into the bushes and kissed him.'

'That's good, I'm glad to hear it. It will mean a lot to him to know that someone loved him and kissed him after he died. It will also mean a lot to him to know he had a proper burial.'

'You can bury him. I don't want to bury him.'

'Very well, I will do so. And if we come back tomorrow morning and the grave is empty and the whole duck family is swimming in the dam, father and mother and babies, with no one missing, then we will know that kissing works, that kissing can raise one from the dead. But if we don't see him, if we don't see the duck family —'

'I don't want them to come back. If they come back Bengi will just throw stones at them again. He is not sorry. He is just pretending. I *know* he is pretending but you won't believe me. You never believe me.'

There is no spade or pickaxe to be found, so he borrows a tyre lever from the truck. The boy leads him to where the carcass lies among the bushes. The feathers have already lost their gloss and ants have got to the eyes. With the lever he chops a hole in the flinty soil. It is not deep enough, he cannot pretend this is a decent burial, but he drops the dead bird in nevertheless and covers it. A webbed foot sticks out stiffly. He collects stones and lays them over the grave. 'There,' he says to the boy. 'It's the best I can do.'

When they visit the spot the next morning the stones are scattered and the duck is gone. There are feathers everywhere. They search but find nothing save the head with its empty eye sockets and one foot. 'I'm sorry,' he says, and tramps off to rejoin the work crew.

Chapter 2

Two more days, and the grape-picking is over; the truck has borne the last binfuls away.

'Who is going to eat all those grapes?' demands David.

'They are not going to be eaten. They are going to be pressed in a wine press and the juice is going to be turned into wine.'

'I don't like wine,' says David. 'It's sour.'

'Wine is an acquired taste. When we are young we don't like it, then when we are older we acquire a taste for it.'

'I am never going to acquire a taste for it.'

'That's what you say. Let's wait and see.'

Having stripped the vineyards bare, they move on to the olive groves, where they spread nets and use long hooks to bring down the olives. The work is more taxing than grape-picking. He looks forward to the midday breaks; he finds the heat of the long afternoons hard to support, and pauses often to drink or just recover his strength. He can hardly believe that only months ago he was working on the docks as a stevedore, carrying heavy loads, barely breaking into a sweat. His back and arms have lost their old strength, his heart beats sluggishly, he is nagged by pain from the rib that was broken.

From Inés, unused as she is to physical labour, he has been expecting complaints and grumbling. But no: she works by his side all day, joylessly but without a murmur. She does not need to be reminded that it was she who decided they should flee Novilla and take up the lives of gypsies. Well, now she has found out how gypsies live: by toiling in other men's fields from sunrise to sunset, all for a day's bread and a few *reales* in their pockets.

But at least the boy is having a good time, the boy for whose sake they fled the city. After a brief, haughty estrangement, he has rejoined Bengi and his tribe — even, it would seem, taken over their leadership. For it is he, not Bengi, who now gives the orders, and Bengi and the others who meekly obey.

Bengi has three younger sisters. They dress in identical calico smocks and wear their hair in identical pigtails tied with identical red ribbons; they join in all the boys' games. At his school in Novilla David had refused to have anything to do with girls. 'They are always whispering and giggling,' he said to Inés. 'They are silly.' Now for the first time he is playing with girls, not seeming to find them silly at all. There is a game he has invented that consists in clambering onto the roof of a shed beside the olive grove and leaping down onto a convenient heap of sand. Sometimes he and the youngest of the sisters take the leap hand in hand, rolling over in a tangle of legs and arms, rising to their feet chortling with laughter.

The little girl, whose name is Florita, follows David like a shadow wherever he goes; he does nothing to discourage her.

During the midday break one of the olive-pickers teases her. 'I see you have a *novio*,' she says. Florita gazes back at her solemnly. Perhaps she does not know the word. 'What is his name? What is the name of your *novio*?' Florita blushes and runs away.

When the girls leap from the roof their smocks open up like the petals of flowers, revealing identical rose-coloured panties.

There are still grapes aplenty from the harvest, whole baskets of them. The children stuff their mouths; their hands and faces are sticky with the sweet juice. All save David, who eats one grape at a time, spits out the seeds, and rinses his hands fastidiously afterwards.

'The others could certainly learn manners from him,' remarks Inés. *My boy*, she wants to add – he, Simón, can see it – *my clever, well-mannered boy. So unlike these other ragamuffins.*

'He is growing up quickly,' he concedes. 'Perhaps too quickly. There are times when I find his behaviour a little too' – he hesitates over the word – 'too *magistral*, too masterful. Or so it seems to me.'

'He is a boy. He has a strong character.'

The gypsy life may not suit Inés, and it does not suit him, but it certainly suits the boy. He has never seen him so active, so full of energy. He wakes up early, eats voraciously, runs around with his friends all day. Inés tries to get him to wear a cap, but the cap is soon lost, never to be found again. Where before he was somewhat pale, he is now as brown as a berry.

It is not little Florita to whom he is closest but Maite, her sister. Maite is seven, a few months older than he. She is the prettiest of the three sisters and the most thoughtful in disposition.

One evening the boy confides in Inés: 'Maite asked me to show her my penis.'

'And?' says Inés.

'She says if I show her my penis she will show me her thing.'

'You should play more with Bengi,' says Inés. 'You shouldn't be playing with girls all the time.'

'We weren't playing, we were talking. She says if I put my penis in her thing she will get a baby. Is it true?'

'No, it's not true,' says Inés. 'Someone should wash that girl's mouth out with soap.'

'She says that Roberto comes to the women's room when they are asleep and puts his penis in her mother's thing.'

Inés casts him, Simón, a helpless glance.

'What grown-up people do may sometimes seem strange,' he intervenes. 'When you are older you will understand better.'

'Maite says her mother makes him put a balloon on his penis so that she won't get a baby.'

'Yes, that is correct, some people do that.'

'Do you put a balloon on your penis, Simón?'

Inés gets up and leaves.

'I? A balloon? No, of course not.'

'So if you don't, can Inés get a baby?'

'My boy, you are talking about sexual intercourse, and sexual intercourse is for married people. Inés and I aren't married.'

'But you can do sexual intercourse even if you aren't married.'

'It is true, you can have sexual intercourse if you are not married. But having babies when you are not married is not a good idea. On the whole.'

'Why? Is it because the babies are *huérfano* babies?'

'No, a baby born to an unmarried mother is not a *huérfano*. A *huérfano* is something quite different. Where did you come across that word?'

'In Punta Arenas. Lots of boys in Punta Arenas are *huérfanos*. Am I a *huérfano*?'

'No, of course not. You have a mother. Inés is your mother. A *huérfano* is a child with no parents at all.'

'Where do *huérfanos* come from if they don't have parents?'

'A *huérfano* is a child whose parents have died and left him alone in the world. Or sometimes the mother has no money to buy food and gives him away to other people to look after. Him or her. Those are the ways you get to be a *huérfano*. You are not a *huérfano*. You have Inés. You have me.'

'But you and Inés are not my real parents, so I am a *huérfano*.'

'David, you arrived on a boat, just as I did, just as the people around us did, the ones who didn't have the luck to be born here. Very likely Bengi and his brother and his sisters arrived on boats too. When you travel across the ocean on a boat, all your memories are washed away and you start a completely new life. That is how it is. There is no before. There is no history. The boat docks at the harbour and we climb down the gang-plank and we are plunged into the here and now. Time begins. The clock starts running. You are not a *huérfano*. Bengi is not a *huérfano*.'

'Bengi was born in Novilla. He told me. He has never been on a boat.'

'Very well, if Bengi and his brother and sisters were born here then their history begins here and they are not *huérfanos*.'

'I can remember the time before I was on the boat.'

'So you have told me already. There are lots of people who say they can remember the life they had before they crossed the ocean. But there is a problem with such memories, and because you are clever I think you can see what the problem is. The problem is that we have no way of telling whether what these people remember are true memories or made-up memories. Because sometimes a made-up memory can feel just as true as a true memory, particularly when we *want* the memory to be true. So, for example, someone may wish to have been a king or a lord before he crossed the ocean, and he may wish it so much that he convinces himself he truly was a king or a lord. Yet the memory is probably not a true memory. Why not? Because being a king is quite a rare thing. Only one person in a million becomes a king. So the chances are that someone who remembers being a king is just making up a story and then forgetting he made it up. And similarly with other memories. We just have no way of telling for sure whether a memory is true or false.'

'But was I born out of Inés' tummy?'

'You are forcing me to repeat myself. Either I can reply, "Yes, you were born out of Inés' tummy," or I can reply, "No, you weren't born out of Inés' tummy." But neither reply will bring us any closer to the truth. Why not? Because, like everyone else who came on the boats, you can't remember and nor can Inés. Unable to remember, all you can do, all she can do, all any of us can do is to make up stories. So, for instance, I can tell you that on my last day in the other life I was among a huge crowd waiting to embark, so huge that they had to telephone the retired pilots and ships' masters and tell them to come to the docks and help out. And in that crowd, I could say, I saw you and your mother – saw you with my own eyes. Your mother was clutching your hand, looking worried, unsure of where to go. Then, I could say, I lost sight of the pair of you in the crowd. When at last it was my turn to step on board, whom did I see but you, all by yourself, clinging to a rail, calling, "Mummy, Mummy, where are you?" So I went over and took you by the hand and said, "Come, little friend, I will help you find your mother." And that was how you and I met.

'That is a story I could tell, about my first vision of you and your mother, as I remember it.'

'But is it *true*? Is it a *true* story?'

'Is it true? I don't know. It *feels* true to me. The more often I tell it to myself, the truer it feels. You feel true, clutching the rail so tightly that I had to loosen your fingers; the crowd at the docks feels true – hundreds of thousands of people, all lost, like you, like me, with empty hands and anxious eyes. The bus feels true – the bus that delivered the superannuated pilots and ships' masters at the docks, wearing the navy-blue uniforms they had brought down from trunks in the attic, still smelling of naphtha. It all feels true from beginning to end. But maybe it feels so true because I have repeated it to myself so often. Does it feel true to you? Do you remember how you were separated from your mother?'

'No.'

'No, of course you don't. But do you not remember because it didn't happen or because you have forgotten? We will never know for sure. That is the way things are. That is what we must live with.'

'I think I am a *huérfano*.'

'And I think you are just saying so because it seems romantic to you to be alone in the world without parents. Well, let me inform you that in Inés you have the best mother in the world, and if you have the best mother in the world you are certainly not a *huérfano*.'

'If Inés has a baby will he be my brother?'

'Your brother or your sister. But Inés isn't going to have a baby because Inés and I are not married.'

'If I put my penis in Maite's thing and she has a baby, will it be a *huérfano*?'

'No. Maite is not going to have a baby of any kind. You and she are too young to make babies, just as you and she are too young to understand why grown-up people get married and have sexual intercourse. Grown-up people get married because they have passionate feelings for each other, in a way that you and Maite don't. You and she can't feel passion because you are still too young. Accept that as a fact and don't ask me to explain why. Passion can't be explained, it can only be experienced. More exactly, it has to be experienced from the inside before it can be understood from the outside. What matters is that you and Maite should not have sexual intercourse because sexual intercourse without passion is meaningless.'

'But is it horrible?'

'No, it isn't horrible, it is just an unwise thing to do, unwise and frivolous. Any more questions?'

'Maite says she wants to marry me.'

'And you? Do you want to marry Maite?'

'No. I don't ever want to get married.'

'Well, you may change your mind about that when the passions arrive.'

'Are you and Inés going to get married?'

He does not reply. The boy trots to the door. 'Inés!' he calls out. 'Are you and Simón going to get married?'

'*Shush!*' comes Inés' angry retort. She re-enters the dormitory. 'That's enough talk. It's time for you to go to bed.'

'Do you have passions, Inés?' asks the boy.

'That is none of your business,' says Inés.

'Why don't you ever want to talk to me?' says the boy. 'Simón talks to me.'

'I do talk to you,' says Inés. 'But not about private matters. Now brush your teeth.'

'I'm not going to have passions,' the boy announces.

'That is what you say today,' says he, Simón. 'But as you grow up you will find that the passions have a life of their own. Now hurry up and brush your teeth, and maybe your mother will read you a good-night story.'

Chapter 3

Roberta, whom on the first day they took to be the owner of the farm, is in fact an employee like them, employed to oversee the workers, to supply them with rations and pay them their wages. She is a friendly person, well liked by all. She takes an interest in the workers' personal lives and brings little treats for the children: sweets, biscuits, lemonade. The farm is owned, they learn, by three sisters known far and wide simply as the Three Sisters, elderly now, and childless, who divide their time between the farm and their residence in Estrella.

Roberta has a long conversation with Inés. 'What are you going to do about your son's schooling?' she asks. 'I can see he is a bright lad. It would be a pity if he ended up like Bengi, who has never been to a proper school. Not that there is anything wrong with Bengi. He is a nice boy, but he has no future. He will just be a farm labourer like his parents, and what kind of life is that, in the long term?'

'David went to a school in Novilla,' says Inés. 'It wasn't a success. He didn't have good teachers. He is a naturally clever child. He found the pace in the classroom too slow. We had to remove him and educate him at home. I am afraid that if we put him in a school here he will have the same experience.'

Inés' account of their dealings with the school system of Novilla is less than wholly truthful. He and Inés had agreed to keep quiet about their entanglements with the authorities in Novilla; but evidently Inés feels free to confide in the older woman, and he does not intervene.

'Does he want to go to school?' asks Roberta.

'No, he doesn't, not after his experiences in Novilla. He is perfectly happy here on the farm. He likes the freedom.'

'It's a wonderful life for a child, but the harvest is coming to an end, you know. And running around on a farm like a wild thing is no preparation for the future. Have you thought of a private teacher? Or of an academy? An academy won't be like a normal school. Maybe an academy would suit a child like him.'

Inés is silent. He, Simón, speaks for the first time. 'We can't afford a private tutor. As for academies, there were no academies in Novilla. At least no one spoke of them. What exactly is an academy? Because if it is just a fancy name for a school for troublesome children, children with ideas of their own, then we wouldn't be interested – would we, Inés?'

Inés shakes her head.

'There are two academies in Estrella,' says Roberta. 'They are not for troublesome children at all. One is the Singing Academy and the other is the Dance Academy. There is also the Atom School; but that is for older children.'

'David likes to sing. He has a good voice. But what happens in these academies besides singing and dancing? Do they hold proper classes? And do they accept such young children?'

'I am no expert on education, Inés. All the families I know in Estrella send their children to normal schools. But I am sure the academies teach the basics — you know, reading and writing and so forth. I can ask the sisters if you like.'

'What about the Atom School?' he asks. 'What do they teach there?'

'They teach about atoms. They watch the atoms through a microscope, doing whatever it is that atoms do. That is all I know.'

He and Inés exchange glances. 'We will keep the academies in mind as a possibility,' he says. 'For the present we are perfectly happy with the life we have here on the farm. Do you think we can stay on after the end of the harvest if we offer the sisters a small rental? Otherwise we will have to go through the rigmarole of registering with the Asistencia and looking for a job and finding a place to live, and we are not ready for that, not yet — are we, Inés?'

Inés shakes her head.

'Let me speak to the sisters,' says Roberta. 'Let me speak to señora Consuelo. She is the most practical. If she says you can stay on the farm, then maybe you can give señor Robles a call. He offers private lessons and doesn't charge much. He does it out of love.'

'Who is señor Robles?'

'He is the water engineer for the district. He lives a few kilometres further up the valley.'

'But why would a water engineer give private lessons?'

'He does all kinds of things besides engineering. He is a man of many talents. He is writing a history of the settlement of the valley.'

'A history. I didn't know that places like Estrella had a history. If you give us a telephone number I will get in touch with señor Robles. And will you remember to speak to señora Consuelo?'

'I will. I am sure she won't mind if you stay here while you look for something more permanent. You must be longing to move into a home of your own.'

'Not really. We are happy with things as they are. For us, living like gypsies is still an adventure – isn't it, Inés?'

Inés nods.

'And the child is happy too. He is learning about life, even if he doesn't go to school. Will there be jobs around the farm that I can do to repay your kindness?'

'Of course. There are always odd jobs.' Roberta pauses thoughtfully. 'One more thing. As I am sure you know, this is the year of the census. The census-takers are very thorough. They call at every farm, even the remotest. So if you are trying to dodge the census – and I am not saying you are – you won't succeed by staying here.'

'We are not trying to dodge anything,' says he, Simón. 'We are not fugitives. We merely want what is best for our child.'

The next day, in the late afternoon, a truck pulls up at the farm and a large, florid-faced man alights. He is greeted by Roberta, who leads him to the dormitory. 'Señor Simón, señora Inés, this is señor Robles. I will leave the three of you to discuss your business.'

Their discussion is brief. Señor Robles, so he informs them, loves children and gets on well with them. He will be happy to introduce young David, of whom he has heard glowing praise from señora Roberta, to the elements of mathematics. If they agree, he will stop at the farm twice a week to give the boy a lesson. He will not accept payment in any form. It will be reward enough to have contact with a bright young mind. He himself, alas, has no children. His wife having passed on, he is alone in the world. If among the children of other fruit-pickers there are any who would like to join David in his lessons, they will be welcome. And the parents, señora Inés and señor Simón, may of course sit in too – that goes without saying.

'You won't find it boring, teaching elementary arithmetic?' asks he, señor Simón, parent.

'Of course not,' says señor Robles. 'For a true mathematician the elements of the science are its most interesting part, and instilling the elements in a young mind the most challenging undertaking – challenging and rewarding.'

He and Inés pass on señor Robles' offer to the few fruit-pickers left on the farm, but when the time comes for the first lesson David is the only student and he, Simón, the only parent in attendance.

'We know what one is,' says señor Robles, opening the class, 'but what is two? That is the question before us today.'

It is a warm, windless day. They are seated under a shady tree outside the dormitory, señor Robles and the boy on opposite sides of a table, he discreetly to one side with Bolívar at his feet.

From his breast pocket señor Robles takes two pens and places them side by side on the table. From another pocket he produces a little glass bottle, shakes out two white pills, and places them beside the pens. 'What do these' – his hand hovers over the pens – 'and these' – his hand hovers over the pills – 'have in common, young man?'

The boy is silent.

'Ignoring their use as writing instruments or medicine, looking at them simply as objects, is there some property that these' – he shifts the pens slightly to the right – 'and these' – he shifts the pills slightly to the left – 'have in common? Any property that makes them alike?'

'There are two pens and two pills,' says the boy.

'Good!' says señor Robles.

'The two pills are the same but the two pens aren't the same because one is blue and one is red.'

'But they are still two, aren't they? So what is the property the pills and the pens have in common?'

'Two. Two for the pens and two for the pills. But they aren't the same two.'

Señor Robles casts him, Simón, an irritated glance. From his pockets he produces another pen, another pill. Now there are three pens on the table, three pills. 'What do these' – he holds a hand over the pens – 'and these' – he holds a hand over the pills – 'have in common?'

'Three,' says the boy. 'But it's not the same three because the pens are different.'

Señor Robles ignores the qualification. 'And they don't have to be pens or pills, do they? I could equally well replace the pens with oranges and the pills with apples, and the answer would be the same: three. Three is what the ones on the left, the oranges, have in common with the ones on the right, the apples. There are three in each set. So what have we learned?' And, before the boy can answer, he informs him what they have learned: 'We have learned that three does not depend on what is in the set, be it apples or oranges or pens or pills. Three is the name of the property that these sets have in common. And' – he whisks away one of the pens, one of the pills – 'three is not the same as two, because' – he opens a hand in which nestle the missing pen, the missing pill – 'I have subtracted an item, one item, from each set. So what have we learned? We have learned about two and about three, and in exactly the same way we can learn about four and five and so on up to a hundred, up to a thousand, up to a million. We have learned something about number, namely that each number is the name of a property shared by certain sets of objects in the world.'

'Up to a million million,' says the boy.

'Up to a million million and beyond,' agrees señor Robles.

'Up to the stars,' says the boy.

'Up to the number of the stars,' agrees señor Robles, 'which may well be infinite, we don't yet know for sure. So what have we achieved thus far in our first lesson? We have found out what a number is, and we have also found out a way of counting – one, two, three, and so forth – a way of getting from one number to the next in a definite order. So let us summarize. Tell me, David, what is two?'

'Two is if you have two pens on the table or two pills or two apples or two oranges.'

'Yes, good, nearly right but not exactly right. Two is what they have in common, apples or oranges or any other object.'

'But it has got to be hard,' says the boy. 'It can't be soft.'

'It can be a hard object or a soft object. Any objects in the world will do, without restriction, so long as there is more than one of them. That is an important point. Every object in the world is subject to arithmetic. In fact every object in the universe.'

'But not water. Or vomit.'

'Water isn't an object. A glass of water is an object, but water in itself is not an object. Another way of saying that is to say that water is not countable. Like air or earth. Air and earth aren't countable either. But we can count bucketfuls of earth, or canisters of air.'

'Is that good?' says the boy.

Señor Robles replaces the pens in his pocket, drops the pills back into the bottle, turns to him, Simón. 'I'll stop by again on Thursday,' he says. 'Then we can move on to addition and subtraction – how we combine two sets to get a sum, or remove elements of a set to get a difference. In the meantime your son can practise his counting.'

'I can already count,' says the boy. 'I can count to a million. I taught myself.'

Señor Robles rises. 'Anyone can count to a million,' he says. 'What is important is to get a grasp of what numbers really are. So as to have a firm foundation.'

'Are you sure you won't stay?' says he, Simón. 'Inés is making tea.'

'Alas, I don't have the time,' says señor Robles, and drives off in a flurry of dust.

Inés emerges with the tea tray. 'Has he gone?' she says. 'I thought he would stay for tea. That was a very short lesson. How did it go?'

'He is coming back next Thursday,' says the boy. 'We are going to do four then. We did two and three today.'

'Won't it take forever if you do just one number at a time?' says Inés. 'Isn't there a quicker way?'

'Señor Robles wants to make sure the foundations are firm,' says he, Simón. 'Once the foundations are firmly laid, we will be ready to erect our mathematical edifice on them.'

'What is an edifice?' says the boy.

'An edifice is a building. This particular edifice will be a tower, I would guess, stretching far into the sky. Towers take time to build. We must be patient.'

'He only needs to be able to do sums,' says Inés, 'so that he won't be at a disadvantage in life. Why does he need to be a mathematician?'

There is silence.

'What do you think, David?' says he, Simón. 'Would you like to go on with these lessons? Are you learning anything?'

'I already know about four,' says the boy. 'I know all the numbers. I told you, but you wouldn't listen.'

'I think we should cancel,' says Inés. 'It is just a waste of time. We can find someone else to teach him, someone who is prepared to teach sums.'

He breaks the news to Roberta ('What a pity!' she says. 'But you are the parents, you know best.') and telephones señor Robles. 'We are immensely grateful to you, señor Robles, for your generosity and your patience, but Inés and I feel the boy needs something simpler, something more practical.'

'Mathematics is not simple,' says señor Robles.

'Mathematics is not simple, I agree, but our plan was never to turn David into a mathematician. We just don't want him to suffer as a consequence of not going to school. We want him to feel confident handling numbers.'

'Señor Simón, I have met your son only once, I am not a psychologist, my background is in engineering, but there is something I must tell you. I suspect young David may be suffering from what they call a cognitive deficit. This means that he is deficient in a certain basic mental capacity, in this case the capacity to classify objects on the basis of similarity. This capacity comes so naturally to us as human beings, ordinary human beings, that we are barely aware we have it. It is the ability to see objects as members of classes that makes language possible. We do not need to see each tree as an individual entity, as animals do, we can see it as an example of the class *tree*. It also makes mathematics possible.

'Why do I raise the topic of classification? I do so because in certain rare cases the faculty is weak or missing. Such people will always have difficulty with mathematics and with abstract language in general. I suspect your son is such a person.'

'Why are you telling me this, señor Robles?'

'Because I believe that you owe it to the boy to have his condition investigated further, and then perhaps to adjust the form that his further education may take. I would urge you to make an appointment with a psychologist, preferably one who specializes in cognitive disorders. The Department of Education will be able to provide you with names.'

'Adjust the form of his education: what do you mean by that?'

'In the simplest terms, I mean that if he is always going to struggle with numbers and abstract concepts, then it may be best if he goes, for example, to a trade school, where he can learn a useful, practical trade like plumbing or carpentry. That is all. I take note that you have decided to cancel our mathematics lessons, and I agree with your decision. I think it is a wise one. I wish you and your wife and son a happy future. Good night.'

'I spoke to señor Robles,' he tells Inés. 'I cancelled the lessons. He thinks David should go to a trade school and learn to be a plumber.'

'I wish that señor Robles was here, so that I could give him a slap in the face,' says Inés. 'I never liked the look of him.'

The next day he drives up the valley to señor Robles' house and at the back door leaves a litre of the farm's olive oil, with a card. 'Thank you from David and his parents,' says the card.

Then he has a serious talk to the boy. 'If we find you another teacher, someone who will teach you just simple sums, not mathematics, will you listen? Will you do as you are told?'

'I did listen to señor Robles.'

'You know perfectly well that you did not listen to señor Robles. You undermined him. You made fun of him. You said silly things on purpose. Señor Robles is a clever man. He has a degree in engineering from a university. You could have learned from him, but instead you decided to be silly.'

'I am not silly, señor Robles is silly. I can do sums already. Seven and nine is sixteen. Seven and sixteen is twenty-three.'

'Why didn't you show him you can do sums while he was here?'

'Because, his way, you first have to make yourself small. You have to make yourself as small as a pea, and then as small as a pea inside a pea, and then a pea inside a pea inside a pea. Then you can do his numbers, when you are small small small small small.'

'And why do you have to be so small to do numbers his way?'

'Because his numbers are not real numbers.'

'Well, I wish you had explained that to him instead of being silly and irritating him and driving him away.'

Chapter 4

Days pass, the winter winds begin to blow. Bengi and his kinfolk take their leave. Roberta has offered to drive them to the bus station, where they will catch the bus to the north and seek work on one of the ranches on the great flatlands. Maite and her two sisters, wearing their identical outfits, come to say goodbye. Maite has a gift for David: a little box she has made of stiff cardboard, painted quite delicately with a design of flowers and tumbling vines. 'It's for you,' she says. Brusquely and without a word of thanks David accepts the box. Maite offers her cheek to be kissed. He pretends not to see. Covered in shame, Maite turns and runs off. Even Inés, who does not like the girl, is pained by her distress.

'Why do you treat Maite so cruelly?' he, Simón, demands. 'What if you never see her again? Why let her carry such a bad memory of you for the rest of her life?'

'I am not allowed to ask you, so you are not allowed to ask me,' says the boy.

'Ask you what?'

'Ask me why.'

He, Simón, shakes his head in bafflement.

That evening Inés finds the painted box tossed in the trash.

They wait to hear more about the academies, the Academy of Singing and the Academy of Dancing, but Roberta appears to have forgotten. As for the boy, he seems to be perfectly happy by himself, dashing about the farm on business of his own or sitting on his bunk absorbed in his book. But Bolívar, who at first would accompany him on all his activities, now prefers to stay at home, sleeping.

The boy complains about Bolívar. 'Bolívar doesn't love me any more,' he says.

'He loves you as much as ever,' says Inés. 'He is just not as young as he used to be. He doesn't find it fun to run around all day as you do. He gets tired.'

'A year for a dog is the same as seven years for us,' says he, Simón. 'Bolívar is middle-aged.'

'When is he going to die?'

'Not any time soon. He still has many years before him.'

'But is he going to die?'

'Yes, he is going to die. Dogs die. They are mortal, like us. If you want to have a pet who lives longer than you, you will have to get yourself an elephant or a whale.'

Later that day, as he is sawing firewood – one of the chores he has undertaken – the boy comes to him with a fresh idea. 'Simón, you know the big machine in the shed? Can we put olives in it and make olive oil?'

'I don't think that will work, my boy. You and I are not strong enough to turn the wheels. In the old days they used an ox. They harnessed an ox to the shaft and he walked in a circle and turned the wheels.'

'And then did they give him olive oil to drink?'

'If he wanted olive oil they gave him olive oil. But usually oxen don't drink olive oil. They don't like it.'

'And did he give them milk?'

'No, it's the cow who gives us milk, not the ox. The ox hasn't anything to give except his labour. He turns the olive press or pulls the plough. In return for that we give him our protection. We protect him from his enemies, the lions and tigers who want to kill him.'

'And who protects the lions and the tigers?'

'No one. Lions and tigers refuse to work for us, so we don't protect them. They have to protect themselves.'

'Are there lions and tigers here?'

'No. Their day is over. Lions and tigers have gone away. Gone into the past. If you want to find lions and tigers, you will have to look in books. Oxen too. The day of the ox is all but over. Nowadays we have machines to do the work for us.'

'They should invent a machine to pick olives. Then you and Inés wouldn't have to work.'

'That's true. But if they invented a machine to pick olives then olive-pickers like us would have no jobs and therefore no money. It is an old argument. Some people are on the side of the machines, some on the side of the hand-pickers.'

'I don't like work. Work is boring.'

'In that case, you are lucky to have parents who don't mind working. Because without us you would starve, and you wouldn't enjoy that.'

'I won't starve. Roberta will give me food.'

'Yes, no doubt – out of the goodness of her heart she will give you food. But do you really want to live like that: on the charity of others?'

'What is charity?'

'Charity is other people's goodness, other people's kindness.'

The boy regards him oddly.

'You can't rely endlessly on other people's kindness,' he pursues. 'You have to give as well as take, otherwise there will be no evenness, no justice. Which kind of person do you want to be: the kind who gives or the kind who takes? Which is better?'

'The kind who takes.'

'Really? Do you really believe so? Is it not better to give than to take?'

'Lions don't give. Tigers don't give.'

'And you want to be a tiger?'

'I don't want to *be* a tiger. I am just telling you. Tigers aren't bad.'

'Tigers aren't good either. They aren't human, so they are outside goodness and badness.'

'Well, I don't want to be human either.'

I don't want to be human either. He recounts the conversation to Inés. 'It disturbs me when he talks like that,' he says. 'Have we made a big mistake, removing him from school, bringing him up outside society, letting him run around wild with other children?'

'He is fond of animals,' says Inés. 'He doesn't want to be like us, sitting and worrying about the future. He wants to be free.'

'I don't think that is what he means by not wanting to be human,' he says. But Inés is not interested.

Roberta arrives bearing a message: they are invited to tea with the sisters, at four o'clock, in the big house. David should come too.

From her suitcase Inés brings out her best dress and the shoes that go with it. She frets over the state of her hair. 'I haven't seen a hairdresser since we left Novilla,' she says. 'I look like a madwoman.' She makes the boy put on his frilled shirt and the shoes with buttons, though he complains they are too small and hurt his feet. She wets his hair and brushes it straight.

Promptly at four o'clock they present themselves at the front door. Roberta leads them down a long corridor to the rear of the house, to a room cluttered with little tables and stools and knick-knacks. 'This is the winter parlour,' says Roberta. 'It gets afternoon sun. Sit down. The sisters will be along shortly. And please, no mention of the ducks – you remember? – the ducks that that other boy killed.'

'Why?' says the boy.

'Because it will upset them. They have soft hearts. They are good people. They want the farm to be a refuge for wildlife.'

While they wait he inspects the pictures on the walls: watercolours, nature scenes (he recognizes the dam on which the ill-fated ducks had swum), prettily done but amateurish.

Two women enter, followed by Roberta bearing a tea tray. 'These are they,' intones Roberta: 'señora Inés and her husband señor Simón and their son David. Señora Valentina and señora Consuelo.'

The women, clearly sisters, are, he would guess, in their sixties, greying, soberly dressed. 'Honoured to meet you, señora Valentina, señora Consuelo,' he says, bowing. 'Allow me to thank you for giving us a place to stay on your beautiful estate.'

'I'm not their son,' says David in a calm, level voice.

'Oh,' says one of the sisters in mock surprise, Valentina or Consuelo, he does not know which is which. 'Whose son are you then?'

'Nobody's,' says David firmly.

'So you are nobody's son, young man,' says Valentina or Consuelo. 'That is interesting. An interesting condition. How old are you?'

'Six.'

'Six. And you don't go to school, I understand. Wouldn't you like to go to school?'

'I have been to school.'

'And?'

Inés intervenes. 'We sent him to school in the last place where we lived, but he had poor teachers there, so we have decided to educate him at home. For the time being.'

'They gave the children tests,' he, Simón, adds, 'monthly tests, to measure their progress. David didn't like being measured, so he wrote nonsense for the tests, which got him into trouble. Got us all into trouble.'

The sister ignores him. 'Wouldn't you like to go to school, David, and meet other children?'

'I prefer to be educated at home,' says David primly.

The other sister, meanwhile, has poured the tea. 'Do you take sugar, Inés?' she asks. Inés shakes her head. 'And you, Simón?'

'Is it tea?' says the boy. 'I don't like tea.'

'Then you need not have any,' says the sister.

'You will be wondering, Inés, Simón,' says the first sister, 'why you have been invited here. Well, Roberta has been telling us about your son, about what a clever boy he is, clever and well spoken, about how he is wasting his time with the fruit-pickers' children when he ought to be learning. We discussed the matter, my sisters and I, and we thought we would put a proposal before you. And if you are wondering, by the way, where the third of the sisters is, since I am aware that we are known all over the district as the Three Sisters, I will tell you that señora Alma is unfortunately indisposed. She suffers from melancholy, and today is one of those days when her melancholy has got the better of her. One of her black days, as she calls them. But she is entirely in accord with our proposal.

'Our proposal is that you enrol your son in one of the private academies in Estrella. Roberta has told you a little about the academies, I believe: the Academy of Singing and the Academy of Dance. We would recommend the Academy of Dance. We are acquainted with the principal, señor Arroyo, and his wife, and can vouch for them. As well as a training in dance they offer an excellent general education. We, my sisters and I, will be responsible for your son's fees as long as he is a student there.'

'I don't like dancing,' says David. 'I like singing.'

The two sisters exchange looks. 'We have had no personal contact with the Academy of Singing,' says Valentina or Consuelo, 'but I think I am correct in saying that they do not offer a general education. Their task is to train people to become professional singers. Do you want to be a professional singer, David, when you grow older?'

'I don't know. I don't yet know what I want to be.'

'You don't want to be a fireman or a train driver like other little boys?'

'No. I wanted to be a lifesaver but they wouldn't let me.'

'Who wouldn't let you?'

'Simón.'

'And why is Simón opposed to you being a lifesaver?'

He, Simón, speaks. 'I am not opposed to him being a lifesaver. I am not opposed to any of his plans or dreams. As far as I am concerned – his mother may feel differently – he can be a lifesaver or a fireman or a singer or the man in the moon, as he chooses. I do not direct his life, I no longer even pretend to advise him. The truth is, he has tired us out with his wilfulness, his mother and me. He is like a bulldozer. He has flattened us. We have been flattened. We have no more resistance.'

Inés gapes at him in astonishment. David smiles to himself.

'What a strange outburst!' says Valentina. 'I haven't heard an outburst like that in years. Have you, Consuelo?'

'Not in years,' says Consuelo. 'Quite dramatic! Thank you, Simón. Now, what do you say to our proposal that young David should be enrolled at the Academy of Dance?'

'Where is this academy?' says Inés.

'In the city, in the heart of the city, in the same building as the art museum. You would not be able to stay here on the farm, unfortunately. It is too far. The travel would be too much. You would have to find accommodation in the city. But you wouldn't want to stay on the farm anyway, now that harvest time is over. You would find it too lonely, too boring.'

'We haven't found it boring at all,' says he, Simón. 'On the contrary, we have flourished. We have enjoyed every minute of our time here. In fact I have come to an agreement with Roberta to help with odd jobs while we stay on in the barracks. There are always odd jobs to be done, even in the off season. Pruning, for example. Cleaning.'

He looks to Roberta for support. She gazes steadily into the distance.

'By the barracks you mean the dormitories,' says Valentina. 'The dormitories will be closed during the winter, so you can't stay there. But Roberta can advise you on where to look for lodgings. And if all else fails there is the Asistencia.'

Inés rises. He follows suit.

'You haven't given us your answer,' says Consuelo. 'Do you need time to discuss the matter? How do you feel, young man? Wouldn't you like to go to the Academy of Dance? You would meet other children there.'

'I want to stay here,' says the boy. 'I don't like dancing.'

'Unfortunately,' says señora Valentina, 'you cannot stay here. Furthermore, since you are very young and have no knowledge of the world, only prejudices, you are in no position to make decisions about your future. My suggestion' – she reaches out, hooks a finger under his chin, raises his head so that he has to look directly at her – 'my suggestion is that you allow your parents Inés and Simón to discuss our offer, and then conform to whatever decision they reach, in a spirit of filial obedience. Understood?'

David meets her gaze evenly. 'What is filial obedience?' he asks.

Chapter 5

Fronted by a long sandstone colonnade, the art museum lies on the north side of the main square in Estrella. As instructed, they pass by the main entrance and make for a narrow doorway on a side street over which there is a sign in florid gold characters – *Academia de la Danza* – and an arrow pointing to a stairway. They ascend to the second floor, pass through swing doors, and find themselves in a large, well-lit studio, empty save for an upright piano in a corner.

A woman enters, tall, slim, dressed all in black. 'Can I help you?' she asks.

'I would like to speak to someone about enrolling my son,' says Inés.

'Enrolling your son in . . .?'

'Enrolling him in your Academy. I believe that señora Valentina has spoken to your director about it. David is my son's name. She assured us that children who enrol in your Academy get a general education. I mean, they don't just dance.' She utters the word *dance* with some disdain. 'It is the general education we are interested in – not so much the dancing.'

'Señora Valentina has indeed spoken to us about your son. But I made it clear to her and I should make it clear to you, señora: this is not a regular school or a substitute for a regular school. It is an academy devoted to the training of the soul through music and dance. If you are looking for a regular education for your child, you will be better served by the public school system.'

The training of the soul. He touches Inés' arm. 'If I may,' he says, addressing this pale young woman, so pale as to seem bloodless – *alabastro* is the word that occurs to him – but beautiful nonetheless, strikingly beautiful – perhaps that is what has provoked Inés' hostility, the beauty, as if of a statue that has come to life and wandered in from the museum – 'if I may . . . We are strangers in Estrella, new arrivals. We have been working on the farm owned by señora Valentina and her sisters, temporarily, while we find our feet here. The sisters have kindly taken an interest in David and have offered financial assistance for him to attend your Academy. They speak very highly of the Academy. They say that you are known to provide an excellent all-round education, that your director, señor Arroyo, is a respected educator. May we make an appointment to see señor Arroyo?'

'Señor Arroyo, my husband, is not available. We are not in session this week. Classes resume on Monday, after the break. But if you want to discuss practical matters you can discuss them with me. First, will your son be coming to us as a boarder?'

'A boarder? We were not told you took in boarders.'

'We have a limited number of places for boarders.'

'No, David will be living at home, will he not, Inés?'

Inés nods.

'Very well. Next, footwear. Does your son have dancing slippers? No? He will need dancing slippers. I will write down the address of the shop where you can buy them. Also lighter, more comfortable clothing. It is important that the body be free.'

'Dancing slippers. We will attend to that. You spoke a moment ago of the soul, the training of the soul. In what direction do you train the soul?'

'In the direction of the good. Of obedience to the good. Why do you ask?'

'For no particular reason. And the rest of the curriculum, besides the dancing? Are there books we need to buy?'

There is something disquieting about the woman's appearance, something he has not been able to put a finger on. Now he recognizes what it is. She has no eyebrows. Her eyebrows have been plucked out or shaved off; or perhaps they have never grown. Below her fair, rather sparse hair, pulled back tightly on her scalp, is an expanse of naked forehead as broad as his hand. The eyes, a blue darker than sky blue, meet his gaze calmly, assuredly. *She sees through me*, he thinks, *through all this talk.* Not as young as he had at first thought. Thirty? Thirty-five?

'Books?' She waves a dismissive hand. 'Books will come later. Everything in its time.'

'And the classrooms,' says Inés. 'Can I see the classrooms?'

'This is our only classroom.' Her gaze sweeps the studio. 'This is where the children dance.' Stepping closer, she takes Inés by the hand. 'Señora, you must understand, this is an academy of dance. First comes the dance. All else is secondary. All else follows later.'

At her touch Inés visibly stiffens. He knows only too well how Inés resists, indeed flinches from, the human touch.

Señora Arroyo turns to the boy. 'David – that is your name?'

He expects the usual challenge, the usual denial ('*It is not my real name*'). But no: the boy raises his face to her like a flower opening.

'Welcome, David, to our Academy. I am sure you will like it here. I am señora Arroyo and I will be looking after you. Now, you heard what I told your parents about the dancing slippers and about not wearing tight clothes?'

'Yes.'

'Good. Then I will be expecting you on Monday morning at eight o'clock sharp. That is when the new quarter starts. Come here. Feel the floor. It's lovely, isn't it? It was laid down especially for dancing, out of planks cut from cedar trees that grow high in the mountains, by carpenters, true crafts-men, who made it as smooth as is humanly possible. We wax it every week until it glows, and every day it is polished again by the students' feet. So smooth and so warm! Can you feel the warmth?'

The boy nods. Never has he seen him so responsive before – responsive, trusting, childlike.

'Goodbye now, David. We will see you on Monday, with your new slippers. Goodbye, señora. Goodbye, señor.' The swing doors close behind them.

'She is tall, isn't she, señora Arroyo,' he says to the boy. 'Tall and graceful too, like a real dancer. Do you like her?'

'Yes.'

'So is it decided then? You will go to her school?'

'Yes.'

'And we can tell Roberta and the three sisters that our quest has been successful?'

'Yes.'

'What do you say, Inés: has our quest been successful?'

'I will tell you what I think when I have seen what kind of education they give.'

Blocking their way to the street is a man with his back to them. He wears a rumpled grey uniform; his cap is pushed back on his head; he is smoking a cigarette.

'Excuse me,' he (Simón) says.

The man, evidently lost in reverie, gives a start, then recovers and with an extravagant sweep of the arm waves them through: 'Señora y señores . . .' Passing him they are enveloped in fumes of tobacco and the smell of unwashed clothes.

In the street, as they hesitate, finding their bearings, the man in grey speaks: 'Señor, are you looking for the museum?'

He turns to face him. 'No – our business was with the Academy of Dance.'

'Ah, the Academy of Ana Magdalena!' His voice is deep, the voice of a true bass. Tossing his cigarette aside, he comes nearer. 'So let me guess: you are going to enrol in the Academy, young man, and become a famous dancer! I hope you will find time one day to come and dance for me.' He shows yellowed teeth in a big, all-enfolding smile. 'Welcome! If you attend the Academy you are going to see a lot of me, so let me introduce myself. I am Dmitri. I work at the museum, where I am Principal Attendant – that is my title, such a grand one! What does a Principal Attendant do? Well, it is the Principal Attendant's duty to guard the museum's pictures and sculptures, to preserve them from dust and natural enemies, to lock them up safely in the evenings and set them free in the mornings. As Principal Attendant I am here every day except Saturdays, so naturally I get to meet all the young folk from the Academy, them and their parents.' He turns to him, Simón. 'What did you think of the estimable Ana Magdalena? Does she impress you?'

He exchanges glances with Inés. 'We spoke to señora Arroyo but nothing is decided yet,' he says. 'We have to weigh up our options.'

Dmitri the liberator of the statues and paintings frowns. 'No need for that. No need to weigh up anything. You would be stupid to refuse the Academy. You would regret it for the rest of your life. Señor Arroyo is a master, a true master. There is no other word for it. It is an honour for us to have him among us in Estrella, which has never been a great city, teaching our children the art of dance. If I were in your son's position I would clamour night and day to be allowed into his Academy. You can forget about your other options, whatever they are.'

He is not sure that he likes this Dmitri, with his smelly clothing and his oily hair. He certainly does not like being harangued by him in public (it is mid-morning, the streets are full of people). 'Well,' he says, 'that is for us to decide, is it not, Inés? And now we must be on our way. Goodbye.' He takes the boy's hand; they leave.

In the car the boy speaks up for the first time. 'Why don't you like him?'

'The museum guard? It's not a question of liking or disliking. He is a stranger. He doesn't know us, doesn't know our circumstances. He should not be sticking his nose into our affairs.'

'You don't like him because he has a beard.'

'That is nonsense.'

'He doesn't have a beard,' says Inés. 'There is a difference between wearing a nice, neat beard and not caring for your appearance. This man doesn't shave, he doesn't wash, he doesn't wear clean clothes. He is not a good example to children.'

'Who is a good example to children? Is Simón a good example?'

There is silence.

'Are you a good example, Simón?' the boy presses.

Since Inés will not stand up for him, he has to stand up for himself. 'I try,' he says. 'I try to be a good example. If I fail, it is

47

not for want of trying. I hope I have, on the whole, been a good example. But you must be the judge of that.'

'You are not my father.'

'No, I am not. But that does not disqualify me – does it? – from setting an example.'

The boy does not reply. In fact he loses interest, switches off, stares abstractedly out of the window (they are passing through the dreariest of neighbourhoods, block after block of boxlike little houses). A long silence falls.

'Dmitri sounds like scimitar,' the boy says suddenly. 'To chop off your head.' A pause. 'I like him even if you don't. I want to go to the Academy.'

'Dmitri has nothing to do with the Academy,' says Inés. 'He is just a doorman. If you want to go to the Academy, if your mind is set on it, you can go. But as soon as they start complaining that you are too clever for them and want to send you to psychologists and psychiatrists, I am taking you out at once.'

'You don't have to be clever to dance,' says the boy. 'When are we going to buy my dancing slippers?'

'We will buy them now. Simón will drive us to the shoe shop right now, to the address the lady gave us.'

'Do you hate her too?' says the boy.

Now it is Inés' turn to stare out of the window.

'I like her,' says the boy. 'She is pretty. She is prettier than you.'

'You should learn to judge people by their inner qualities,' says he, Simón. 'Not just by whether they are pretty or not. Or whether they have a beard.'

'What are inner qualities?'

'Inner qualities are qualities like kindness and honesty and a sense of justice. You must surely have read about them in *Don*

Quixote. There are a multitude of inner qualities, more than I can name off the top of my head, you would have to be a philosopher to know the whole list, but prettiness is not an inner quality. Your mother is just as pretty as señora Arroyo, only in a different way.'

'Señora Arroyo is kind.'

'Yes, I agree, she seems kind. She seemed to take a liking to you.'

'So she has inner qualities.'

'Yes, David, she is kind as well as being pretty. But prettiness and kindness are not connected. Being pretty is an accident, a matter of luck. We can be born pretty or we can be born plain, we have no say in it. Whereas being kind is not an accident. We are not born kind. We learn to be kind. We become kind. That is the difference.'

'Dmitri has inner qualities too.'

'Dmitri may well have inner qualities, I may have been too hasty in judging him, I concede that point. I simply didn't observe any of his inner qualities, not today. They were not on display.'

'Dmitri is kind. What does *estimable* mean? Why did he say *the estimable Ana Magdalena*?'

'Estimable. You must surely have come across the word in *Don Quixote*. To esteem someone is to respect and honour him or her. However, Dmitri was using the word ironically. He was making a kind of joke. *Estimable* is a word that is usually applied to older people, not to someone of señora Arroyo's age. For instance, if I called you *estimable young David* it would sound funny.'

'*Estimable old Simón.* That's funny too.'

'If you say so.'

Dancing slippers, as it turns out, come in only two colours, gold and silver. The boy refuses both.

'Is it for señor Arroyo's Academy?' the shop assistant asks.

'Yes.'

'All the children at the Academy are outfitted with our slippers,' says the assistant. 'All of them wear either gold or silver, without exception. If you turn up wearing black slippers or white slippers, young man, you will get very strange looks indeed.'

The assistant is a tall, stooping man with a moustache so thin it might be drawn on his lip in charcoal.

'Do you hear the gentleman, David?' says he, Simón. 'It's gold or silver or dancing in your socks. Which is it to be?'

'Gold,' says the boy.

'Gold it is,' he tells the assistant. 'How much?'

'Forty-nine *reales*,' says the assistant. 'Let him try on this pair for size.'

He glances at Inés. Inés shakes her head. 'Forty-nine *reales* for a child's slippers,' she says. 'How can you charge such a price?'

'They are made of kidskin. They are not ordinary slippers. They are designed for dancers. They have built-in support for the arch.'

'Forty *reales*,' says Inés.

The man shakes his head. 'Very well, forty-nine,' he, Simón, says.

The man seats the boy, removes his shoes, slides the dancing slippers onto his feet. They fit snugly. He pays the man his forty-nine *reales*. The man packs the slippers in their box and gives the box to Inés. In silence they leave the shop.

'Can I carry them?' says the boy. 'Did they cost a lot of money?'

'A lot of money for a pair of slippers,' says Inés.

'But is it a lot of money?'

He waits for Inés to reply, but she is silent. 'There is no such thing as a lot of money in itself,' he says patiently. 'Forty-nine *reales* is a lot of money for a pair of slippers. On the other hand, forty-nine *reales* would not be a lot of money for a car or a house. Water costs almost nothing here in Estrella, whereas if you were in the desert, dying of thirst, you would give everything you owned for just a sip of water.'

'Why?' says the boy.

'Why? Because staying alive is more important than anything else.'

'Why is staying alive more important than anything?'

He is about to answer, about to produce the correct, patient, educative words, when something wells up inside him. Anger? No. Irritation? No: more than that. Despair? Perhaps: despair in one of its minor forms. Why? Because he would like to believe he is guiding the child through the maze of the moral life when, correctly, patiently, he answers his unceasing *Why* questions. But where is there any evidence that the child absorbs his guidance or even hears what he says?

He stops where he is on the busy sidewalk. Inés and the boy stop too, and stare at him in puzzlement. 'Think of it in this way,' he says. 'We are tramping through the desert, you and Inés and I. You tell me you are thirsty and I offer you a glass of water. Instead of drinking the water you pour it out in the sand. You say you thirst for answers: *Why this? Why that?* I, because I am patient, because I love you, offer you an answer each time, which you pour away in the sand. Today, at last, I am tired of offering you water. *Why is staying alive important?* If life does not seem important to you, so be it.'

Inés raises a hand to her mouth in dismay. As for the boy, his face sets in a frown. 'You say you love me but you don't love me,' he says. 'You just pretend.'

'I offer you the best answers I have and you throw them away like a child. Don't be surprised if I lose patience with you sometimes.'

'You are always saying that. You are always saying I am a child.'

'You are a child, and a silly child too, sometimes.'

A woman of middle age, a shopping basket on her arm, has stopped to listen. She whispers something to Inés that he does not catch. Inés shakes her head hurriedly.

'Come, let's go,' says Inés, 'before the police come and take us away.'

'Why are the police going to take us away?' says the boy.

'Because Simón is behaving like a madman while we stand here listening to his nonsense. Because he is being a public nuisance.'

Chapter 6

Monday arrives, and it falls to him to convey the boy to his new school. They get there well before eight o'clock. The studio doors are open but the studio itself is empty. He sits down on the piano stool. Together they wait.

A door opens at the back and señora Arroyo enters, dressed as before in black. Ignoring him, she sweeps across the floor, stops before the boy, takes his hands in her own. 'Welcome, David,' she says. 'I see you have brought a book. Will you show me?'

The boy offers her his *Don Quixote*. She examines it with a frown, pages through it, returns it to him.

'And do you have your dancing slippers?'

The boy takes the slippers out of their cotton bag.

'Good. Do you know what we call gold and silver? We call them the noble metals. Iron and copper and lead we call the slave metals. The noble metals are above, the slave metals are below. Just as there are noble metals and slave metals, there are noble numbers and slave numbers. You will learn to dance the noble numbers.'

'They are not real gold,' says the boy. 'It's just a colour.'

'It is just a colour, but colours have meaning.'

'I'll leave now,' says he, Simón. 'I will be back to fetch you this afternoon.' He kisses the boy on the crown of his head. 'Goodbye, my boy. Goodbye, señora.'

With time to kill, he wanders into the art museum. The walls are rather sparsely hung. *Zafiro Gorge at Sunset. Composition I. Composition II. The Drinker.* The artists' names mean nothing to him.

'Good morning, señor,' says a familiar voice. 'How do we impress you?'

It is Dmitri, sans cap, so dishevelled he might just have got out of bed.

'Interesting,' he replies. 'I am not an expert. Is there an Estrella school of painting, an Estrella style?'

Dmitri ignores the question. 'I was watching when you brought your son. A big day for him, his first day with the Arroyos.'

'Yes.'

'And you must have had a chance to speak to señora Arroyo, Ana Magdalena. Such a dancer! So graceful! But childless, alas. She wants to have children of her own but she can't. It is a source of distress to her, of anguish. You wouldn't think it, to look at her, would you – anguish? You would think she was one of the serene angels who live on nectar. A little sip now and again, nothing more, thank you. But then there are señor Arroyo's children from his first marriage, whom she mothers. And the boarders too. So much love to give. Have you met señor Arroyo? No? Not yet? A great man, a true idealist who lives only for his music. You will see. Unfortunately he does not always have his feet on the ground, if you understand my meaning. Head in the clouds. So it's Ana Magdalena who has to do the hard work, taking the youngsters through their dances, feeding the boarders, running a household, seeing to the affairs of the Academy. And she does it all! Splendidly! Not a word of complaint! Cool as a cucumber! A woman in a thousand. Everyone admires her.'

'And all of these are housed on the same premises – the Dance Academy, the boarding establishment, the Arroyo household?'

'Oh, there is plenty of space. The Academy occupies the entire upper floor. Where are you from, señor, you and your family?'

'From Novilla. We lived in Novilla until recently, until we moved north.'

'Novilla. I've never been there. I came straight to Estrella and have been here ever since.'

'And you have worked in the museum all that time?'

'No, no, no – I have had more jobs than I can remember. That is my nature: a restless nature. I started out as a porter in the produce market. Then I had a spell working on the roads, but I didn't like it. For a long while I worked in the hospital. Terrible. Terrible hours. But moving too – the sights you see! Then came the day my life changed. No exaggeration. Changed for the better. I was hanging about on the square, minding my business, when she walked past. I couldn't believe my eyes. Thought it was an apparition. So beautiful. Unearthly. I jumped up and followed her – followed like a dog. For weeks I hung around the Academy, just for a glimpse of her. Of course she paid me no attention. Why should she? An ugly fellow like me. Then I saw a notice advertising a job at the museum, a cleaner, bottom of the ladder, and to cut a long story short I started work here and have been here ever since. Promoted first to Attendant and then last year to Principal Attendant. Because of my diligence and my punctuality.'

'I'm not sure I understand. You are referring to señora Arroyo?'

'Ana Magdalena. Whom I worship. I am not ashamed to confess to it. Wouldn't you do the same if you worshipped a woman — follow her to the ends of the earth?'

'The museum is hardly the ends of the earth. How does señor Arroyo feel about your worshipping of his wife?'

'Señor Arroyo is an idealist, as I told you. His mind is elsewhere, in the celestial sphere where the numbers spin.'

He has had enough of this conversation. He did not ask for this man's confidences. 'I must leave, I have business to attend to,' he says.

'I thought you wanted to see the Estrella school of painters.'

'Another day.'

Hours yet before the school day ends. He buys a newspaper, sits down at a cafe on the square, orders a cup of coffee. On the front page is a photograph of an elderly couple with a gigantic cucurbit from their garden. It weighs fourteen kilograms, says the report, breaking the previous record by almost a kilogram. On page two a crime report lists the theft of a lawnmower from a shed (unlocked) and vandalism at a public toilet (a washbasin smashed). The deliberations of the municipal council and its various subcommittees figure largely: the subcommittee on public amenities, the subcommittee on roads and bridges, the subcommittee on finances, the subcommittee charged with organizing the forthcoming theatre festival. Then there are the sports pages, which preview a high point of the football season, the forthcoming clash between Aragonza and North Valley.

He scans the Employment Offered columns. Bricklayer. Mason. Electrician. Bookkeeper. What is he looking for? Light labour, perhaps. Gardening. No demand for stevedores, of course.

He pays for his coffee. 'Is there an Office of Relocations in the city?' he asks the waitress. 'Of course,' she says, and gives him directions.

The relocations centre in Estrella is not nearly as grand as the one in Novilla – nothing but a cramped little bureau on a side street. Behind the desk sits a pale-faced, rather mournful-looking young man with a scraggly beard.

'Good day,' says he, Simón. 'I am a new arrival here in Estrella. For the past month or so I have been employed in the valley doing casual labour – fruit-picking mainly. Now I am looking for something more permanent, preferably in the city.'

The clerk fetches a card tray and sets it down on his desk. 'It looks like a lot, but most of the cards are duds,' he confides. 'The trouble is, people don't let us know when a position is filled. How about this: Optima Dry Cleaners. Do you know anything about dry-cleaning?'

'Nothing, but let me take the address. Do you have anything that is more physical – outdoor work, perhaps?'

The clerk ignores his question. 'Stockman at a hardware store. Does that interest you? No experience needed, just a head for figures. Do you have a head for figures?'

'I am not a mathematician, but I can count.'

'As I said, I can't promise the position is still open. You see how the ink is faded?' He holds the card up to the light. 'That tells you how old the card is. How about this one? Typist in a law office. Can you type? No? Then there is this one: cleaner at the art museum.'

'That position has been filled. I met the man who filled it.'

'Have you considered retraining? That may be your best option: enrol for a course that retrains you for a new profession. As long as you are in training you continue to get your unemployment allowance.'

'I'll think about it,' he says. He does not mention that he has not registered for unemployment.

Three o'clock approaches. He makes his way back to the Academy. At the doorway is Dmitri. 'Come to fetch your son?' says Dmitri. 'I make a point of being here when the young ones come out. Free at last! So excited, so full of joy! I wish I could feel that kind of joy again, just for a minute. I remember nothing of my childhood, you know, not a minute. A complete blank. I mourn the loss. It grounds you, your childhood. Gives you roots in the world. I am like a tree that has been uprooted by the tempest of life. Do you know what I mean? Your boy is lucky to have a childhood of his own. How about you? Did you have a childhood?'

He shakes his head. 'No, I arrived fully formed. They took one look at me and marked me down as middle-aged. No childhood, no youth, no memories. Washed clean.'

'Well, no use pining. At least we have the privilege of mixing with the young ones. Maybe some of their angel dust will rub off on us. Hark! End of dancing for the day. Now they will be saying their thanks. They always end the day with a prayer of thanks.'

Together they listen. A faint droning sound that tails off into silence. Then the doors of the Academy burst open and the children come clattering down the stairway, girls and boys, fair and dark. 'Dmitri! Dmitri!' they cry, and in a moment Dmitri is surrounded. He dips into his pockets and brings forth handfuls of sweets, which he tosses in the air. The children fall on them. 'Dmitri!'

Last to emerge, hand in hand with señora Arroyo, eyes cast down, unusually subdued, is David, wearing his gold slippers.

'Goodbye, David,' says señora Arroyo. 'We will see you in the morning.'

The boy does not respond. When they get to the car he climbs into the back seat. In a minute he is asleep, and does not wake until they reach the farm.

Inés is waiting with sandwiches and cocoa. The boy eats and drinks. 'How was your day?' she asks at last. No reply. 'Did you dance?' He nods abstractedly. 'Will you show us later how you danced?'

Without answering the boy clambers onto his bunk and curls into a ball.

'What is wrong?' Inés whispers to him, Simón. 'Did something happen?'

He tries to reassure her. 'He is a bit dazed, that is all. He has been among strangers all day.'

After supper the boy is more forthcoming. 'Ana Magdalena taught us the numbers,' he tells them. 'She showed us Two and Three and you were wrong, Simón, and señor Robles was wrong too, you were both wrong, the numbers *are* in the sky. That is where they live, with the stars. You have to call them before they will come down.'

'Is that what señora Arroyo told you?'

'Yes. She showed us how to call down Two and Three. You can't call down One. One has to come by himself.'

'Will you show us how you call down these numbers?' says Inés.

The boy shakes his head. 'You have to dance. You have to have music.'

'What if I switch on the radio?' he, Simón, suggests. 'Maybe there will be music to dance to.'

'No. It has to be special music.'

'And what else happened today?'

'Ana Magdalena gave us biscuits and milk. And raisins.'

'Dmitri told me you say a prayer at the end of the day. Who do you pray to?'

'It's not a prayer. Ana Magdalena makes the arc sound and we have to get in harmony with it.'

'What is the arc?'

'I don't know, Ana Magdalena won't let us see it, she says it is secret.'

'Most mysterious. I'll ask when next I see her. But it seems that you had a good day. And all because out of the goodness of their hearts señora Alma and señora Consuelo and señora Valentina took an interest in you. An academy of dance where you learn how to call down numbers from the stars! And where you get biscuits and milk from the hands of a pretty lady! How fortunate we are to have ended up here in Estrella! Don't you agree? Don't you feel lucky? Don't you feel blessed?'

The boy nods.

'I certainly feel that way. I think we must be the luckiest family in the world. Now it is time to brush your teeth and go to bed and get a good night's sleep so that in the morning you will be ready to dance again.'

The days assume a new pattern. At six thirty he wakes the boy and gives him breakfast. By seven they are in the car. There is little traffic on the roads; well before eight he drops him off at the Academy. Then he parks the car on the square and spends the next seven hours hunting desultorily for employment or inspecting apartments or – more often – simply sitting in a cafe reading the newspaper, until it is time to pick up the boy and bring him home.

To his and Inés' enquiries about his schooldays the boy responds briefly and reluctantly. Yes, he likes señor Arroyo. Yes, they are learning songs. No, they have not had reading lessons. No, they do not do sums. About the mysterious arc that señora Arroyo sounds at the end of the day he will say nothing.

'Why are you always asking me what I did today?' he says. 'I don't ask you what you did. Anyway, you don't understand.'

'What don't we understand?' says Inés.

'You don't understand anything.'

After that they stop interrogating him. Let him tell his story in his own good time, they say to themselves.

One evening he, Simón, unthinkingly blunders into the women's dormitory. Inés, on her knees on the floor, looks up with displeasure. The boy, wearing only underpants and the golden dancing slippers, stops in mid-motion.

'Go away, Simón!' exclaims the boy. 'You are not allowed to watch!'

'Why? What is it that I shouldn't watch?'

'He is practising something complicated,' says Inés. 'He needs to concentrate. Go away. Close the door.'

Surprised, puzzled, he retreats, then hovers at the door listening. There is nothing to hear.

Later, when the boy is asleep, he questions Inés. 'What was going on that was too private for me to see?'

'He was practising his new steps.'

'But what is secret about that?'

'He thinks you won't understand. He thinks you will make fun of him.'

'Given that we send him to an academy of dance, why should I make fun of his dancing?'

'He says you don't understand the numbers. He says you are hostile. Hostile to the numbers.'

She shows him a chart the boy has brought home: intersecting triangles, their apices marked with numerals. He can make no sense of it.

'He says this is how they learn numbers,' says Inés. 'Through dance.'

The next morning, on the way to the Academy, he brings up the subject. 'Inés showed me your dance chart,' he says. 'What are the numbers for? Are they the positions of your feet?'

'It's the stars,' says the boy. 'It's astrology. You close your eyes while you dance and you can see the stars in your head.'

'What about counting the beats? Doesn't señor Arroyo count the beats for you while you dance?'

'No. You just dance. Dancing is the same as counting.'

'So señor Arroyo just plays and you just dance. It doesn't sound like any dance lesson I am familiar with. I am going to ask señor Arroyo whether I can sit in on one of his lessons.'

'You can't. You are not allowed. Señor Arroyo says no one is allowed.'

'Then when will I ever see you dancing?'

'You can see me now.'

He glances at the boy. The boy is sitting still, his eyes closed, a slight smile on his lips.

'That is not dancing. You can't dance while you are sitting in a car.'

'I can. Look. I am dancing again.'

He shakes his head in bafflement. They arrive at the Academy. Out of the shadows of the doorway emerges Dmitri. He ruffles the boy's neatly brushed hair. 'Ready for the new day?'

Chapter 7

Inés has never liked getting up early. However, after three weeks on the farm with little to do but chat to Roberta and await the child's return, she rouses herself early enough one Monday morning to join them on their ride to the city. Her first destination is a hairdresser. Then, feeling more herself, she stops at a women's outfitters and buys herself a new dress. Chatting to the cashier, she learns that they are looking for a saleslady. On an impulse she approaches the proprietor and is offered the position.

The need to make the move from the farm to the city suddenly becomes urgent. Inés takes over the hunt for accommodation, and within days has found an apartment. The apartment itself is featureless, the neighbourhood dreary, but it is within walking distance of the city centre and has a park nearby where Bolívar can exercise.

They pack up their belongings. For the last time he, Simón, wanders out into the fields. It is dusk, the magic hour. The birds chatter in the trees as they settle for the night. From far away comes the tinkle of sheep-bells. Are they right, he wonders, to leave this garden place that has been so good to them?

They say their goodbyes. 'We hope to see you back for the harvest,' says Roberta. 'That's a promise,' says he, Simón. To señora

Consuelo (señora Valentina is busy, señora Alma is struggling with her demons) he says: 'I cannot tell you how thankful we are to you and your sisters for your great generosity'; to which señora Consuelo replies: 'It is nothing. In another life you will do the same for us. Goodbye, young David. We look forward to seeing your name in lights.'

On the first night in their new home they have to sleep on the floor, since the furniture they ordered has not been delivered. In the morning they buy some basic kitchenware. They are running short of money.

He, Simón, takes a job, paid by the hour, delivering advertising material to households. With the job comes a bicycle, a heavy, creaking machine with a large basket bolted above the front wheel. He is one of four delivery men (he rarely crosses paths with the other three); his assigned area is the north-east quadrant of the city. During school hours he winds through the streets of his quadrant stuffing pamphlets into letter boxes: piano lessons, cures for baldness, hedge trimming, electrical repairs (competitive rates). It is, to a degree, interesting work, good for the health and not unpleasant (though he has to push the bicycle up the steeper streets). It is a way of getting to know the city, also a way of meeting people, making new contacts. The sound of a rooster crowing leads him to the backyard of a man who keeps poultry; the man undertakes to supply him with a pullet each week, at a price of five *reales*, and for an additional *real* to slaughter and dress the bird too.

But winter is upon them, and he dreads the rainy days. Though he is equipped with a capacious oilskin cape and a mariner's oilskin hat, the rain nonetheless finds its way through. Cold and sodden, he is sometimes tempted to dump his pamphlets and return the bicycle to the depot. He is tempted, but he does not give in. Why not? He is not sure. Perhaps because he feels a certain obligation to the city that has offered them a new life, even though it is not clear to him how a city, which has no sensation, no feelings, can benefit from the distribution among its citizens of advertisements for twenty-four-piece cutlery sets in handsome presentation boxes at low low prices.

He thinks of the Arroyos, husband and wife, to whose upkeep he is in small measure contributing by pedalling around in the rain. Though he has not yet had an opportunity to distribute advertisements for their Academy, what the couple offer – dancing to the stars as a substitute for learning one's multiplication tables – is not different in nature from what is offered by the lotion that miraculously brings hair follicles back to life or the vibrating belt that miraculously dissolves body fat, molecule by molecule. Like Inés and himself, the Arroyos must have arrived in Estrella with nothing but the barest belongings; they too must have passed a night sleeping on newspapers or the equivalent; they too must have scraped a living together until their Academy got going. Maybe, like him, señor Arroyo had to spend a while stuffing pamphlets into letter boxes; maybe Ana Magdalena of the alabaster complexion had to go down on her knees and wash floors. A city criss-crossed by the paths of immigrants: if they did not all live in hope, if they did not each have their quantum of hopefulness to add to the great sum, where would Estrella be?

David brings home a Notice to Parents. There is to be an open evening at the Academy. Señor and señora Arroyo will address the parents on the educational philosophy behind the Academy, students will give a performance, after which there will be light refreshments. Parents are encouraged to bring interested friends along. Proceedings will commence at seven.

The audience, on the evening, is disappointingly thin, no more than twenty. Of the chairs that have been set out many remain empty. Taking their place in the front row, he and Inés can hear the young performers whispering and giggling behind the curtain drawn across the far end of the studio.

Wearing a dark evening dress with a shawl over her bare shoulders, señora Arroyo emerges. For a long moment she stands in silence before them. Again he is struck by her poise, her calm beauty.

She speaks. 'Welcome, all of you, and thank you for coming out on a cold, wet evening. Tonight I am going to tell you a little about the Academy and what my husband and I hope to achieve for our students. For that it will be necessary to give you a brief outline of the philosophy behind the Academy. Those of you who are familiar with it, please bear with me.

'As we know, from the day when we arrive in this life we put our former existence behind us. We forget it. But not entirely. Of our former existence certain remnants persist: not memories in the usual sense of the word but what we can call shadows of memories. Then, as we become habituated to our new life, even these shadows fade, until we have forgotten our origins entirely and accept that what our eyes see is the only life there is.

'The child, however, the young child, still bears deep impresses of a former life, shadow recollections which he lacks words to express. He lacks words because, along with the world we have lost, we have lost a language fit to evoke it. All that is left of that primal language is a handful of words, what I call transcendental words, among which the names of the numbers, *uno, dos, tres,* are foremost.

'*Uno-dos-tres*: is this just a chant we learn at school, the mindless chant we call *counting*; or is there a way of seeing through the chant to what lies behind and beyond it, namely the realm of the numbers themselves – the noble numbers and their auxiliaries, too many to count, as many as the stars, numbers born out of the unions of noble numbers? We, my husband and I and our helpers, believe there is such a way. Our Academy is dedicated to guiding the souls of our students toward that realm, to bringing them in accord with the great underlying movement of the universe, or, as we prefer to say, the dance of the universe.

'To bring the numbers down from where they reside, to allow them to manifest themselves in our midst, to give them body, we rely on the dance. Yes, here in the Academy we dance, not in a graceless, carnal, or disorderly way, but body and soul together, so as to bring the numbers to life. As music enters us and moves us in dance, so the numbers cease to be mere ideas, mere phantoms, and become real. The music evokes its dance and the dance evokes its music: neither comes first. That is why we call ourselves an academy of music as much as an academy of dance.

'If my words this evening seem obscure, dear parents, dear friends of the Academy, that only goes to show how feeble words are. Words are feeble – that is why we dance. In the dance we call the numbers down from where they live among the aloof stars. We surrender ourselves to them in dance, and while we dance, by their grace, they live among us.

'Some of you – I can see from your looks – remain sceptical. *What are these numbers she talks of that dwell among the stars?* you murmur among yourselves. *Do I not use numbers every day when I do business or buy groceries? Are numbers not our humble servants?*

'I reply: The numbers you have in mind, the numbers we use when we buy and sell, are not true numbers but simulacra. They are what I call ant numbers. Ants, as we know, have no memory. They are born out of the dust and die into the dust. Tonight, in the second part of the show, you will see our younger students playing the parts of ants, performing the ant operations that we call the lower arithmetic, the arithmetic we use in household accounts and so forth.'

Ants. The lower arithmetic. He turns to Inés. 'Can you make sense of this?' he whispers. But Inés, lips compressed, eyes narrowed, watching Ana Magdalena intently, refuses to answer.

Out of the corner of his eye, half hidden in the shadow of the doorway, he espies Dmitri. What interest can Dmitri have in the dance of numbers, Dmitri the bear? But of course it is the person of the speaker that interests him.

'Ants are by nature law-abiding creatures,' Ana Magdalena is saying. 'The laws they obey are the laws of addition and subtraction. That is all they do, day in and day out, during every waking hour: carry out their mechanical, twofold law.

'In our Academy we do not teach the law of the ant. I know that some of you are concerned about that fact – the fact that we do not teach your children to play ant games, adding numbers to numbers and so forth. I hope you now understand why. We do not want to turn your children into ants.

'Enough. Thank you for your attention. Please welcome our performers.'

She gives a sign and steps aside. Dmitri, wearing his museum uniform, which for once is neatly buttoned, strides forward and hauls the curtains open, first the left curtain, then the right. At the same moment, from above, come the muted tones of a pipe organ.

Onstage a single figure is revealed, a boy of perhaps eleven or twelve, wearing golden slippers and a white toga that leaves one shoulder bare. Arms raised above his head, he gazes into the distance. While the organist, who can only be señor Arroyo, plays a set of flourishes, he maintains this pose. Then, in time to the music, he begins his dance. The dance consists in gliding from point to point on the stage, sometimes slowly, sometimes swiftly, coming to a near halt at each point but never actually halting. The pattern of the dance, the relation of each point to the next, is obscure; the movements of the boy are graceful but without variety. He, Simón, soon loses interest, closes his eyes, and concentrates on the music.

The upper notes of the organ are tinny, the lower notes without resonance. But the music itself takes possession of him. Calm descends; he can feel something within him – his soul? – take up the rhythm of the music and move in time to it. He falls into a mild trance.

The music grows more complex, then simple again. He opens his eyes. A second dancer has appeared onstage, so similar in looks to the first that he must be a younger brother. He too occupies himself in gliding from one invisible point to another. Now and then their two paths cross, but there never seems any danger that they will collide. No doubt they have rehearsed so often that they know each other's moves by heart; yet there seems more to it than that, a logic that dictates their passage, a logic that he cannot quite grasp, though he feels on the edge of doing so.

The music comes to a close. The two dancers attain their end points and return to their static poses. Dmitri hauls the left curtain closed, then the right. There is ragged applause from the audience, in which he joins. Inés too is clapping.

Ana Magdalena comes forward again. There is a radiance to her which – he is quite prepared to believe – has been drawn out by the dance, or the music, or the dance and music together; indeed, he feels a certain radiance in himself.

'What you have just seen are the Number Three and the Number Two, danced by two of our senior students. To close this evening's performance our junior students will perform the ant dance I earlier referred to.'

Dmitri draws the curtains open. Before them, arrayed in a column, are eight children, girls and boys, wearing singlets and shorts and green caps with waving antennae to denote their ant nature. David is at the head of the column.

Señor Arroyo, at the organ, plays a march, emphasizing its mechanical rhythm. Taking big steps rightward and leftward, backward and forward, the ants re-form themselves from a column of eight into a matrix of four rows in two columns. They hold their positions for four measures, marching on the spot; then they re-form themselves into a new matrix of two rows in four columns. They hold that position, marching; then they transform themselves into a single row, eight long. They hold their positions, marching; then suddenly they break ranks and, as the music abandons its staccato rhythm and becomes simply one massive, inharmonious chord after another, flit across the stage with their arms held out like wings, nearly bumping into one another (and in one case actually bumping together and falling to the floor in a paroxysm of giggles). Then the steady rhythm of the march reasserts itself and swiftly the ants reassemble in their original column of eight.

Dmitri draws the curtains closed and stands there beaming. The assembly claps loudly. The music does not stop. Dmitri whisks open the curtains to reveal the insects still marching in column. Redoubled applause.

'What do you think of it?' he says to Inés.

'What do I think? I think: As long as he is happy, that is all that matters.'

'I agree. But what did you think of the speech? What did you think —'

David interrupts, rushing up to them flushed and excited, still wearing the floppy antennae. 'Did you see me?' he demands.

'Of course we saw you,' says Inés. 'You made us feel very proud. You were the leader of the ants.'

'I was the leader, but the ants aren't good, they just march. Next time Ana Magdalena says I can dance a proper dance. But I have to do lots of practice.'

'That's good. When is next time?'

'The next concert. Can I have some cake?'

'As much as you like. No need to ask. The cake is for all of us.'

He looks around, searching for señor Arroyo. He is curious to meet the man, to find out whether he too believes in a higher realm where the numbers dwell, or whether he just plays the organ and leaves the transcendental stuff to his wife. But señor Arroyo is nowhere to be seen: the scattering of men in the room are clearly parents like himself.

Inés is in conversation with one of the mothers. She beckons him over. 'Simón, this is señora Hernández. Her son was also an ant. Señora, this is my friend Simón.'

Amigo: friend. Not a word Inés has used before. Is that what he is, what he has become?

'Isabella,' says señora Hernández. 'Please call me Isabella.'

'Inés,' says Inés.

'I was complimenting Inés on your son. He is a very confident performer, isn't he?'

'He is a very confident child,' says he, Simón. 'He has always been like that. As you can imagine, it is not easy to teach him.'

Isabella gives him a puzzled look.

'He is confident but his confidence is not always well founded,' he continues, beginning to flounder. 'He believes he has powers he does not really have. He is still very young.'

'David taught himself to read,' says Inés. 'He can read *Don Quixote*.'

'In a condensed version, for children,' he says, 'but yes, it is true, he taught himself to read, without any help.'

'They are not keen on reading here at the Academy,' says Isabella. 'They say reading can come later. While they are young it is just dance, music and dance. Still, she is persuasive, isn't she, Ana Magdalena. Speaks very well. Didn't you think so?'

'What of the higher realm from which the numbers descend to us, the holy Number Two and the holy Number Three – did you understand that bit?' he says.

A little boy who must be Isabella's son sidles up, his lips ringed with chocolate. She finds a tissue and wipes his mouth, to which he submits patiently. 'Let us take off these funny ears and give them back to Ana Magdalena,' she says. 'You can't come home looking like an insect.'

The evening is over. Ana Magdalena stands at the door bidding goodbye to the parents. He shakes her cool hand. 'Please convey my thanks to señor Arroyo,' he says. 'I am sorry we didn't have a chance to meet him. He is a fine musician.'

73

Ana Magdalena nods. For an instant the blue eyes fix on his. *She sees straight through me*, he thinks with a jolt. *Sees through me and doesn't like me.*

It hurts him. It is not something he is used to, being disliked, and being disliked moreover on no grounds. But perhaps it is not a personal dislike. Perhaps the woman dislikes the fathers of all her students, as rivals to her authority. Or perhaps she simply dislikes men, all save the invisible Arroyo.

Well, if she dislikes him he dislikes her too. It surprises him: he does not often take a dislike to a woman, particularly a beautiful woman. And this woman is beautiful, no doubt about that, with the kind of beauty that stands up to the closest scrutiny: perfect features, perfect skin, perfect figure, perfect bearing. She is beautiful yet she repels him. She may be married, but he associates her nevertheless with the moon and its cold light, with a cruel, persecutory chastity. Is it wise to be giving their boy – any boy, indeed any girl – into her hands? What if at the end of the year the child emerges from her grasp as cold and persecutory as herself? For that is his judgement on her – on her religion of the stars and her geometric aesthetic of the dance. Bloodless, sexless, lifeless.

The boy has fallen asleep on the back seat of the car, his stomach full of cake and lemonade. Nevertheless, he is wary of speaking his thoughts to Inés: even in deepest sleep the child seems to hear what is going on around him. So he holds his tongue until the child is safely tucked away in bed.

'Inés, are you sure we have done the right thing?' he says. 'Should we not look around for a school that is a little less . . . extreme?'

Inés says nothing.

'I couldn't make sense of that lecture of the señora's,' he presses on. 'What I did understand I found a bit crazy. She isn't a teacher, she is a preacher. She and her husband have made up a religion and now they are hunting for converts. David is too young, too impressionable to be exposed to that kind of thing.'

Inés speaks. 'When I was a teacher we had señor C the postman who whistles and el G the cat who purrs and el T the train who hoots. Each letter had its own personality and its own sound. We made up words by putting letters together one after another. That is how you teach small children to read and write.'

'You were a teacher?'

'We used to run classes at La Residencia for the children of the domestics.'

'You never told me that.'

'Each letter of the alphabet had a personality. Now she is giving the numbers personalities too, Ana Magdalena. *Uno, dos, tres.* Making them come alive. That is how you teach small children. It's not religion. I'm going to bed. Good night.'

Five of the pupils at the Academy are boarders, the rest are day students. The boarders stay with the Arroyos because they come from districts of the province too far-flung to commute from. These five, together with the young usher and Señor Arroyo's two sons, are given proper sit-down lunches, which Ana Magdalena prepares. The day students bring their own lunches. Each evening Inés packs David's lunch box for the next day and puts it in the refrigerator: sandwiches, an apple or a banana, plus a little treat, a chocolate or a cookie.

One evening, as she is preparing his lunch box, David speaks: 'Some girls at school won't eat meat. They say it is cruel. Is it cruel, Inés?'

'If you don't eat meat you won't get strong. You won't grow.'

'But is it cruel?'

'No, it is not cruel. Animals don't feel anything when they are slaughtered. They don't have feelings in the way that we do.'

'I asked señor Arroyo if it is cruel and he said animals can't do syllogisms so it isn't cruel. What does syllogisms mean?'

Inés is nonplussed. He, Simón, intervenes. 'What he means, I think, is that animals don't think logically, as we do. They can't make logical inferences. They don't understand that they are being packed off to the butcher even when all the evidence points that way, so they aren't frightened.'

'But does it hurt?'

'Being slaughtered? No, not if the butcher is skilful. Just as it doesn't hurt when you go to the doctor, if the doctor is skilful.'

'So it is not cruel, is it.'

'No, it is not particularly cruel. A big, strong ox hardly feels it. To the ox it is like a pinprick. And then there is no more feeling at all.'

'But why do they have to die?'

'Why? Because they are like us. We are mortal, so are they, and mortal beings have to die. That was what señor Arroyo had in mind when he made his joke about syllogisms.'

The boy shakes his head impatiently. 'Why do they have to die to give us their meat?'

'Because that is what happens when you cut an animal up: it dies. If you cut off a lizard's tail he will grow a new tail. But an ox is not like a lizard. If you cut off an ox's tail he won't grow a new one. If you cut off his leg he will bleed to death. David, I don't want you to brood about these things. Oxen are good creatures. They wish us well. In their own language they say: *If young David needs to eat my flesh so that he can grow strong and healthy, then I willingly give it to him.* Isn't that so, Inés?'

Inés nods.

'Then why don't we eat people?'

'Because it is disgusting,' says Inés. 'That's why.'

Chapter 8

Since Inés has never in the past shown an interest in fashion, he does not expect her to stay long at Modas Modernas. But he is wrong. She revels in her success as saleslady, particularly with the older clientele, who appreciate her patience with them. Discarding the wardrobe she brought with her from Novilla, she herself begins to wear newer fashions bought at a discount or borrowed from the shop.

With Claudia, the owner, a woman of her age, she strikes up a quick friendship. They lunch at a cafe around the corner, or buy sandwiches and eat them in the stockroom, where Claudia unburdens herself about her son, who has fallen into bad company and is on the verge of dropping out of school; also, in less specific terms, about her errant husband. Whether Inés unburdens herself in turn Inés does not say – at least not to him, Simón.

In preparation for the new season Claudia goes on a buying expedition to Novilla, leaving Inés in charge of the shop. Her sudden promotion arouses the ire of the cashier, Inocencia, who has been with Modas Modernas since its birth. It is a relief to all when Claudia returns.

He, Simón, listens nightly to Inés' stories of the ups and downs of fashion, of troublesome or over-fastidious customers, of the unwished-for rivalry with Inocencia. About such meagre adventures as befall him on his delivery rounds Inés remains incurious.

On the next of her trips to Novilla Claudia invites Inés to accompany her. Inés asks him, Simón, what he thinks. Should she go? What if she is recognized and taken in by the police? He scoffs at her fears. On the scale of heinousness, he says, the crime of aiding and abetting a minor in the practice of truancy surely figures near the bottom. David's file will by now have been buried under mountains of other files; and even if it has not, the police surely have better things to do than comb the streets for delinquent parents.

So Inés accepts Claudia's invitation. Together they catch the overnight train to Novilla and spend the day in a distributor's warehouse in the industrial quarter of the city making their selection. During a break Inés telephones La Residencia and speaks to her brother Diego. Without preliminaries Diego demands the car back (he calls it *his* car). Inés refuses, but offers to pay him half its value if he will let her take it over. He asks for two-thirds; but she digs in her heels and he capitulates.

She asks to speak to her other brother, Stefano. Stefano is no longer at La Residencia, Diego informs her. He has gone to live in the city with his girlfriend, who is expecting a baby.

With Inés away or preoccupied with goings-on at Modas Modernas, it falls to him, Simón, to attend to David's needs. Besides accompanying him to the Academy in the mornings and fetching him home in the afternoons, he takes on the task of preparing his meals. His own command of the art of cooking is rudimentary, but fortunately the boy is so hungry these days that he eats whatever is put before him. He gobbles down huge helpings of mashed potato with green peas; he looks forward eagerly to roast chicken at the weekends.

He is growing fast. He will never be tall, but his limbs are well knit and his energy is boundless. After school he rushes off to join in football games with other boys from the apartment block. Though he is the youngest, his determination and his toughness win him the respect of older, bigger boys. His style of running – shoulders hunched, head lowered, elbows tucked into his sides – may be eccentric, but he is quick on his feet, hard to knock over.

At the beginning he, Simón, used to keep Bolívar on a leash while the boy was playing, for fear the dog might race onto the field and attack anyone who threatened his young master. But Bolívar has soon come to learn that running around after a ball is just a game, a human game. Now he is content to sit quietly on the sidelines, indifferent to the football, enjoying the mild warmth of the sun and the rich medley of smells in the air.

According to Inés, Bolívar is seven years old, but he, Simón, wonders whether the dog is not older. Certainly he is in the latter phase of his life, the phase of decline. He has begun to put on weight; though he is an intact male, he seems to have lost interest in bitches. He has become less approachable too. Other dogs are wary of him. He has only to lift his head and give a muted growl to send them slinking off.

He, Simón, is the sole spectator of the scrappy afternoon football games, games whose action is continually interrupted by arguments among the players. One day a deputation of older boys approaches him to ask if he will referee. He declines: 'I'm too old and unfit,' he says. This is not entirely true; but in retrospect he is glad he refused and suspects David is glad too.

He wonders who the boys from the apartment block think he is: David's father? His grandfather? An uncle? What story has David told them? That the man who watches their games shares a home with him and his mother, though he sleeps alone? Is David proud of him or ashamed of him or both proud and ashamed; or is a six-year-old, soon to be seven, too young to have ambivalent feelings?

At least the boys respect the dog. The first day he arrived with the dog they gathered in a circle around him. 'His name is Bolívar,' David announced. 'He is an Alsatian. He won't bite you.' Bolívar the Alsatian gazed calmly into the distance, allowing the boys to revere him.

In the apartment he, Simón, behaves more like a lodger than an equal member of the family. He takes care to keep his room neat and tidy at all times. He does not leave his toiletries in the bathroom, or his coat on the rack by the front door. How Inés explains his role in her life to Claudia and the wider world he does not know. She has certainly never referred to him, in his hearing, as her husband; if she prefers to present him as a gentleman boarder, he is happy to play along.

Inés is a difficult woman. Nonetheless, he finds in himself a growing admiration for her, and a growing affection too. Who would have thought she would put La Residencia behind her, and the easy life she lived there, and devote herself with such single-mindedness to the fortunes of this wilful child!

'Are we a family, you and Inés and I?' asks the boy.

'Of course we are a family,' he duly replies. 'Families take many forms. We are one of the forms a family can take.'

'But do we have to be a family?'

He has made a resolution not to give in to irritation, to take the boy's questions seriously even when they are merely idle.

'If we wanted, we could be less of a family. I could move out and find lodgings of my own and see you only now and again. Or Inés could fall in love and get married and take you to live with her new husband. But those are roads neither of us wants to follow.'

'Bolívar doesn't have a family.'

'We are Bolívar's family. We look after Bolívar and Bolívar looks after us. But no, you are right, Bolívar does not have a family, a dog family. He used to have a family when he was little, but then he grew up and found he didn't need a family any longer. Bolívar prefers to live by himself and meet other dogs in the street, casually. You may make a similar decision when you grow up: to live by yourself without a family. But while you are still young you need us to look after you. So we are your family: Inés and Bolívar and I.'

If we wanted, we could be less of a family. Two days after this conversation the boy announces, out of the blue, that he wants to become a boarder at the Academy.

He, Simón, tries to discourage him. 'Why would you want to move to the Academy when you have such a nice life here?' he says. 'Inés will miss you terribly. I will miss you.'

'Inés won't miss me. Inés never recognized me.'

'Of course she did.'

'She says she didn't.'

'Inés loves you. She holds you in her heart.'

'But she didn't recognize me. Señor Arroyo recognizes me.'

'If you go to señor Arroyo you will no longer have a room of your own. You will have to sleep in a dormitory with the other children. When you feel lonely in the middle of the night you will have no one to go to for comfort. Señor Arroyo and Ana

Magdalena certainly won't let you climb into their bed. There will be no one to play football with in the afternoons. For supper you will get carrots and cauliflower, which you hate, instead of mashed potatoes and gravy. And what of Bolívar? Bolívar won't know what has happened. *Where is my young master?* Bolívar will say. *Why has he abandoned me?*'

'Bolívar can visit me,' says the boy. 'You can bring him.'

'It's a big decision, becoming a boarder. Can't we leave it until the next quarter, and give ourselves time to think it over properly?'

'No. I want to be a boarder now.'

He speaks to Inés. 'I don't know what Ana Magdalena could have promised him,' he says. 'I think it is a bad idea. He is far too young to leave home.'

To his surprise, Inés disagrees. 'Let him go. He will soon be begging to come home again. It will teach him a lesson.'

It is the last thing he would have expected of her: to give up her precious son to the Arroyos.

'It will be expensive,' he says. 'Let us at least discuss it with the sisters, see how they feel. It is, after all, their money.'

Though they have not been invited to the sisters' residence in Estrella, they have been careful to maintain the link with Roberta on the farm, and to pay the occasional call when the sisters are there, as a token that they have not forgotten their generosity. On these visits David is unusually forthcoming about the Academy. The sisters have heard him expound on the noble numbers and the auxiliary numbers and watched him perform some of the movements from the simpler dances, the Two and the Three, dances which if done justly call down their respective noble numbers from the stars. They have been charmed by his physical grace and impressed by the gravity with which he presents the unusual teachings of the Academy. But on this new visit the boy is faced with a challenge of another kind: to explain to them why he wants to leave home and live with the Arroyos.

'Are you sure that señor and señora Arroyo will have room for you?' asks Consuelo. 'As I understand it – correct me if I am wrong, Inés – there are just the two of them, and they have quite a complement of boarders as well as children of their own. What have you got against living at home with your parents?'

'They don't understand me,' says the boy.

Consuelo and Valentina exchange glances. '*My parents don't understand me,*' says Consuelo ruminatively. 'Where have I heard those words before? Pray tell me, young man: why is it so important that your parents should understand you? Is it not enough that they are good parents?'

'Simón doesn't understand the numbers,' says the boy.

'I don't understand numbers either. I leave that sort of thing to Roberta.'

The boy is silent.

'Have you thought carefully about this, David?' asks Valentina. 'Is your mind made up? Are you sure that after a week with the Arroyos you won't change your mind and ask to come home?'

'I won't change my mind.'

'Very well,' says Consuelo. She glances at Valentina, at Alma. 'You can have your wish and become a boarder at the Academy. We will discuss the fees with señora Arroyo. But your complaint about your parents, that they don't understand you, pains us. It seems to be asking a lot that they should not only be good parents but understand you as well. I certainly don't understand you.'

'Nor I,' says Valentina. Alma is silent.

'Aren't you going to thank señora Consuelo and señora Valentina and señora Alma?' says Inés.

'Thank you,' says the boy.

The next morning, instead of going to Modas Modernas, Inés accompanies them to the Academy. 'David says he wants to become a boarder here,' she tells Ana Magdalena. 'I don't know who put the idea in his head, and I'm not asking you to tell. I just want to know: Do you have room for him?'

'Is this true, David? You want to board with us?'

'Yes,' says the boy.

'And you are opposed, señora?' says Ana Magdalena. 'If you are opposed to the idea, why not simply say so?'

She is addressing Inés, but he, Simón, is the one who replies. 'We don't oppose this latest desire of his for the simple reason that we don't have the strength,' he says. 'With us David always gets his way, in the end. That is the kind of family we are: one master and two servants.'

Inés does not find this amusing. Nor does Ana Magdalena. But David smiles serenely.

'Girls like security,' says Ana Magdalena, 'but for boys it is different. For boys, some boys, leaving home is a great adventure. However, David, I must warn you, if you come and live with us you won't be master any longer. In our home señor Arroyo is the master and the boys and girls listen to what he says. Do you accept that?'

'Yes,' says the boy.

'But just during the week,' says Inés. 'At weekends he comes home.'

'I will write down a list of the things you should pack for him,' says Ana Magdalena. 'Don't worry. If I see he is lonely and pining for his parents I will give you a call. Alyosha will keep an eye on him too. Alyosha is sensitive to such things.'

'Alyosha,' says he, Simón. 'Who is Alyosha?'

'Alyosha is the man who takes care of the boarders,' says Inés. 'I told you. Weren't you listening?'

'Alyosha is the young man who helps us,' says Ana Magdalena. 'He is a product of the Academy, so he knows our way of doing things. The boarders are his special responsibility. He takes his meals with them and has a room of his own off the dormitory. He is very sensitive, very good-natured, very sympathetic. I will introduce you to him.'

The transition from day student to boarder proves to be the simplest of matters. Inés buys a little suitcase into which they pack a few toiletries and changes of clothing. The boy adds *Don Quixote*. The next morning he matter-of-factly kisses Inés goodbye and marches off down the street with him, Simón, trailing behind carrying the suitcase.

Dmitri is, as usual, waiting at the door. 'Aha, so the young master is coming to assume residence,' says Dmitri, taking over the suitcase. 'A great day, to be sure. A day for singing and dancing and killing the fatted calf.'

'Goodbye, my boy,' says he, Simón. 'Be good, and I will see you on Friday.'

'I am good,' says the boy. 'I am always good.'

He watches as Dmitri and the boy disappear up the staircase. Then, on an impulse, he follows. He arrives in the studio in time to catch a glimpse of the boy trotting off to the interior reaches of the apartment, holding Ana Magdalena's hand. A feeling of loss rolls through him like a fog. Tears come, which he tries in vain to hide.

Dmitri puts a consoling arm around his shoulder. 'Be calm,' says Dmitri.

Instead of being calm he bursts into sobs. Dmitri draws him to his breast; he offers no resistance. He allows himself a huge sob, another, a third, inhaling with deep, shuddering breaths the smells of tobacco smoke and serge. *Letting go*, he thinks: *I am letting go. It is excusable, in a father.*

Then the time for tears is over. He pulls himself free, clears his throat, whispers a word that is meant to be a word of gratitude but comes forth as a kind of gargle, and rushes down the stairs.

At home, that evening, he tells Inés of the episode, an episode that in retrospect seems stranger and stranger – more than strange, bizarre.

'I don't know what got into me,' he says. 'After all, it is not as if the child is being taken away and locked up in a prison. If he feels lonely, if he doesn't get along with this Alyosha man, he can, as Ana Magdalena says, be home in half an hour. So why was I so heartbroken? And in front of Dmitri, of all people! Dmitri!'

But Inés' mind is elsewhere. 'I should have packed his warm pyjamas,' she says. 'If I give them to you, will you take them tomorrow?'

Next morning he hands over to Dmitri the pyjamas in a brown paper packet with David's name written on it. 'Warm clothing, from Inés,' he says. 'Don't give it to David himself, he is too scatterbrained. Give it to Ana Magdalena, or better, give it to the young man who looks after the boarders.'

'Alyosha. I will give it to him without fail.'

'Inés frets that David might be cold at night. That is her nature – to fret. By the way, let me apologize for the spectacle I made of myself yesterday. I don't know what got into me.'

'It was love,' says Dmitri. 'You love the boy. It broke your heart to see him turn his back on you like that.'

'Turn his back? You misunderstand. David is not turning his back on us. Far from it. Boarding at the Academy is just temporary, a whim of his, an experiment. When he gets bored with it, or unhappy, he will come home again.'

'Parents always feel heartsore when their young flee the nest,' says Dmitri. 'It's natural. You have a soft heart, I can see that. I have a soft heart too, despite the rough exterior. No need to be ashamed. It is our nature, yours and mine. It is how we were born. We are softies.' He grins. 'Not like that Inés of yours. *Un corazón de cuero.*'

'You have no idea what you are talking about,' he says stiffly. 'There has never been a more devoted mother than Inés.'

'*Un corazón de cuero,*' repeats Dmitri. 'A heart of leather. If you don't believe me, wait and see.'

He stretches out the day's bicycle round for as long as he can, pedalling slowly, dawdling on street corners. The evening yawns before him like a desert. He finds a bar and orders a *vino de paja*, the rough wine he acquired a taste for on the farm. By the time he leaves he is feeling pleasantly befuddled. But before long the oppressive gloom returns. *I must find something to do!* he tells himself. *One cannot live like this, killing time!*

Un corazón de cuero. If anyone is hard of heart it is David, not Inés. Of Inés' love for the child, and his own, there can be no doubt. But is it good for the child that, out of love, they give in so easily to his wishes? Maybe in the institutions of society there resides a blind wisdom. Maybe, instead of treating the boy like a little prince, they should return him to the public schools and let his teachers tame him, turn him into a social animal.

His head aching, he returns to the apartment, shuts himself in his room, and falls asleep. When he wakes it is evening and Inés is home.

'I'm sorry,' he says, 'I was exhausted, I haven't made supper.'

'I have already eaten,' says Inés.

Chapter 9

In the weeks that follow, the fragility of their domestic set-up becomes more and more apparent. Simply put, with the child gone there is no reason why Inés and he should be living together. They have nothing to say to each other; they have next to nothing in common. Inés fills in the silences with chatter about Modas Modernas to which he barely listens. When he is not on his bicycle rounds he keeps to his room, reading the newspaper or dozing. He does not shop, does not cook. Inés begins staying out late, he presumes with Claudia, though she offers no information. Only during the boy's weekend visits is there any semblance of family life.

Then one Friday, when he arrives at the Academy to pick up the boy, he finds the doors locked. After a long hunt he tracks down Dmitri in the museum.

'Where is David?' he demands. 'Where are the children? Where are the Arroyos?'

'They have gone swimming,' says Dmitri. 'Didn't they tell you? They have gone on a trip to Lake Calderón. It's a treat for the boarders, now that the weather is warming up. I would have liked to go too, but alas, I have my duties.'

'When will they be back?'

'If the weather stays fine, on Sunday afternoon.'

'Sunday!'

'Sunday. Don't worry. Your boy will have a wonderful time.'

'But he can't swim!'

'Lake Calderón is the most placid sheet of water in all the wide world. No one has ever drowned there.'

This is the news with which Inés is greeted when she comes home: that the boy has gone off to Lake Calderón on an outing, that they will not see him this weekend.

'And where is Lake Calderón?' she demands.

'Two hours' drive to the north. According to Dmitri, Lake Calderón is an educational experience not to be missed. The children are taken out in boats with glass bottoms to see the under-water life.'

'Dmitri. So now Dmitri is an expert on education.'

'We can drive to Lake Calderón first thing in the morning, if you like. Just to make sure everything is in order. We can say hello to David; if he is unhappy we can bring him back.'

This is what they do. They drive out to Lake Calderón with Bolívar snoozing on the back seat. The sky is cloudless, the day promises to be hot. They miss the turn-off; it is noon before they find the little settlement on the lake, with its single rooming house and its one shop selling ice cream and plastic sandals and fishing tackle and bait.

'I am looking for the place where school groups go,' he says to the girl behind the counter.

'*El centro recreativo*. Follow the road along the lake front. It is about a kilometre further on.'

El centro recreativo is a low, sprawling building giving onto a sandy beach. Disporting themselves on the beach are scores of people, men and women, adults and children, all in the nude. Even at a distance he has no difficulty in recognizing Ana Magdalena.

'Dmitri said nothing about this – this nudism,' he says to Inés. 'What shall we do?'

'Well, I am certainly not taking off my clothes,' she replies.

Inés is a good-looking woman. She has no reason to be ashamed of her body. What she does not say is: *I am not taking off my clothes in front of you.*

'Then let me be the one,' he says. While the dog, set free, lopes off toward the beach, he retires to the back seat and divests himself of his clothes.

Picking his way delicately over the stones, he arrives on the sandy beach just as a boat full of children comes in. A young man with a sweep of dark hair like a raven's wing holds it steady while the children tumble out, splashing in the shallow water, whooping and laughing, naked, David among them. With a start the boy recognizes him. 'Simón!' he calls out, and comes running. 'Guess what we saw, Simón! We saw an eel, and it was eating a baby eel, the baby eel's head was sticking out of the big eel's mouth, it was so funny, you should have seen it! And we saw fishes, lots of fishes. And we saw crabs. That's all. Where is Inés?'

'Inés is waiting in the car. She isn't feeling well, she has a headache. We came to find out what your plans are. Do you want to come home with us or do you want to stay?'

'I want to stay. Can Bolívar stay too?'

'I don't think so. Bolívar isn't used to strange places. He might wander off and get lost.'

'He won't get lost. I will look after him.'

'I don't know. I'll discuss it with Bolívar and see what he wants to do.'

'All right.' And without a further word the boy turns and scampers off after his friends.

The boy does not seem to find it strange that he, Simón, should be standing here in the nude. And indeed his own self-consciousness is evaporating fast among all these naked folk, young and old. But he is aware that he has avoided looking directly at Ana Magdalena. Why? Why is it she alone before whom he feels his nakedness? He has no sexual feeling for her. He is simply not her equal, sexual or otherwise. Yet it is as if something would flash from his eyes if he were to look straight at her, something like an arrow, hard as steel and unmistakable, something he cannot afford.

He is not her equal: of that he is sure. If she were blindfolded and put on exhibition, like one of the statues in Dmitri's museum or like an animal in a cage in a zoo, he could spend hours gazing at her, rapt in admiration at the perfection she represents of a certain kind of creaturely form. But that is not the whole story, not by far. It is not just that she is young and vital while he is old and spent; not just that she is, so to speak, carved out of marble while he is, so to speak, put together from clay. Why did that phrase come at once to mind: *not her equal*? What is the more fundamental difference between the two of them that he senses but cannot put his finger on?

A voice speaks behind him, her voice: 'Señor Simón.' He turns and reluctantly raises his eyes.

On her shoulders there is a dusting of sand; her breasts are rosy, burnt by the sun; at her crotch there is a patch of fur, the lightest shade of brown, so fine that it is near to invisible.

'Are you here alone?' she says.

High shoulders, a long waist. Long legs, firmly muscled, a dancer's legs.

'No – Inés is waiting in the car. We were concerned about David. We were told nothing about this outing.'

She frowns. 'But we sent a note to all the parents. Didn't you receive it?'

'I know of no note. Anyway, all is well that ends well. The children seem to be having a good time. When will you be bringing them back?'

'We haven't decided yet. If the weather stays fine, we may be here the whole weekend. Have you met my husband? Juan, this is señor Simón, David's father.'

Señor Arroyo, master of music and director of the Academy of Dance: this is not how he expected to meet him, in the nude. A large man, not corpulent, not exactly, but no longer young: his flesh, at throat and breast and belly, has begun to sag. His complexion, the whole complexion of his body, even of his bald skull, is a uniform brick red, as if the sun were his natural element. His idea it must have been, this excursion to the beach.

They shake hands. 'It is your dog?' says señor Arroyo, gesturing.

'Yes.'

'A handsome beast.' His voice is low and easy. Together they contemplate the handsome beast. Gazing over the water, Bolívar pays them no heed. A pair of spaniels edge up to him, take turns to smell his genitals; he does not deign to smell theirs.

'I was explaining to your wife,' he, Simón, says. 'As a result of some or other failure of communication, we did not learn in advance about this outing. We thought David would be coming home for the weekend, as usual. That is why we are here. We were a little anxious. But all is well, I see, so we will be leaving now.'

Señor Arroyo regards him with what seems an amused curl of the lip. He does not say, *A failure of communication? Please explain.*

He does not say, *I am sorry you have had a wasted trip.* He does not say, *Would you like to stay for lunch?* He says nothing. No small talk.

Even his eyelids have a baked hue. And then the blue eyes, paler than his wife's.

He collects himself. 'May I ask, how is David getting on with his studies?'

The heavy head nods once, twice, thrice. Now there is a definite smile on the lips. 'Your son has – what shall I call it? – a confidence that is unusual in someone so young. He is not afraid of adventures – adventures of the mind.'

'No, he is not afraid. And he sings well too. I am no musician but I can hear it.'

Señor Arroyo raises a hand and languidly brushes the words away. 'You have done well,' he says. 'You are the one, are you not, who has taken responsibility for raising him. So he tells me.'

His heart swells. So that is what the boy tells people: that he, Simón, is the one who has raised him! 'David has had a varied education, if I may put it that way,' he says. 'You say he is confident. That is true. At times it is more than confidence. He can be headstrong. With some of his teachers that has not gone down well. But for you and señora Arroyo he has the greatest respect.'

'Well, if that is so then we must do our best to deserve it.'

Without his noticing it, señora Arroyo, Ana Magdalena, has slipped away. Now she re-emerges into his field of vision, receding down the lakeshore, tall, graceful, with a cluster of naked children gambolling around her.

'I should be leaving,' he says. 'Goodbye.' And then: 'The numbers, two and three and so forth – I have been struggling to understand your system. I listened carefully to the lecture that señora Arroyo gave, I question David, but I confess I still have difficulty.'

Señor Arroyo raises an eyebrow and waits.

'Counting does not play a great part in my life,' he plunges on. 'I mean, I count apples and oranges like everyone else. I count money. I add and subtract. The ant arithmetic your wife spoke about. But the dance of the two, the dance of the three, the noble numbers and the auxiliary numbers, calling down the stars – that stuff eludes me. Do you ever get beyond two and three in your teaching? Do the children ever get to study proper mathematics – x and y and z? Or is that for later?'

Señor Arroyo is silent. The midday sun beats down on them.

'Can you give me some clue, some fingerhold?' he says. 'I want to understand. Genuinely. I genuinely wish to understand.'

Señor Arroyo speaks. 'You wish to understand. You address me as if I were the sage of Estrella, the man with all the answers. I am not. I do not have answers for you. But let me say a word about answers in general. In my opinion, question and answer go together like heaven and earth or like man and woman. A man goes out and scours the world for the answer to his one great question, *What is it that I lack?* Then one day, if he is lucky, he finds his answer: woman. Man and woman come together, they *are one* – let us resort to that expression – and out of their oneness, their union, comes a child. The child grows up until one day the question comes to him, *What is it that I lack?*, and so the cycle is resumed. The cycle resumes because in the question already lies the answer, like an unborn child.'

'Therefore?'

'Therefore, if we wish to escape the cycle, perhaps we should be scouring the world not for the true answer but for the true question. Perhaps that is what we lack.'

'And how does that help me, señor, to understand the dances you teach my son, the dances and the stars that the dances are supposed to call down, and the place of the dances in his education?'

'Yes, the stars . . . We continue to be puzzled by the stars, even old men like you and me. *Who are they? What do they say to us? What are the laws by which they live?* For a child it is easier. The child does not need to think, for the child can dance. While we stand paralysed, gazing on the gap that yawns between us and the stars – *What an abyss! How will we ever cross it?* – the child simply dances across.'

'David is not like that. He is full of anxiety about gaps. Sometimes paralysed. I have seen it. It is a phenomenon not uncommon among children. A syndrome.'

Señor Arroyo ignores his words. 'The dance is not a matter of beauty. If I wanted to create beautiful figures of movement I would employ marionettes, not children. Marionettes can float and glide as human beings cannot. They can trace patterns of great complexity in the air. But they cannot dance. They have no soul. It is the soul that brings grace to the dance, the soul that follows the rhythm, each step instinct with the next step and the next.

'As for the stars, the stars have dances of their own, but their logic is beyond us; their rhythms too. That is our tragedy. And then there are the wandering stars, the ones who don't follow the dance, like children who don't know arithmetic. *Las estrellas errantes, niños que ignoran la aritmética*, as the poet wrote. To the stars it is given to think the unthinkable, the thoughts that are beyond you and me: the thoughts *before eternity* and *after eternity*, the thoughts *from nothing to one* and *from one to nothing*, and so forth. We mortals have no dance for *from nothing to one*. So, to return to your question about the mysterious x and whether our students at the Academy will ever learn the answer to x, my answer is: Lamentably, I don't know.'

He waits for more but there is no more. Señor Arroyo has had his say. It is his turn. But he, Simón, is lost. He has nothing to offer.

'Be comforted,' says señor Arroyo. 'You came here not to find out about x but because you were concerned for the welfare of your child. You can be assured. He is well. Like other children, young David has no interest in x. He wants to be in the world, to experience this being-alive that is so new and exciting. Now I must go and give my wife a hand. Goodbye, señor Simón.'

He finds his way back to the car. Inés is not there. He dresses hurriedly, whistles for Bolívar. 'Inés!' he says, addressing the dog. 'Where is Inés? Find Inés!'

The dog leads him to Inés, seated not far away under a tree on a little knoll overlooking the lake.

'Where is David?' she says. 'I thought he was coming home with us.'

'David is having a good time, he wants to be with his friends.'

'So when will we see him again?'

'That depends on the weather. If it continues fine they will stay the whole weekend. Don't fret, Inés. He is in good hands. He is happy. Isn't that all that counts?'

'So we are going back to Estrella?' Inés gets up, dusts off her dress. 'I am surprised at you. Doesn't this whole business make you feel sad? First he demands to leave home, now he doesn't even want to spend the weekend with us.'

'It would have happened sooner or later. He has an independent nature.'

'You call it independence but to me it looks as if he is totally under the thumb of the Arroyos. I saw you having a chat with el señor. What was that about?'

'He was explaining his philosophy to me. The philosophy behind the Academy. The numbers and the stars. Calling down the stars and so forth.'

'Is that what you call it: philosophy?'

'No, I don't call it philosophy. Privately I call it claptrap. Privately I call it a load of mystical rubbish.'

'Then why don't we pull ourselves together and remove David from their Academy?'

'Remove him and send him where? To the Academy of Singing, where they will have some nonsensical philosophy of their own to peddle? *Breathe in. Empty your mind. Be one with the cosmos.* To the city schools? *Sit still. Recite after me: one and one is two, two and one is three.* The Arroyos may be full of nonsense, but at least it is harmless nonsense. And David is happy here. He likes the Arroyos. He likes Ana Magdalena.'

'Yes, Ana Magdalena . . . I suppose you have fallen in love with her. You can confess. I won't laugh.'

'In love? No, nothing like that.'

'But you find her attractive.'

'I find her beautiful, in the way that a goddess is beautiful, but I don't find her attractive. It would be – what shall I say? – irreverent to be attracted to her. Maybe even dangerous. She could strike a man dead.'

'Strike you dead! Then you should take precautions. Wear armour. Carry a shield. You told me that the man from the museum, Dmitri, is infatuated with her. Have you warned him she can strike him dead too?'

'No, I haven't. I am not friends with Dmitri. We don't exchange confidences.'

'And the young man – who is he?'

'The young man who went out with the children in the boat? That is Alyosha, the usher, the one who looks after the boarders. He seems nice.'

'You seem to find it easy, being without clothes in front of strangers.'

'Surprisingly easy, Inés. Surprisingly easy. One slips back into being an animal. Animals are not naked, they are simply themselves.'

'I noticed you and your dangerous goddess being yourselves together. That must have been exciting.'

'Don't mock me.'

'I am not mocking you. But why can't you be frank with me? Anyone can see that you have fallen for her, just like Dmitri. Why not admit it instead of talking in circles?'

'Because it is not true. Dmitri and I are different people.'

'Dmitri and you are both men. That's enough for me.'

Chapter 10

The trip to the lake marks a further cooling in relations between Inés and himself. Soon afterwards she informs him that she will be taking a week's leave in order to spend time in Novilla with her brothers. She misses her brothers, is thinking of inviting them to Estrella.

'Your brothers and I have never got on well together,' he says. 'Particularly Diego. If they are going to be staying with you, maybe I should move out.'

Inés does not protest.

'Give me time to find a place of my own,' he says. 'I would prefer not to announce it to David, not yet. Do you agree?'

'Couples get divorced every day and the children come through,' says Inés. 'David will have me, he will have you, we just won't be living together.'

He knows the city's north-east by now like the back of his hand. Without difficulty he finds a room for himself with an ageing couple. The facilities are rudimentary, the electricity tends to cut out unpredictably, but the room is cheap and has its own entrance and is within reach of the city centre. While Inés is at work he removes his belongings from the apartment and installs himself in his new home.

Though he and Inés put on a show of spousal amity for the boy, he is not for a moment deceived. 'Where is your stuff, Simón?' he demands; whereupon he, Simón, has to admit that, for the time being, he has moved out to make way for Diego and perhaps Stefano too.

'Is Diego going to be my uncle or my father?' asks the boy.

'He will be your uncle, as he has always been.'

'And you?'

'I will be what I have always been. I do not change. Things change around me but I am unchanging. You will see.'

If the boy is distressed by the rupture between Inés and him, Simón, he shows no sign of it. On the contrary, he is ebullient, full of stories about his life at the Academy. Ana Magdalena has a waffle machine and makes waffles for the boarders every morning. 'You must buy a waffle machine, Inés, it's brilliant.' Alyosha has taken over the reading of their bedtime stories, and is reading them a story about three brothers and their quest for the sword Madragil, which is also brilliant. Behind the museum Ana Magdalena has a garden with an enclosure where she keeps rabbits and chickens and a lamb. One of the rabbits is naughty and keeps burrowing his way out. Once they found him hiding in the basement of the museum. His favourite among the animals is the lamb, whose name is Jeremiah. Jeremiah does not have a mother, so he has to drink cowsmilk out of a bottle with a rubber teat. Dmitri lets him hold the bottle for Jeremiah.

'Dmitri?'

Dmitri, it turns out, is the one charged with looking after the Academy's menagerie, just as Dmitri is the one charged with bringing wood from the cellar for the big oven and with swabbing the bathroom after the children have had their shower.

'I thought Dmitri worked for the museum. Do the people at the museum know that Dmitri is also employed by the Academy?'

'Dmitri doesn't want money. He does it for Ana Magdalena. He will do anything for her because he loves her and worships her.'

'Loves her and worships her: is that what he says?'

'Yes.'

'Well, that's nice. That's admirable. My concern is that Dmitri may be performing these services for love and worship during time when he is being paid by the museum to guard their pictures. But that is enough about Dmitri. What more can you tell us? Do you like being a boarder? Did we make the right decision?'

'Yes. When I have bad dreams I wake Alyosha up and he lets me sleep in his bed.'

'Is it just you who sleeps in Alyosha's bed?' asks Inés.

'No, anyone who has bad dreams can sleep with Alyosha. He says so.'

'And Alyosha? Whose bed does Alyosha sleep in when he has bad dreams of his own?'

The boy is not amused.

'What about the dancing?' asks he, Simón. 'How is your dancing coming on?'

'Ana Magdalena says I am the best dancer of all.'

'That's nice. When can I persuade you to do a dance for me?'

'Never, because you don't believe in it.'

You don't believe in it. What does he have to believe in before the boy will dance for him? The mumbo-jumbo about the stars?

They eat together – Inés has cooked supper – then it is time for him to take his leave. 'Good night, my boy. I'll come by in the morning. We can take Bolívar for a walk. Maybe there will be a football game in the park.'

'Ana Magdalena says, if you are a dancer you mustn't play football. She says you can strain your muscles.'

'Ana Magdalena knows about lots of things but she doesn't know about football. You are a strong boy. You won't hurt yourself playing football.'

'Ana Magdalena says I mustn't.'

'Very well, I won't force you to play football. But please explain one thing to me. You never obey me, you hardly ever obey Inés, yet you do exactly what Ana Magdalena tells you. Why so?'

There is no reply.

'All right. Good night. I will see you in the morning.'

He trudges back to his lodgings in a bad mood. There was once a time when the boy gave himself heart and soul to Inés, or at least to Inés' vision of him as the little prince in hiding; but those days seem to be over. For Inés it must be dispiriting to find herself supplanted by señora Arroyo. As for him, what place is left for him in the boy's life? Perhaps he should follow the example of Bolívar. Bolívar has all but completed the move into the twilight of a dog's life. He has grown a paunch; sometimes, as he settles down to sleep, he lets loose a sad little sigh. Yet if Inés were so thoughtless as to introduce a puppy into the household – a puppy meant to grow up and take the place of their present guardian – Bolívar would close his jaws around his junior rival's neck and give him a shake until the neck bone snapped. Perhaps that is the kind of father he should become: idle, selfish, and dangerous. Perhaps the boy will respect him then.

Inés leaves on the promised trip to Novilla; for the time being the boy is again his responsibility. On Friday afternoon he is waiting outside the Academy. The bell rings, the students pour out, but there is no sign of David.

He climbs the stairs. The studio is empty. Beyond it an unlit corridor leads to a series of rooms panelled in dark wood, empty of furniture. He passes through a dim space, a dining hall perhaps, with long, battered-looking tables and a sideboard stacked with crockery, and finds himself at the foot of another flight of stairs. From above comes the murmur of a male voice. He ascends, knocks at a closed door. The voice pauses. Then: 'Come in.'

He is in a spacious room lit by skylights, evidently the boarders' dormitory. Seated side by side on one of the beds are Ana Magdalena and Alyosha. A dozen children cluster around them. He recognizes the two Arroyo boys who had danced at the concert, but David is not there.

'I apologize for intruding,' he says. 'I am hunting for my son.'

'David is at his music lesson,' says Ana Magdalena. 'He will be free at four o'clock. Would you like to wait? You can join us. Alyosha is reading us a story. Alyosha, children, this is señor Simón, David's father.'

'I am not intruding?' he says.

'You are not intruding,' says Ana Magdalena. 'Sit down. Joaquín, tell señor Simón what has happened thus far.'

You are not intruding. Sit down. In Ana Magdalena's voice, in her whole bearing, there is an unexpected friendliness. Has the change come about because they were naked together? Was that all that was needed?

Joaquín, the elder of the Arroyo boys, speaks. 'There is a fisherman, a poor fisherman, and one day he catches a fish and he cuts it open and in its stomach he finds a gold ring. He rubs the ring and –'

'To make it sparkle.' It is his younger brother who interrupts him. 'He rubs the ring to make it sparkle.'

'He rubs the ring to make it sparkle and a genie appears and the genie says, "Each time you rub the magic ring I will appear and grant you a wish, you have three wishes, so what is your first wish?" That's all.'

'All-powerful,' says Ana Magdalena. 'Remember, the genie says he is all-powerful and can grant any wish. Alyosha, go on reading.'

He has not looked properly at Alyosha before. The young man has fine, rather beautiful black hair which he combs straight back from his temples, and a complexion as delicate as a girl's. There is no sign that he shaves. He casts his dark, long-lashed eyes down and, in a surprisingly resonant voice, reads.

'Not believing the genie's words, the fisherman decided to test him. "I wish for a hundred fishes to take to the fish market and sell," he said.

'Instantly a great wave broke on the beach and left a hundred fishes at his feet, leaping and flapping as they expired.

'"What is your second wish?" asked the genie.

'Emboldened, the fisherman replied, "I wish for a beautiful girl to be my wife."

'Instantly there appeared, kneeling before the fisherman, a girl so beautiful that she took his breath away. "I am yours, my lord," said the girl.

'"And what is your final wish?" said the genie.

'"I wish to be king of the world," said the fisherman.

'Instantly the fisherman found himself clothed in a robe of golden samite, with a gold crown on his head. An elephant appeared, which lifted him with its trunk and seated him on a throne upon its back. "You have had your final wish. You are king of the world," said the genie. "Farewell." And he vanished in a puff of smoke.

'It was late in the day. The beach was deserted, save for the fisherman and his beautiful bride-to-be and the elephant and the hundred dying fish. "We shall proceed to my village," said the fisherman in his most kingly voice. "Proceed!" But the elephant did not stir. "Proceed!" shouted the fisherman even more loudly; still the elephant did not heed him. "You! Girl!" shouted the king. "Fetch a stick and beat this elephant to make him proceed!" Obediently the girl fetched a stick and beat the elephant until the elephant began to walk.

'As the sun was setting they arrived at the fisherman's village. His neighbours clustered around, marvelling at the elephant and the beautiful girl and the fisherman himself, seated on his throne with the crown on his head. "Behold, I am king of the world, and this is my queen!" said the fisherman. "To show my bounty, on the morrow you shall have a feast of a hundred fishes." The villagers rejoiced and helped the king down from the elephant; he retired to his humble dwelling where he spent the night in the arms of his beautiful bride.

'As soon as day dawned, the villagers set off for the beach to fetch the hundred fishes. But when they arrived they saw nothing but fish bones, for during the night wolves and bears had come down to the beach and gorged themselves. So the villagers came back saying, "O king, wolves and bears have devoured the fishes, catch more fishes for us, we are hungry."

'Out of the folds of his robe the fisherman fetched the gold ring. He rubbed it and rubbed it, but no genie appeared.

'Then the villagers grew angry, saying, "What kind of king are you who cannot feed us?"

'"I am king of all the world," replied the fisherman made king. "If you refuse to recognize me I will remove myself." He turned to his bride of the night. "Bring the elephant," he commanded. "We are departing from this ungrateful village."

'But during the night the elephant had wandered off, throne and all, and no one knew where to find him.

'"Come!" said the fisherman to his bride. "We will walk."

'But his bride refused. "Queens don't walk," she pouted. "I want to ride like a queen on *un palafrén blanco* with a retinue of maidens preceding me beating tambourines."'

The door opens and Dmitri tiptoes into the room followed by David. Alyosha pauses in his reading. 'Come, David,' says Ana Magdalena. 'Alyosha is reading us the story of the fisherman who would be king.'

While David takes a seat by her side Dmitri remains at the door, squatting, with his cap in his hands. Ana Magdalena frowns and gives an abrupt little wave as if ordering him out, but he pays no attention.

'Go on, Alyosha,' says Ana Magdalena, 'and listen carefully, children, because when Alyosha has finished I am going to ask you what we can learn from the story of the fisherman.'

'I know the answer,' says David. 'I have read the story already by myself.'

'You may have read the story, David, but the rest of us have not,' says Ana Magdalena. 'Alyosha, go on.'

'"You are my bride, you will obey me," said the fisherman.

'Haughtily the girl tossed her head. "I am a queen, I do not walk, I ride on *un palafrén*," she repeated.'

'What is a *palafrén*, Alyosha?' asks one of the children.

'A *palafrén* is a horse,' says David. 'Isn't that so, Alyosha?'

Alyosha nods. '"I ride on *un palafrén*."'

'Without a word the king turned his back on his bride and strode off. For many miles he walked until he came to another village. The villagers gathered around him, marvelling at his crown and his samite robe.

'"Behold, I am king of the world," said the fisherman. "Bring me food to eat, for I am hungry."

'"We will bring you food," replied the villagers, "but if you are a king as you say, where is your retinue of followers?"

'"I do not need a retinue of followers to be king," said the fisherman. "Do you not see the crown upon my head? Do as I say. Bring me a feast."

'Then the villagers laughed at him. Instead of bringing him a feast, they knocked the crown off his head and tugged off his samite robe until he stood before them in the humble garb of a fisherman. "You are a pretender!" cried the villagers. "You are just a fisherman! You are no better than us! Go back to where you came from!" And they beat him with staves until he ran away. And thus ended the story of the fisherman who would be king.'

'And thus ended the story,' echoes Ana Magdalena. 'An interesting story, is it not, children. What do you think we can learn from it?'

'I know,' says David, and gives him, Simón, a little sidelong smile as if to say, *Do you see how clever I am here in the Academy?*

'You may know, David, but that is because you have read the story before,' says Ana Magdalena. 'Let us give other children a chance.'

'What happened to the elephant?' The speaker is the younger of the Arroyo boys.

'Alyosha, what happened to the elephant?' says Ana Magdalena.

'The elephant was swept up into the skies by a great whirlwind and deposited back in his forest home, where he lived happily ever after,' says Alyosha evenly.

A look passes from his eyes to hers. For the first time it occurs to him that something might be going on between them, between the director's alabaster-pure wife and the handsome young usher.

'What can we learn from the story of the fisherman?' repeats Ana Magdalena. 'Was the fisherman a good man or a bad man?'

'He was a bad man,' says the younger Arroyo boy. 'He beat the elephant.'

'He didn't beat the elephant, his bride beat the elephant,' says the older Arroyo boy, Joaquín.

'But he made her do it.'

'The fisherman was bad because he was selfish,' says Joaquín. 'He only thought about himself when he was given the three wishes. He should have thought about other people.'

'So what do we learn from the story of the fisherman?' says Ana Magdalena.

'That we should not be selfish.'

'Do we agree, children?' says Ana Magdalena. 'Do we agree with Joaquín that the story warns us against being selfish, that if we are too selfish we will end up being chased away into the desert by our neighbours? David, did you want to say something.'

'The villagers were wrong,' says David. He looks around, lifting his chin in a challenging way.

'Explain,' says Ana Magdalena. 'Give your reasons. Why were the villagers wrong?'

'He was king. They should have bowed down before him.'

From Dmitri, squatting on his heels at the doorway, comes the sound of slow handclapping. 'Bravo, David,' says Dmitri. 'Spoken like a master.'

Ana Magdalena frowns at Dmitri. 'Don't you have duties?' she says.

'Duties to statues? The statues are dead, every one of them, they can take care of themselves.'

'He wasn't a real king,' says Joaquín, who seems to be growing in confidence. 'He was a fisherman pretending to be king. That's what the story says.'

'He was king,' says David. 'The genie made him king. The genie was all-powerful.'

The two boys glare at each other. Alyosha intervenes. 'How do we come to be king?' he asks. 'That is the true question, is it not? How does any of us come to be king? Do we have to meet a genie? Do we have to cut open a fish and find a magic ring?'

'You first have to be a prince,' says Joaquín. 'You can't be a king if you haven't been a prince first.'

'You can,' says David. 'He had three wishes and it was his third wish. The genie made him king of the world.'

Again, from Dmitri, comes slow, resounding handclapping. Ana Magdalena ignores him. 'So what do *you* think we can learn from the story, David?' she asks.

The boy takes a deep breath, as if about to speak, then abruptly shakes his head.

'What?' repeats Ana Magdalena.

'I don't know. I can't see it.'

'Time for us to go, David,' he says, and rises. 'Thank you, Alyosha, for the reading. Thank you, señora.'

This is the boy's first visit to the cramped room where he, Simón, now lives. He makes no comment on it, but drinks his orange juice and eats his biscuits. Then, with Bolívar shadowing them, they go for a walk, exploring the neighbourhood. The neighbourhood is not interesting, just one street after another of narrow-fronted residences. It is Friday evening, however, and people coming home from the week's labour glance curiously at the small boy and the big dog with the cold yellow eyes.

'This is my territory,' says he, Simón. 'This is where I deliver my messages, to all the streets around here. It is not a grand job, but being a stevedore wasn't a grand job either. Each of us finds the level that suits us best, and this is my level.'

They halt at an intersection. Bolívar pads past them into the road. A burly man on a bicycle swerves to avoid him, glances back angrily. 'Bolívar!' exclaims the boy. Lazily Bolívar returns to his side.

'Bolívar behaves as if he were king,' says he, Simón. 'He behaves as if he had met a genie. He thinks everyone should give way before him. He ought to think again. Maybe his wishes are all used up. Or maybe his genie was just made of smoke.'

'Bolívar is king of the dogs,' says the boy.

'Being king of the dogs won't save him from being run over by a car. The king of the dogs is just a dog, in the end.'

For whatever reason, the boy is not his usual lively self. At the table, over their meal of mashed potato and gravy and peas, his eyelids droop. Without protest he settles into his bed on the sofa.

'Sleep tight,' he, Simón, whispers, kissing him on the brow.

'I'm getting tiny-tiny-tiny,' the boy says in a croaky, half-asleep voice. 'I'm getting tiny-tiny-tiny and I'm falling.'

'Let yourself fall,' he whispers. 'I am here to watch over you.'

'Am I a ghost, Simón?'

'No, you are not a ghost, you are real. You are real and I am real. Now sleep.'

In the morning he seems more perky. 'What are we going to do today?' he says. 'Can we go to the lake? I want to sail in the boat again.'

'Not today. We can make an excursion to the lake when Diego and Stefano are here, when we show them the sights. How about a football match instead? I'll buy a newspaper and see who is playing.'

'I don't want to watch football. It's boring. Can we go to the museum?'

'All right. But is it really the museum you want to visit or is it Dmitri? Why do you like Dmitri so much? Is it because he gives you sweets?'

'He talks to me. He tells me things.'

'He tells you stories?'

'Yes.'

'Dmitri is a lonely man. He is always looking for someone to tell his stories to. It's a bit pathetic. He should find himself a girlfriend.'

'He is in love with Ana Magdalena.'

'Yes, so he told me, so he tells anyone who will listen to him. Ana Magdalena must find it embarrassing.'

'He has pictures of women with no clothes on.'

'Well, it doesn't surprise me. That is what men do when they are lonely, some men. They collect pictures of beautiful women and dream of what it would be like to be with them. Dmitri is lonely and he doesn't know what to do about his loneliness, so when he isn't following señora Arroyo around like a dog he looks at pictures. We can't blame him, but he should not be showing his pictures to you. It's not nice, and it will make Inés cross if she hears about it. I'll speak to him. Does he show them to other children as well?'

The boy nods.

'What else can you tell me? What do you and he talk about?'

'About the other life. He says he is going to be with Ana Magdalena in the other life.'

'Is that all?'

'He says I can be with them in the other life.'

'You and who else?'

'Just me.'

'I will definitely speak to him. I will speak to Ana Magdalena too. I am not happy about Dmitri. I don't think you should be seeing so much of him. Now finish your breakfast.'

'Dmitri says he has lust. What is lust?'

'Lust is a condition that grown-ups suffer from, my boy, usually grown men like Dmitri who are by themselves too much without a wife or a girlfriend. It is a kind of ache, like a headache or a stomach ache. It makes them have fantasies. It makes them imagine things that aren't true.'

'Does Dmitri suffer from lust because of Ana Magdalena?'

'David, Ana Magdalena is a married woman. She has a husband of her own to love. She can be a friend to Dmitri but she can't love him. Dmitri needs a woman who will love him for himself. As soon as he finds a woman who loves him he will be cured of all his woes. He won't need to look at pictures anymore, and he won't need to tell every passer-by how much he worships the lady upstairs. But I am sure he is grateful to you for listening to his stories, for being a good friend to him. I am sure it has helped him.'

'He told another boy he is going to kill himself. He is going to shoot a bullet through his head.'

'Which boy was that?'

'Another boy.'

'I don't believe it. The boy must have misunderstood. Dmitri isn't going to kill himself. Besides, he doesn't have a gun. On Monday morning, when I take you to school, I'll have a chat to Dmitri and ask him what is wrong and what we can do to help. Maybe, when we all go to the lake, we can invite Dmitri along. Shall we do that?'

'Yes.'

'Until then, I don't want you to see Dmitri in private. Do you understand? Do you understand what I am saying?'

The boy is silent, refuses to meet his gaze.

'David, do you understand what I am saying? This is a serious matter. You don't know Dmitri. You don't know why he takes you into his confidence. You don't know what is going on in his heart.'

'He was crying. I saw him. He was hiding in the closet and crying.'

'Which closet?'

'The closet with the brooms and stuff.'

'Did he tell you why he was crying?'

'No.'

'Well, when there is something weighing on our heart it often does us good to cry. There is probably something weighing on Dmitri's heart, and now that he has cried his heart is less burdened. I'll talk to him. I'll find out what is wrong. I'll get to the bottom of it.'

Chapter 11

He is as good as his word. On Monday morning, after delivering David to his class, he seeks out Dmitri. He finds him in one of the exhibition rooms, standing on a chair, using a long feather duster to dust a framed painting high on the wall. The painting shows a man and a woman dressed rather formally in black sitting on a lawn in sylvan surroundings, with a picnic cloth spread before them, while in the background a herd of cattle graze peacefully.

'Do you have a moment, Dmitri?' he says.

Dmitri descends and faces him.

'David tells me that you have been inviting children from the Academy into your room. He also tells me you have been show-ing him pictures of naked women. If this is true, I want you to put a stop to it at once. Otherwise there will be serious consequences for you, which I don't need to spell out. Do you understand me?'

Dmitri tilts his cap back. 'You think I am violating these chil-dren's pretty young bodies? Is that what you are accusing me of?'

'I am not accusing you of anything. I am sure your relations with the children are entirely blameless. But children imagine things, they exaggerate things, they talk among themselves, they talk to their parents. The whole business could turn nasty. Surely you see that.'

A young couple wander into the exhibition room, the first visitors of the day. Dmitri returns the chair to its proper place in a corner, then sits down on it, holding the feather duster erect like a spear. 'Entirely blameless,' he says in a low voice. 'You say that to my face: *entirely blameless*? Surely you joke, Simón. Is that your name: Simón?'

The young couple cast them a glance, whisper together, leave the room.

'Next year, Simón, I will celebrate my forty-fifth year in this life. Yesterday I was a stripling and today, in the blink of an eye, I am forty-four, with whiskers and a big belly and a bad knee and everything else that goes with being forty-four. Do you really believe that one can reach such an advanced age and still be *entirely blameless*? Would you say that of yourself? Are you entirely blameless?'

'Please, Dmitri, no speeches. I came to make a request, a polite request. Stop inviting children from the Academy into your room. Stop showing them dirty pictures. Also, stop talking to them about their teacher, señora Arroyo, and your feelings for her. They don't understand.'

'And if I don't stop?'

'If you don't stop I will report you to the museum authorities and you will lose your job. It is as simple as that.'

'As simple as that . . . Nothing in this life is simple, Simón – you ought to know that. Let me tell you about this job of mine. Before I came to the museum I worked in the hospital. Not as a doctor, I hasten to say, I was always the stupid one, never passed my exams, no good at book learning. Dmitri the dumb ox. No, I wasn't a doctor, I was an orderly, doing the jobs no one else wanted to do. For seven years, on and off, I was a hospital orderly. I have told you about it already, if you remember. I don't regret those years. I saw a lot of life, a lot of life and a lot of death. So much death that in the end I had to walk away, couldn't face it anymore. I took this job instead, where there is nothing to do but sit around all day, yawning, waiting for the bell to ring for closing time. If it wasn't for the Academy upstairs, if it wasn't for Ana Magdalena, I would have perished long ago of boredom.

'Why do you think I chat to your little boy, Simón, and to other little ones? Why do you think I play games with them and buy them sweets? Is it because I want to corrupt them? Is it because I want to violate them? No. Believe it or not, I play with them in the hope that some of that fragrance and innocence of theirs will rub off on me, so that I won't turn into a sullen, lonely old man sitting in a corner like a spider, no good to anyone, superfluous, unde-sired. Because what good am I by myself, and what good are you by yourself – yes, you, Simón! – what good are we by ourselves, tired, used-up old men like us? We might as well lock ourselves in the lavatory and put a bullet through our heads. Don't you agree?'

'Forty-four isn't old, Dmitri. You are in the prime of life. You don't need to haunt the corridors of the Arroyos' dance academy. You could get married, you could have children of your own.'

'I could. I could indeed. You think I don't want to? But there is a catch, Simón, there is a catch. The catch is señora Arroyo. I am *encaprichado* with her. Are you familiar with the word? No? You will find it in books. Infatuated. You know it, she knows it, every-one knows it, it is no secret. Even señor Arroyo knows, whose head is up in the clouds most of the time. I am infatuated with señora Arroyo, crazy about her, *loco*, that is the beginning and the end of it. You say, *Give her up, look elsewhere*. But I won't. I am too stupid to do that – too stupid, too simple-minded, too old-fashioned, too faithful. Like a dog. I am not ashamed to say it. I am

Ana Magdalena's dog. I lick the ground where her foot has trod. On my knees. And now you want me to abandon her, just like that, abandon her and find a replacement. *Gentleman, responsible, steady employment, no longer young, seeks respectable widow with view to marriage. Write box 123, include photograph.*

'It won't work, Simón. It is not the woman in box 123 whom I love but Ana Magdalena Arroyo. What kind of husband would I make for box 123, what kind of father, as long as I bear Ana Magdalena's image in my heart? And those children you wish on me, those children of my own: do you think they will love me, children engendered from the loins of indifference? Of course not. They will hate and despise me, which will be exactly what I deserve. Who needs an absent-hearted father?

'So thank you for your considered and considerate advice, but unfortunately I cannot follow it. When it comes to life's great choices, I follow my heart. Why? Because the heart is always right and the head is always wrong. Do you understand?'

He begins to see why David is captivated by this man. No doubt there is an element of posturing in all this talk of extravagant, unrequited love, as well as a perverse kind of boasting. Mockery too: from the beginning he has felt he is singled out for these confidences only because Dmitri regards him as a eunuch or a moon-dweller, alien to the earthly passions. But the performance is a powerful one nonetheless. How wholehearted, how grand, how *true* Dmitri must appear to a boy of David's age, compared with a dry old stick like himself!

'Yes, Dmitri, I understand. You make yourself clear, all too clear. Let me make myself clear too. Your relations with señora Arroyo are your business, not mine. Señora Arroyo is a grown woman, she can take care of herself. But children are a different matter. The

Arroyos are running a school, not an orphanage. You cannot take over their students and adopt them into a family of your own. *They are not your children*, Dmitri, just as señora Arroyo is not your wife. I want you to stop inviting David, my child, the child for whose welfare I am responsible, into your room and showing him dirty pictures. My child or any other child. If you don't put a stop to it I will see to it that you are dismissed. That is all.'

'A threat, Simón? Are you issuing threats?' Dmitri rises from his chair, still holding the feather duster. 'You, a stranger from nowhere, threatening me? Do you think I have no power here?' His lips open in a smile that reveals his yellowed teeth. Lightly he shakes the feathers in his, Simón's, face. 'Do you think I have no friends in higher places?'

He, Simón, steps back. 'What I think is of no consequence to you,' he says coldly. 'I have said what I had to say. Good morning.'

That night it begins to rain. It rains all day too, without interruption or promise of interruption. The bicycle messengers are unable to go out on their rounds. He stays in his room, killing time, listening to music on the radio, dozing, while water drips into a bucket from a leak in the roof.

On the third day of the rains the door to his room bursts open and David stands before him, his clothes sodden, his hair plastered to his scalp.

'I ran away,' he announces. 'I ran away from the Academy.'

'You ran away from the Academy! Come, close the door, take off those wet clothes, you must be icy cold. I thought you liked it at the Academy. Has something happened?' While he talks he fusses around the boy, undressing him, wrapping him in a towel.

'Ana Magdalena is gone. And Dmitri too. They are both gone.'

'I'm sure there is some explanation. Do they know you are here? Does señor Arroyo know? Does Alyosha know?'

The boy shakes his head.

'They will be worried. Let me make you something warm to drink, then I will go out and telephone to say you are safe.'

Donning his yellow oilskin and yellow mariner's cap he goes out into the downpour. From the telephone booth on the street corner he calls the Academy. There is no reply.

He returns to the room. 'No one answers,' he says. 'I will have to go there myself. Wait for me here. Please, please don't run away.'

This time he goes by bicycle. It takes him fifteen minutes, through the downpour. He arrives drenched to the bone. The studio is empty, but in the cavernous dining hall he finds David's comrades the boarders seated at one of the long tables with Alyosha reading to them. Alyosha breaks off and stares at him enquiringly.

'I am sorry to interrupt,' he says. 'I telephoned but there was no reply. I have come to tell you that David is safe. He is at home with me.'

Alyosha blushes. 'I'm sorry. I have been trying to keep everyone together, but sometimes I lose track. I thought he was upstairs.'

'No, he is with me. He said something about Ana Magdalena being gone.'

'Yes, Ana Magdalena is away. We are having a break from classes until she comes back.'

'And when will that be?'

Alyosha shrugs helplessly.

He pedals back to the cottage. 'Alyosha says they are having a break from classes,' he tells the boy. 'He says Ana Magdalena will be back soon. She hasn't run away at all. That is just a nonsense story.'

'It is not nonsense. Ana Magdalena has run away with Dmitri. They are going to be gypsies.'

'Who told you that?'

'Dmitri.'

'Dmitri is a dreamer. He has always dreamed of running away with Ana Magdalena. Ana Magdalena has no interest in him.'

'You never listen to me! They have run away. They are going to have a new life. I don't want to go back to the Academy. I want to go with Ana Magdalena and Dmitri.'

'You want to leave Inés and be with Ana Magdalena?'

'Ana Magdalena loves me. Dmitri loves me. Inés doesn't love me.'

'Of course Inés loves you! She can't wait to get back from Novilla so that she can be with you again. As for Dmitri, he doesn't love anyone. He is incapable of love.'

'He loves Ana Magdalena.'

'He has a passion for Ana Magdalena. That's a different thing. Passion is selfish. Love is unselfish. Inés loves you in an unselfish way. So do I.'

'It's boring being with Inés. It's boring being with you. When is it going to stop raining? I hate the rain.'

'I am sorry to hear you are so bored. As for the rain, I am unfortunately not the emperor of the heavens, so there is nothing I can do to stop it.'

Estrella has two radio stations. He switches to the second station just as the announcer is reporting the closure of the agricultural fair on account of the 'unseasonable' weather. That news is fol-lowed by a long recital of bus services that have been curtailed, and of schools that are suspending classes. 'Estrella's two academies will be closing their gates too, the Academy of Singing and the Academy of Dance.'

'I told you,' says the boy. 'I am never going back to the Academy. I hate it there.'

'A month ago you loved the Academy. Now you hate it. Maybe, David, it is time for you to learn that there are not only two feelings you can have, love and hate, that there are many other feelings too. If you decide to hate the Academy and turn your back on it, you will soon find yourself in one of the public schools, where your teachers won't read you stories about genies and elephants but make you do sums all day, sixty-three divided by nine, seventy-two divided by six. You are a lucky boy, David, lucky and much indulged. I think you should wake up to that fact.'

Having said his say, he goes out in the rain and calls the Academy. This time Alyosha picks up the telephone. 'Alyosha! It is Simón again. I have just heard on the radio that the Academy is going to be closed until the rain stops. Why didn't you tell me? Let me speak to señor Arroyo.'

A long silence. Then: 'Señor Arroyo is busy, he can't come to the telephone.'

'Señor Arroyo, the director of your Academy, is too busy to speak to parents. Señora Arroyo has abandoned her duties and cannot be found. What is going on?'

Silence. From outside the booth a young woman casts him an exasperated look, mouths words, taps her wristwatch. She has an umbrella, but it is flimsy, no proof against the squalls of rain that sweep down on her.

'Alyosha, listen to me. We are coming back, David and I. We are coming at once. Leave the door unlocked. Goodbye.'

He has given up trying to keep dry. They ride to the Academy together, the boy sitting on the crossbar of the heavy old bicycle, peering out from under the yellow oilskin, shouting with pleasure and lifting his feet high as they plough through sheets of water. The traffic lights are not working, the streets are almost empty. On the town square the stallholders have long since packed up and gone home.

A car stands outside the entrance to the Academy. A child whom he recognizes as one of David's classmates sits in the back, his face pressed to the window, while his mother tries to lift a suitcase into the trunk. He goes to her aid.

'Thank you,' she says. 'You are David's father, aren't you? I remember you from the concert. Shall we get out of the rain?'

He and she retreat to the entranceway, while David clambers into the car with his friend.

'Terrible, isn't it?' says the woman, shaking the water from her hair. He recognizes her, remembers her name: Isabella. In her raincoat and high heels she is rather elegant, rather attractive. Her eyes are restless.

'You mean the weather? Yes, I've never known rain like this before. It's like the end of the world.'

'No, I meant the business of señora Arroyo. So unsettling for the children. It had such a good reputation, the Academy. Now I begin to wonder. What are your plans for David? Will you be keeping him here?'

'I don't know. His mother and I need to talk. What exactly do you mean about señora Arroyo?'

'Haven't you heard? They have broken up, the Arroyos, and she has decamped. I suppose one could have foreseen it, the younger woman and the older man. But in the middle of the term, with no warning to the parents. I don't see how the Academy can go on functioning. That is the disadvantage of these small operations – they depend so much on individuals. Well, we must be off. How are we going to separate the children? You must be proud of David. Such a clever boy, I hear.'

She raises the collar of her raincoat, braves the rain, raps on the window of the car. 'Carlos! Carlitos! We are leaving now! Goodbye, David. Maybe you can come and play one day soon. We will give your parents a ring.' A quick wave and she drives off.

The doors to the studio stand open. As they mount the stairs they hear organ music, a swift bravura passage played over and over again. Alyosha is waiting for them, his face strained. 'Is it still raining out there?' he says. 'Come, David, give us a hug.'

'Don't be sad, Alyosha,' says the boy. 'They have gone to a new life.'

Alyosha gives him, Simón, a puzzled glance.

'Dmitri and Ana Magdalena,' the boy patiently explains. 'They have gone to a new life. They are going to be gypsies.'

'I am totally confused, Alyosha,' says he, Simón. 'I hear one story after another, and I don't know which to believe. It is imperative that I speak to señor Arroyo. Where is he?'

'Señor Arroyo is playing,' says Alyosha.

'So I hear. Nevertheless, may I speak to him?'

The quick, brilliant passage he had heard is now being woven together with a heavier passage in the bass that seems obscurely related to it. There is no sorrow in the music, no pensiveness, nothing to suggest that the musician has been abandoned by his beautiful young wife.

'He has been at the keyboard since six this morning,' says Alyosha. 'I don't think he wants to be interrupted.'

'Very well, I have time, I will wait. Can you see to it that David puts on dry clothes? And may I use the telephone?'

He calls Modas Modernas. 'This is Inés' friend Simón. Can someone please pass on a message to Inés in Novilla? Tell her there is a crisis at the Academy and she should come home without delay . . . No, I don't have a number for her . . . Just say *a crisis at the Academy*, she will understand.'

He sits down and waits for Arroyo. If he were not so exasperated he might be able to enjoy the music, the ingenious way in which the man interweaves motifs, the harmonic surprises, the logic of his resolutions. A true musician, no doubt about that, consigned to the role of schoolteacher. No wonder he is disinclined to face irate parents.

Alyosha returns bearing a plastic bag containing the boy's wet clothes. 'David is saying hello to the animals,' he reports.

Then the boy comes rushing in. 'Alyosha! Simón!' he shouts. 'I know where he is! I know where Dmitri is! Come!'

They follow the boy down the back stairs into the vast, dimly lit basement of the museum, past racks of scaffolding, past canvases stacked pell-mell against the walls, past a clutch of marble nudes roped together, until they come to a little cubicle in a corner, made of sheets of plywood nailed together in a slapdash way, roofless. 'Dmitri!' the boy shouts, and beats on the door. 'Alyosha is here, and Simón!'

There is no reply. Then he, Simón, notices the door to the cubicle is sealed with a padlock. 'There is no one in there,' he says. 'It is locked from the outside.'

'He *is* there!' says the boy. 'I can hear him! Dmitri!'

Alyosha drags one of the scaffolding panels across and leans it against a wall of the cubicle. He ascends, peers in, hastily descends.

Before anyone can stop him David has scaled the scaffolding too. At the top he visibly freezes. Alyosha climbs up and brings him down.

'What is it?' asks he, Simón.

'Ana Magdalena. Go. Take David with you. Call an ambulance. Say there has been an accident. Tell them to come quickly.' Then his legs buckle and he kneels on the floor. His face is pale. 'Go, go, go!' he says.

Everything that follows happens in a rush. The ambulance arrives, then the police. The museum is cleared of visitors; a guard is placed at the entrance; the stairway to the basement is barred. With the two Arroyo boys and the remaining boarders in tow, Alyosha retreats to the top floor of the building. Of señor Arroyo there is no sign: the organ loft is empty.

He approaches one of the police officers. 'May we leave?' he asks.

'Who are you?'

'We are the people who discovered . . . who discovered the body. My son David is a student here. He is very upset. I would like to take him home.'

'I don't want to go home,' announces the boy. He has a set, stubborn look; the shock that had silenced him seems to have worn off. 'I want to see Ana Magdalena.'

'That is certainly not going to happen.'

A whistle sounds. Without a word the officer abandons them. At the same moment the boy takes off across the studio, running with his head down like a little bull. He, Simón, catches up with him only at the foot of the stairs, where two ambulancemen, bearing a stretcher draped in a white sheet, are trying to get past a knot of people. The sheet catches, uncovering for a moment the deceased señora Arroyo as far down as her naked bosom. The left side of her face is blue, almost black. Her eyes are wide open. Her upper lip is drawn back in a snarl. Swiftly the ambulancemen replace the sheet.

A uniformed police officer takes the boy by the arm, restraining him. 'Let me go!' he shouts, struggling to be free. 'I want to save her!'

The police officer lifts him effortlessly into the air and holds him there, kicking. He, Simón, does not intervene, but waits until the stretcher has been lodged in the ambulance and the doors have slammed shut.

'You can let him go now,' he says to the officer. 'I will take over. He is my son. He is upset. She was his teacher.'

He has neither the energy nor the spirit to ride the bicycle. Side by side he and the boy trudge through the monotonous rain back to the cottage. 'I'm getting wet again,' complains the boy. He drapes the oilskin over him.

They are greeted at the door by Bolívar, in his usual stately fashion. 'Sit close to Bolívar,' he instructs the boy. 'Let him warm you. Let him give you some of his heat.'

'What is going to happen to Ana Magdalena?'

'She will be at the hospital by now. I am not going to talk about it any further. It has been enough for one day.'

'Did Dmitri kill her?'

'I have no idea. I don't know how she died. Now, there is something I want you to tell me. That little room where we found her – was that the room where Dmitri took you to show you pictures of women?'

'Yes.'

Chapter 12

The next day, the first day of clear skies after the big rains, Dmitri turns himself in. He presents himself at the front desk of police headquarters. 'It was I,' he announces to the young woman behind the desk, and when she fails to understand produces the morning's newspaper and taps the headline 'DEATH OF BALLERINA', with a photograph of Ana Magdalena, head and shoulders, beautiful in her rather icy way. 'It was I who killed her,' he says. 'I am the guilty one.'

In the hours that follow he writes for the police a full and detailed account of what happened: how, on a pretext, he persuaded Ana Magdalena to accompany him to the basement of the museum; how he forced himself on her and afterwards strangled her; how he locked the body in the cubicle; how for two days and two nights he wandered the streets of the city, indifferent to cold and rain, mad, he writes, though mad with what he does not say (with guilt? with grief?), until, coming upon the newspaper on a news-stand, with the photograph whose eyes, as he puts it, pierced him to the soul, he came to his senses and gave himself up, 'resolved to pay his debt'.

All of this comes out at the first hearing, which is held amid intense public interest, nothing so extravagant having occurred in Estrella within living memory. Señor Arroyo is not present at the hearing: he has bolted the doors of the Academy and will speak to no one. He, Simón, tries to attend, but the throng outside the tiny courtroom is packed so tight that he gives up. From the radio he learns that Dmitri has admitted his guilt and refused legal assistance, even though the magistrate has explained to him that this is neither the time nor the place to enter a plea. 'I have done the worst thing in the world, I have killed the person I love,' he is reported to have said. 'Lash me, hang me, break my bones.' From the courtroom he has been conveyed back to his cell, enduring on the way a barrage of gibes and insults from onlookers.

Responding to his call, Inés has returned from Novilla, accompanied by her elder brother, Diego. David moves back into the apartment with them. Since there are no classes to attend, he is free to play football with Diego all day. Diego, he reports, is 'brilliant' at football.

He, Simón, meets Inés for lunch. They discuss what is to be done about David. 'He seems his normal self, he seems to have got over the shock,' he tells her, 'but I have my doubts. No child can be exposed to a sight like that and not suffer after-effects.'

'He should never have gone to that Academy,' says Inés. 'We should have hired a tutor, like I said. What a calamity those Arroyos have turned out to be!'

He demurs. 'It was hardly señora Arroyo's fault that she was murdered, or her husband's, for that matter. One can cross paths with a monster like Dmitri anywhere. To look on the positive side, at least David has learned a lesson about adults and where their passions can lead them.'

Inés sniffs. 'Passions? Do you call rape and murder passions?'

'No, rape and murder are crimes, but you cannot deny that Dmitri was driven to them by passion.'

'So much the worse for passion,' says Inés. 'If there were less passion around the world would be a safer place.'

They are in a cafe across the street from Modas Modernas, with tables packed tightly together. Their neighbours, two well-dressed women who may well belong to Inés' clientele, have fallen silent and are listening in to what has begun to sound like a quarrel. Therefore he withholds what he had been about to say (*Passion*, he had been about to say – *what do you know about passion, Inés?*) and remarks instead: 'Let us not stray into deep water. How is Diego? What does he think of Estrella? How long will he be staying? Is Stefano going to join you?'

No, he learns, Stefano will not be coming to Estrella. Stefano is entirely under the thumb of his girlfriend, who does not want him to leave her. As for Diego, he has not formed a favourable impression of Estrella. He calls it *atrasada*, backward; he cannot understand what Inés is doing here; he wants her to come back to Novilla with him.

'And might you do that?' he asks. 'Might you move back to Novilla? I need to know because where David goes I go.'

Inés does not reply, plays with her teaspoon.

'What about the shop?' he says. 'How will Claudia feel if you suddenly abandon her?' He leans closer across the table. 'Tell me honestly, Inés, are you still as devoted to David as ever?'

'What do you mean, *am I still devoted?*'

'I mean, are you still the boy's mother? Do you still love him or are you growing away from him? Because, I must warn you, I cannot be both father and mother.'

Inés rises. 'I have to get back to the shop,' she says.

★ ★ ★

The Academy of Singing is a very different place from the Academy of Dance. Housed in an elegant glass-fronted building, it is situated on a leafy square in the most expensive quarter of the town. He and David are ushered into the office of señora Montoya, the vice-principal, who greets them coolly. Following the closure of the Academy of Dance, she informs him, the Academy of Singing has received a small flood of applications from ex-students. David's name can be added to the list, but his prospects are not favourable: preference will be given to the applicants who have had formal instruction in music. Furthermore, he, Simón, should take note that fees at the Academy of Singing are considerably higher than at the Academy of Dance.

'David took music lessons with señor Arroyo himself,' he says. 'He has a good voice. Will you not give him a chance to prove himself? He excelled at dancing. He could excel at singing too.'

'Is that what he wants to be in life: a singer?'

'David, you heard the señora's question. Do you want to be a singer?'

The boy does not reply, but stares evenly out of the window.

'What do you want to do with your life, young man?' asks señora Montoya.

'I don't know,' says the boy. 'It depends.'

'David is six years old,' says he, Simón. 'One can't expect a six-year-old to have a life plan.'

'Señor Simón, if there is one trait that unites all students at our Academy, from the youngest to the oldest, it is a passion for music. Do you have a passion for music, young man?'

'No. Passions are bad for you.'

'Indeed! Who told you that – that passions are bad for you?'

'Inés.'

'And who is Inés?'

'Inés is his mother,' he, Simón, intervenes. 'I think you mis-understood Inés, David. She was referring to physical passion. A passion for singing is not a physical passion. Why don't you sing for señora Montoya, so that she can hear what a good voice you have? Sing that English song you used to sing to me.'

'No. I don't want to sing. I hate singing.'

He takes the boy to visit the three sisters on their farm. They are as warmly received as ever, and treated to little iced cakes and Roberta's home-made lemonade. The boy sets off on a cir-cuit of the stables and the stalls, reacquainting himself with old friends. During his absence he, Simón, relates the story of the interview with señora Montoya. 'A passion for music,' he says: 'imagine asking a six-year-old whether he has a passion for music. Children may have enthusiasms but they can't yet have passions.'

He has grown to like the sisters. To them he feels he can pour out his heart.

'I have always thought the Academy of Singing a rather pre-tentious institution,' says Valentina. 'But they have high standards, there is no doubt about that.'

'If by some miracle David were to be admitted, would you be prepared to assist with his fees?' He repeats the figure he has been given.

'Of course,' says Valentina without hesitation. Consuelo and Alma nod in agreement. 'We are fond of David. He is an excep-tional child. He has a great future ahead of him. Though not necessarily on the operatic stage.'

'How is he coping with the shock, Simón?' asks Consuelo. 'He must have found it terribly distressing.'

'He has dreams about señora Arroyo. He had grown very close to her, which surprised me, because I found her rather cold, cold and forbidding. But he took to her from the beginning. There must have been some quality he found in her that I missed.'

'She was very beautiful. Very classical. Didn't you find her beautiful?'

'Yes, she was beautiful. But to a small boy beauty is hardly a consideration.'

'I suppose not. Tell me: do you think she was blameless in the whole sad affair?'

'Not wholly. There had been a long history between her and Dmitri. Dmitri was obsessed with her, he worshipped the ground she trod on. So he told me, so he told everyone who would listen to him. Yet she treated him without consideration. She treated him like dirt, in fact. I saw it myself. Is it any wonder that he went berserk in the end? Of course I am not trying to excuse him . . .'

David comes back from his tour. 'Where is Rufo?' he demands.

'He was ill, we had him put to sleep,' answers Valentina. 'Where are your shoes?'

'Roberta made me take them off. Can I see Rufo?'

'Putting someone to sleep is a euphemism, my boy. Rufo is dead. Roberta is going to find us a puppy who will grow up to be a watchdog in his place.'

'But where is he?'

'I can't say. I don't know. We left that to Roberta to take care of.'

'She didn't treat him like dirt.'

'I'm sorry – who didn't treat whom like dirt?'

'Ana Magdalena. She didn't treat Dmitri like dirt.'

'Have you been eavesdropping? That's not nice, David. You shouldn't eavesdrop.'

'She didn't treat him like dirt. She was just pretending.'

'Well, you know better than I do, I am sure. How is your mother?'

He, Simón, intervenes. 'I am sorry Inés can't be here, but she has a brother visiting from Novilla. He is staying in our apartment. I have moved out for the time being.'

'His name is Diego,' says the boy. 'He hates Simón. He says Simón is *una manzana podrida*. He says Inés should run away from Simón and come back to Novilla. What does it mean, *una manzana podrida*?'

'A rotten apple.'

'I know, but what does it *mean*?'

'I don't know. Do you want to tell him, Simón, what *una manzana podrida* is, since you are the *manzana* in question?'

The three sisters dissolve in laughter.

'Diego has been cross with me for a long time for taking his sister away from him. In his view of things, he and Inés and their younger brother were living happily together until I appeared on the scene and stole Inés. Which is entirely false, of course, a complete misrepresentation of the facts.'

'Oh? And what is the truth?' says Consuelo.

'I didn't steal Inés. Inés has no feelings for me. She is David's mother. She watches over him, and I watch over the two of them. That is all.'

'Very strange,' says Consuelo. 'Very unusual. But we believe you. We know you and we believe you. We don't think you are *una manzana podrida* at all.' Her sisters nod in agreement. 'Therefore you, young man, should go back to this brother of Inés and inform him that he has made a big mistake about Simón. Will you do that?'

'Ana Magdalena had a passion for Dmitri,' says the boy.

'I don't think so,' says he, Simón. 'It was the other way around. It was Dmitri who had the passion. It was his passion for Ana Magdalena that led him to do bad things.'

'You always say that passion is bad,' says the boy. 'Inés too. You both hate passion.'

'Not at all. I don't hate passion, that is a complete untruth. Nevertheless, one can't ignore the bad consequences of passion. What do you think, Valentina, Consuelo, Alma: is passion good or bad?'

'I think passion is good,' says Alma. 'Without passion the world would stop going round. It would be a dull and empty place. In fact' – she looks to her sisters – 'without passion we wouldn't be here at all, not one of us. Nor the pigs nor the cows nor the chickens. We are all here because of passion, someone's passion for someone else. You hear it in the springtime, when the air is thick with bird calls, each bird searching for a mate. If that isn't passion, what is? Even the molecules. We wouldn't have water if oxygen didn't have a passion for hydrogen.'

Of the three sisters it is Alma he likes best, though not with a passion. She has no trace of her sisters' good looks. She is short, even dumpy; her face is round and pleasant but without character; she wears little wire-rimmed glasses that do not suit her. Is she a full sister to the other two or only a half-sister? He does not know them well enough to ask.

'You don't think there are two kinds of passion, Alma, good passion and bad passion?' says Valentina.

'No, I think there is just one kind of passion, the same everywhere. What are your thoughts, David?'

'Simón says I am not allowed to have thoughts,' says the boy. 'Simón says I am too young. He says I have to be old like him before I can have thoughts.'

'Simón is full of nonsense,' says Alma. 'Simón is turning into a shrivelled old *manzana*.' Again the sisters dissolve in laughter. 'Pay no attention to Simón. Tell us what *you* think.'

The boy steps to the middle of the floor and without preamble, in his socks, begins to dance. At once he, Simón, recognizes the dance. It is the same dance that the elder Arroyo boy performed at the concert; but David is doing it better, with more grace and authority and conviction, even though the other boy was the son of the master of the dance. The sisters watch in silence, absorbed, as the boy traces his complex hieroglyph, avoiding with ease the fussy little tables and stools of the parlour.

You dance for these women yet you won't dance for me, he thinks. *You dance for Inés. What do they have that I do not?*

The dance comes to its end. David does not take a bow – that is not the way of the Academy – but for a moment he does stand erect and still before them with his eyes closed and a rapt little smile on his lips.

'Bravo!' says Valentina. 'Was that a dance of passion?'

'It is a dance to call down Three,' says the boy.

'And passion?' says Valentina. 'Where does passion come into the picture?'

The boy does not answer but, in a gesture that he, Simón, has not seen before, places three fingers of his right hand over his mouth.

'Is this a charade?' asks Consuelo. 'Must we guess?'

The boy does not stir, but his eyes sparkle mischievously.

'I understand,' says Alma.

'Then perhaps *you* can explain it to us,' says Consuelo.

'There is nothing to explain,' says Alma.

When he told the sisters the boy was having dreams of Ana Magdalena, it was less than the whole truth. In all their time together, first with him, then with Inés, the boy had been able to fall asleep at night without a fuss, to sleep deeply and wake up bright and full of energy. But since the discovery in the basement of the museum there has been a change. Now he regularly appears at Inés' bedside during the night, or at his bedside when he is visiting him, whimpering, complaining of bad dreams. In his dreams Ana Magdalena appears to him, blue from head to foot and carrying a baby which is 'tiny, tiny, tiny, as tiny as a pea'; or else she opens her hand and the baby is revealed in her palm, curled up like a little blue slug.

He tries his best to console the boy. 'Ana Magdalena loved you very much,' he says. 'That is why she visits you in your dreams. She comes to say goodbye and to tell you not to have any more dark thoughts because she is at peace in the next life.'

'I had a dream about Dmitri too. His clothes were all wet. Is Dmitri going to kill me, Simón?'

'Of course not,' he reassures him – 'why would he want to do that? Besides, it is not the real Dmitri you are seeing, just a Dmitri made of smoke. Wave your hands like this' – he waves his hands – 'and he will go away.'

'But did his penis make him kill people? Did his penis make him kill Ana Magdalena?'

'Your penis doesn't make you do things. Something else entered Dmitri to make him do what he did, something strange that none of us understand.'

'I'm not going to have a penis like Dmitri when I grow up. If my penis grows big I am going to cut it off.'

He reports the conversation to Inés. 'He seems to be under the impression that grown-ups are trying to kill each other when they make love, that strangling is the culmination of the act. He also seems to have seen Dmitri naked at some time. Everything is confused in his mind. If Dmitri says he loves him, it means he wants to rape him and strangle him. How I wish we had never laid eyes on the man!'

'The mistake was in sending him to their so-called Academy in the first place,' says Inés. 'I never trusted that Ana Magdalena.'

'Have a little charity,' he says. 'She is dead. We are alive.'

He bids Inés have more charity, but was there not, in truth, something strange about Ana Magdalena – stranger than strange, inhuman? Ana Magdalena and her pack of children, like a wolf mother with her cubs. Eyes that saw straight through you. Even in the all-devouring fire, hard to believe those eyes will ever be consumed.

'When I die will I go blue like Ana Magdalena?' asks the boy.

'Of course not,' he replies. 'You will go straight to the next life. You will be a bright new person there. It will be exciting. It will be an adventure, just as this life has been an adventure.'

'But if I don't go to the next life, will I go blue?'

'Trust me, my boy, there will always be a next life. Death is nothing to be afraid of. It is over in a flash, then the next life begins.'

'I don't want to go to the next life. I want to go to the stars.'

Chapter 13

The courts of justice in Estrella have as their mandate the recovery, rehabilitation and salvation (*recuperación, rehabilitación y salvación*) of offenders: so much he has learned from his fellow bicycle messengers. From this it follows that there are two kinds of trial at law: the long kind, in which the accused contests the charge and the court must determine his guilt or innocence; and the short kind, in which the accused admits his guilt and the task of the court is to prescribe the appropriate remedial penalty.

Dmitri has, from the first, admitted his guilt. He has signed his name to not one but three confessions, each more copious than the previous, relating in detail how he violated and then strangled Ana Magdalena Arroyo. He has been given every opportunity to minimize his transgression (*Had he been drinking on the fatal night? Had the victim died by misadventure in the course of erotic play?*) but has refused them all. What he did was inexcusable, he says, unforgivable. Whether what he did is forgivable or unforgivable is not for him to decide, reply his interrogators; what he must say is *why* he did what he did. This is the point at which the third confession comes to an abrupt stop. 'The accused refused to cooperate further,' report his interrogators. 'The accused became foul-mouthed and violent.'

Proceedings are set for the last day of the month, when Dmitri will appear before a judge and two assessors for sentencing.

Two days before the trial a pair of uniformed officers knock at the door of his, Simón's, rented room and deliver a message: Dmitri has requested to see him.

'Me?' he says. 'Why should he want to see me? He barely knows me.'

'No idea,' say the officers. 'Please come with us.'

They drive him to the police cells. It is six in the evening; a change of shift is taking place, prisoners in the cells are about to receive their supper; he has to kick his heels for quite a while before he is led into an airless room with a vacuum cleaner in one corner and two mismatched chairs, where Dmitri – his hair neatly cut, wearing sharply ironed khaki trousers and a khaki shirt and sandals, looking considerably smarter than in his old days as a museum attendant – awaits him.

'How are you, Simón?' Dmitri greets him. 'How is the fair Inés, and how is that youngster of yours? I think of him often. I loved him, you know. I loved them all, the little dancers from the Academy. And they loved me. But it is gone now, all gone.'

He, Simón, is irritated enough at being called out to visit the man; being treated to this sentimental patter brings him to a boil. 'You bought their affection with sweets,' he says. 'What do you want from me?'

'You are cross, and I can see why. I have done a terrible thing. I have brought grief to many hearts. My behaviour has been inexcusable, inexcusable. You are right to turn your back on me.'

'What do you want, Dmitri? Why am I here?'

'You are here, Simón, because I trust you. I have cast my mind over all my acquaintance, and you are the one I trust most. Why do I trust you? Not because I know you well – I don't know you well, just as you don't know me well. But I trust you. You are a trustworthy man, a man worthy of trust. Anyone can see that. And you are discreet. I myself am not discreet but I admire discretion in others. If I had another life I would choose to be a discreet, trustworthy man. But this is the life I have, the life allotted to me. I am, alas, what I am.'

'Get to the point, Dmitri. Why am I here?'

'If you go down to the storage area of the museum, if you stand at the bottom of the stairs and look to your right, you will see three grey filing cabinets against the wall. The filing cabinets are locked. I used to have a key, but the people here took it away from me. However, the cabinets are easy enough to break into. Push a screwdriver into the crack above the lock and give it a smart blow. The metal strip that holds the drawers shut will buckle. You will see for yourself once you try. It is easy.

'In the bottom drawer of the middle cabinet – *the bottom drawer of the middle cabinet* – you will find a small case of the kind that schoolchildren use. It contains papers. I want you to burn them. Burn the whole lot, without looking at them. Can I trust you to do that?'

'You want me to go to the museum and break open a filing cabinet and steal papers and destroy them. What other criminal acts do you want me to commit on your behalf because you cannot commit them yourself because you are behind bars?'

'Trust me, Simón. I trust you, you must trust me. That little case has nothing to do with the museum. It belongs to me. It contains private possessions. In a few days I am going to be sentenced, and who knows what the sentence will be? Never again, in all likelihood, will I see Estrella, never again pass through the doors of the museum. In the city I used to call my own I will be forgotten, consigned to oblivion. And that will be right, right and just and good. I don't want to be remembered. I don't want to linger on in the popular memory just because the newspapers happened to get their hands on my most private possessions. Do you understand?'

'I understand but I do not approve. I will not do as you request. Instead I will do the following. I will go to the director of the museum and I will say, "Dmitri, who used to work here, tells me there are private possessions of his on the premises, papers and so forth. He has asked me to recover them and restore them to him in jail. Do I have your permission to do so?" If the director agrees, I will bring the papers to you. Then you can dispose of them as you wish. So much I will do for you, but nothing illegal.'

'No, Simón, no, no, no! You can't bring them here, it is too risky! No one must see those papers, not even you!'

'The last thing in the world I want is to see these so-called private papers of yours. I am sure they consist of nothing but filth.'

'Yes! Exactly! Filth! Which is why they must be destroyed! So that there shall be less filth in the world!'

'No. I refuse to do it. Find someone else.'

'There is no one else, Simón, no one I trust. If you do not help me, no one will. It will be only a matter of time before someone finds them and sells them to the newspapers. Then scandal will erupt again, and all the old wounds will be reopened. You can't allow that to happen, Simón. Think of the children who befriended me and brightened my days. Think of your youngster.'

'Scandal indeed. The truth is, you don't want your collection of filthy pictures to be made public because you want people to think well of you. You want them to think of you as a man of passion, not as a criminal with an appetite for pornography. I am leaving now.' He raps on the door, which is opened at once. 'Good night, Dmitri.'

'Good night, Simón. No hard feelings, I hope.'

The day of the trial arrives. The *crime passionnel* at the museum is a talking point all over Estrella, as he has learned during his bicycle rounds. Though he makes sure he is at the courthouse well ahead of time, there is already a press of people at the doors. He pushes his way into the foyer, where he is confronted with a large printed notice: *Change of venue. The sitting of the court scheduled for 8.30 a.m. has been rescheduled. It will be held at 9.30 a.m. in the Teatro Solar.*

The Teatro Solar is the largest theatre in Estrella. On the way there he falls into conversation with a man who has with him a child, a little girl not much older than David.

'Going to the trial?' says the man.

He nods in reply.

'A big day,' says the man. The child, dressed all in white with a red ribbon in her hair, flashes him a smile.

'Your daughter?' he says.

'My eldest,' replies the man.

He glances around and notices several other children in the crowd pressing toward the theatre.

'Do you think it is a good idea to bring her along?' he asks. 'Isn't she a bit young for this kind of thing?'

'A good idea? It depends,' says the man. 'If there is a lot of legal palaver and she gets bored I may have to take her home. But I am hoping it will be short and to the point.'

'I have a son of about the same age,' he says. 'I must say I would never think of bringing him along.'

'Well,' says the man, 'I suppose there are different points of view. As I see it, a big event like this can be educative – bring it home to youngsters how dangerous it can be to get involved with their teachers.'

'The man on trial was never, as far as I know, a teacher,' he replies tartly. Then they are at the entrance to the theatre, and father and daughter are swallowed up in the crowd.

The stalls have already filled up, but he finds a place on the balcony in sight of the stage, where a long bench covered in green baize has been set up, presumably for the judges.

Nine-thirty arrives and passes. The auditorium is becoming hot and stuffy. New arrivals press in behind till he is jammed tight against the rail. Below, people are sitting in the passages. An enterprising young man is going up and down selling bottled water.

Then there is movement. The lights over the stage come on. Led by a uniformed officer, Dmitri emerges, shackled at the ankles. Blinded, he stops and stares out over the audience. His escort seats him in a small roped-off space.

All is still. From the wings emerge the three judges, or rather the presiding judge and his two assessors, wearing red robes. With a great heave the crowd comes to its feet. The theatre has a capacity for, he would guess, two hundred; but there are at least twice as many present.

The crowd settles. The judge-in-chief says something inaudible. The officer guarding Dmitri leaps forward and adjusts the microphone.

'You are the prisoner known as Dmitri?' says the judge. He nods to the officer, who sets before Dmitri a microphone of his own.

'Yes, Your Honour.'

'And you are accused of violating and killing one Ana Magdalena Arroyo on the fifth day of March this year.'

It is not a question but a statement. Nonetheless Dmitri replies: 'The violation and the murder took place on the night of the fourth of March, Your Honour. This error in the record I have pointed out before. The fourth of March was Ana Magdalena's last day on earth. It was a terrible day, terrible for me but even more terrible for her.'

'And you have confessed your guilt on both charges.'

'Three times. I have confessed three times. I am guilty, Your Honour. Sentence me.'

'Patience. Before you are sentenced you will have the right to address the court, a right which I hope you will make use of. First you will have an opportunity to exculpate yourself, then later you will have an opportunity to plead in mitigation. Do you understand what those terms mean: exculpation, mitigation?'

'I understand the terms perfectly, Your Honour, but they have no relevance to my case. I do not exculpate myself. I am guilty. Judge me. Sentence me. Come down on me with the full weight of the law. I will not murmur, I promise.'

There is a rustle among the crowd below. 'Judge him!' comes a cry. 'Be quiet!' comes an answering cry. There are murmurs, low hisses.

The judge glances questioningly at his colleagues, first at the one, then at the other. He raises his gavel and brings it down once, twice, thrice. The rustling ceases, silence falls.

'I address myself to all of you who have taken the trouble to come here today to see justice done,' he says. 'I remind you most earnestly that justice is not done in haste, nor by acclamation, and certainly not by setting aside the protocols of the law.' He turns to Dmitri. 'Exculpation. You say that you cannot or will not exculpate yourself. Why not? Because, you say, your guilt is undeniable. I ask: Who are you to pre-empt these proceedings and decide the question before this court, which is precisely the question of your guilt?

'*Your* guilt: let us take a moment to ponder that phrase. What does it mean, what does it ever mean, to speak of *my guilt* or *your guilt* or *our guilt* in respect of some action or other? What if we were not ourselves, or not fully ourselves, when the action in question was performed? Was the action then *ours*? Why, when people have performed heinous deeds, do they commonly say afterwards, *I cannot explain why I did what I did, I was beside myself, I was not myself*? You stand before us today and assert your guilt. You claim your guilt is undeniable. But what if, at the moment when you make that claim, you are not yourself or fully yourself? These are only some of the issues which the court has a duty to raise and then settle. It is not up to you, the accused, the man in the very eye of the storm, to seal them off.

'You say further that you do not want to save yourself. But your salvation is not a matter that rests in your hands. If we, your judges, do not do our best to save you, following scrupulously the letter of the law, then we will have failed to save the law. Of course we have a responsibility to society, a grave and onerous responsibility, to shield it from rapists and murderers. But we have an equal responsibility to save you the accused from yourself, in the event that you are or were not yourself, as the law understands being oneself to be. Am I clear?'

Dmitri is silent.

'So much for the matter of exculpation, where you refuse to plead. I move on to the matter of mitigation, where again you say you will refuse to offer a plea. Let me tell you, as one man speaking to another, Dmitri: I can understand that you may wish to act honourably and accept without murmur the sentence pronounced on you. I can understand that you should not wish to shame yourself in public by seeming to crawl before the law. But that is the very reason why we have lawyers. When you instruct a lawyer to plead on your behalf you allow him to take on himself whatever shame the plea brings with it. As your representative he crawls on your behalf, so to speak, leaving your precious dignity intact. So let me ask you: Why have you refused to have a lawyer?'

Dmitri clears his throat. 'I spit on lawyers,' he says, and spits on the floor.

The first assessor intervenes. 'Our presiding judge has raised the possibility that you may not be yourself, as being oneself is understood by the law. To what he has said let me add that spitting in a court of law is not something one does when one is oneself.'

Dmitri stares at him fixedly, baring his teeth like an animal at bay.

'The court can appoint a lawyer for you,' continues the assessor. 'It is not too late for that. It is within the court's powers to do so. We can appoint a lawyer and postpone this sitting to give that officer time to acquaint himself fully with the case and decide on your best course of action.'

There is a low murmur of disappointment from the crowd.

'Judge me now!' cries Dmitri. 'If you don't, I will cut my throat. I will hang myself. I will beat my brains out. You won't be able to stop me.'

'Be careful,' says the assessor. 'My colleague has already recognized your wish to be seen to behave honourably. But you do not behave honourably when you threaten the court. On the contrary, you behave like a madman.'

Dmitri is about to reply, but the judge-in-chief raises a hand. 'Be silent, Dmitri. We will all join you in silence. We will be silent together and allow our passions to cool. After which we will deliberate in a calm and reasoned way the question of how to proceed.'

The judge folds his hands and closes his eyes. His colleagues do likewise. People all around begin folding their hands and closing their eyes. Reluctantly he, Simón, follows their example. The seconds tick by. Somewhere behind him a baby whimpers. *Allow our passions to cool*, he thinks: what passion do I feel except a passion of irritation?

The judge-in-chief opens his eyes. 'So,' he says. 'It is not contested that the deceased Ana Magdalena met her end as a result of the actions of the accused Dmitri. The court now calls upon Dmitri to tell his story, the story of the fourth of March as seen through his eyes; and for the purposes of the record let it be known that Dmitri's narrative will be designated a plea in exculpation. Speak, Dmitri.'

'When the fox has the goose by the throat,' says Dmitri, 'he does not say, "Dear goose, as a sign of my grace I am going to give you a chance to persuade me you are not a goose after all." No, he bites off her head and tears open her breast and eats her heart. You have me by the throat. Go on. Bite off my head.'

'You are not a beast, Dmitri, nor are we beasts. You are a man and we are men, entrusted with the task of achieving justice or at least an approximation to justice. Join us in that task. Put your trust in the law, in the tried and tested protocols of the law. Tell us your story, beginning with the deceased Ana Magdalena. Who was Ana Magdalena to you?'

'Ana Magdalena was a teacher of dance and the wife of the principal of the Academy of Dance. The Academy of Dance occupied the floor above the museum, where I worked. I saw her every day.'

'Go on.'

'I loved Ana Magdalena. I loved her from the very first moment I saw her. I venerated her. I worshipped her. I kissed the ground she trod on. But she would have nothing to do with me. She found me uncouth. She laughed at me. So I killed her. I violated her and then afterwards strangled her. That is all.'

'That is not all, Dmitri. You venerated Ana Magdalena, you worshipped her, yet you raped her and strangled her. We find that hard to comprehend. Help us. When the woman one loves spurns one, one's feelings are hurt, but surely one does not react by turning upon her and killing her. There must have been some added cause, something that happened on the day in question that drove you to action. Tell us more fully what happened that day.'

Even from where he stands he, Simón, can see the flush of rage that creeps over Dmitri's face, the intensity with which he grips the microphone. 'Sentence me!' he bellows. 'Be over with it!'

'No, Dmitri. We are not here to obey your commands. We are here to render justice.'

'You cannot render justice! You cannot measure my guilt! It is not measurable!'

'On the contrary, that is exactly why we are here: to measure your guilt and decide on a sentence that fits it.'

'Like a hat to fit a head!'

'Yes, like a hat to fit your head. To render justice not only to you but to your victim.'

'The woman you call my victim does not care what you do. She is dead. She is gone. No one can bring her back.'

'On the contrary, Dmitri, Ana Magdalena is not gone. She is with us today, here, in this theatre. She haunts us, you most of all. She will not go away until she is satisfied that justice has been done. Therefore tell us what happened on the fourth of March.'

There is a distinct snap as the casing of the microphone in Dmitri's hands cracks. Tears well from his clenched eyes like water squeezed from a stone. He shakes his head slowly from side to side. Strangled words emerge: 'I can't! I won't!'

The judge pours a glass of water and motions to the guard to take it to Dmitri. He sips noisily.

'Can we proceed, Dmitri?' asks the judge.

'No,' says Dmitri, and now the tears flow freely. 'No.'

'Then we will take a break to allow you to recover yourself. We will reconvene this afternoon at two p.m.'

There is a growl of dissatisfaction from the spectators. The judge bangs sharply with his gavel. 'Silence!' he commands. 'This is not an entertainment! Bethink yourselves!' And he stalks offstage, followed first by the two assessors, then by the guard, propelling Dmitri before him.

He, Simón, joins the crowd flowing down the stairs. In the foyer he is astonished to come upon Inés' brother Diego, and with him David.

'What are you doing here?' he demands of the boy, ignoring Diego.

'I wanted to come,' says the boy. 'I wanted to see Dmitri.'

'I am sure Dmitri finds it humiliating enough without having children from the Academy here to gape at him. Did Inés give you permission to come?'

'He wants to be humiliated,' says the boy.

'No, he doesn't. This is not something a child can understand. Dmitri doesn't want to be treated like a lunatic. He wants to be left with his dignity.'

A stranger, a thin, bird-like young man carrying a satchel, has been listening in. Now he intervenes. 'But surely the man must be sick in the head,' he says. 'How could anyone commit such a crime unless his mind is twisted? And he keeps demanding the heaviest sentence. What normal person would do that?'

'What counts as the heaviest sentence here in Estrella?' asks Diego.

'The salt mines. Hard labour in the salt mines for the term of one's life.'

Diego laughs. 'So you still have salt mines!'

The young man is puzzled. 'Yes, we have salt mines. What is so strange about that?'

'Nothing,' says Diego. But he continues to smile.

'What is a salt mine?' asks the boy.

'It is where they dig up salt. Like a gold mine where they dig up gold.'

'Is that where Dmitri is going?'

'It is where they send the bad apples,' says Diego.

'Can we visit him? Can we go to the salt mine?'

'Let us not get ahead of ourselves,' says he, Simón. 'I don't believe the judge will send Dmitri to the salt mines. That is my sense of the way things are going. I believe he will rule that Dmitri has a sickness of the head and send him to a hospital to be cured. So that in a year or two he can re-emerge a brand-new man with a brand-new head.'

'You don't sound as if you think much of psychiatry,' says the young man with the satchel. 'I am sorry, I haven't introduced myself. My name is Mario. I am a student at the law school. That is why I am here today. It is an intriguing case. It raises some of the most basic issues. For instance, it is the mission of the court to rehabilitate offenders, but how far should the court exert itself to rehabilitate an offender who does not want to be rehabilitated, like this man Dmitri? Maybe he should be offered a choice: rehabilitation via the salt mines or rehabilitation via the psychiatric hospital. On the other hand, should an offender be allowed any role in his sentencing? In legal circles the resistance to such a course has always been strong, as you can imagine.'

Diego, he can see, is beginning to fret. He knows Diego, knows that he is bored by what he calls clever talk. 'It's a nice day, Diego,' he says. 'Why don't you and David find something more interesting to do?'

'No!' says the boy. 'I want to stay!'

'It was his idea to come here, not mine,' says Diego. 'I could not care less what happens to this Dmitri person.'

'You don't care but I care!' says the boy. 'I don't want Dmitri to get a new head! I want him to go to the salt mine!'

The trial recommences at two p.m. Re-gathered, the audience is considerably smaller than before. He and Diego and the boy have no trouble finding seats.

Dmitri is brought back onto the stage, followed by the judge and assessors.

'I have before me a report from the director of the museum where you, Dmitri, were employed,' says the judge. 'He writes that you have always performed your duties faithfully and that, until these recent events, he had every reason to think of you as an honest man. I also have a report from Dr Alejandro Toussaint, a specialist in nervous diseases, who was commissioned by the court to evaluate your state of mind. Dr Toussaint reports that he was unable to carry out his evaluation because of violent and uncooperative behaviour on your part. Do you wish to comment?'

Dmitri is stonily silent.

'Finally I have a report from the police doctor on the events of the fourth of March. He writes that completed sexual intercourse took place, that is to say, intercourse ending in ejaculation of the male seed, and that this took place while the deceased was still alive. Subsequently the deceased was strangled, manually. Do you contest any of this?'

Dmitri is silent.

'You may ask why I rehearse these last distasteful facts. I do so to make it clear that the court is fully aware of how terrible a crime you have committed. You violated a woman who trusted you and then killed her in the most pitiless way. I shudder, we all shudder, to think what she went through during her last minutes. What we lack is some understanding of why you committed this senseless, gratuitous act. Are you an erring human being, Dmitri, or do you belong to some other species, without a soul, without a conscience? I urge you again: explain yourself to us.'

'I belong to a foreign species. I have no place on this earth. Do away with me. Kill me. Grind me under your heel.'

'That is all you will say?'

Dmitri is silent.

'It is not enough, Dmitri, not enough. But you will not be required to speak again. This court has bent over backwards in its efforts to do you justice and you have resisted at every step. Now you must bear the consequences. My colleagues and I will retire to confer.' He addresses the guard. 'Remove the accused.'

There is an uneasy stir among the crowd. Should they stay? How long is the whole business going to take? Yet no sooner have people begun to drift from the auditorium than Dmitri is led back onto the stage and the judges return to their seats.

'Stand, Dmitri,' says the judge. 'In accordance with the powers invested in me, I will now pronounce sentence. I will be brief. You offer no plea in mitigation of sentence. On the contrary, you demand that we proceed against you with the utmost rigour. The question before us is, does this demand come from your heart, out of contrition for your heinous actions, or from a deranged mind?

'It is a difficult question to answer. In your demeanour there is no sign of contrition. To the bereaved husband of your victim you have uttered no word of apology. You present yourself as a being without a conscience. My colleagues and I have every reason to send you away to the salt mines and close the book on you.

'On the other hand, this is your first transgression. You have been a good worker. You treated the deceased with respect until the day you turned on her. What malign force took control of you on that day remains a mystery to us. You have resisted every effort on our part to understand.

'Our sentence is as follows. You will be removed from here to the hospital for the criminally insane and detained there. The medical authorities will review your case once a year and report to this court. Depending on those reports, you may or may not be called before the court at some future date for review of your sentence. That is all.'

Something like a collective sigh goes up from the citizenry. Is the sigh for Dmitri? Are they sorry for him? It is hard to believe so. The judges file offstage. Dmitri, his head bowed, is removed.

'Goodbye, Diego,' says he, Simón. 'Goodbye, David. What are your plans for the weekend? Am I going to see you?'

'Can we talk to Dmitri?' asks the boy.

'No. That is not possible.'

'I want to!' And without warning he races down the aisle and clambers onto the stage. In haste he and Diego follow, through the wings and down a dark passage. At the end of the passage they come upon Dmitri and his guard, who is peering through a half-opened door onto the street.

'Dmitri!' the boy shouts.

Ignoring his chains, Dmitri hoists the boy aloft and hugs him. Half-heartedly the guard tries to separate them.

'Won't they let you go to the salt mines, Dmitri?' says the boy.

'No, it's not the salt mines for me, it's the madhouse. But I will escape, never fear. I'll escape and catch the first bus to the salt mines. I'll say, *Dmitri here, reporting for duty, sir*. They won't dare to refuse me. So don't worry, young man. Dmitri is still master of his fate.'

'Simón says they are going to chop off your head and give you a new one.'

The door is flung open and light floods in. 'Come on!' says the guard. 'The van is here.'

'The van is here,' says Dmitri. 'Time for Dmitri to go.' He kisses the boy full on the lips and sets him down. 'Goodbye, my young friend. Yes, they want to give me a new head. It's the price of forgiveness. They forgive you but then they chop off your head. Beware of forgiveness, that's what I say.'

'I don't forgive you,' says the boy.

'That's good! Take a lesson from Dmitri: don't ever let them forgive you, and don't ever listen when they promise you a new life. The new life is a lie, my boy, the biggest lie of all. There is no next life. This is the only one there is. Once you let them chop off your head, that's the end of you. Just darkness and darkness and nothing but darkness.'

Out of the blinding sunlight two men in uniform emerge and haul Dmitri down the steps. As they are about to bundle him into the back of their van, he turns and calls out: 'Tell Simón to burn you know what! Tell him I will come and cut his throat if he doesn't!' Then the door slams shut and the van drives off.

'What was that last bit about?' says Diego.

'It's nothing. He left some stuff behind that he wants me to destroy. Pictures he cut out of magazines – that sort of thing.'

'Ladies with no clothes on,' says the boy. 'He let me see them.'

Chapter 14

He is shown into the office of the director of the museum. 'Thank you for agreeing to see me,' he says. 'I come at the request of an employee of yours, Dmitri, who would like to save both himself and the museum from potential embarrassment. On your premises, he tells me, there is a collection of obscene pictures that belongs to him. He would like them to be destroyed before the newspapers get hold of them. Will you permit this?'

'Obscene pictures . . . You have seen these pictures, señor Simón?'

'No, but my son has. My son is a student at the Academy of Dance.'

'And you say these pictures have been stolen from our collection?'

'No, no, they are not that kind of picture. They are photographs of women cut out of pornographic magazines. I can show you. I know exactly where to find them – Dmitri told me.'

The director brings out a bunch of keys, leads the way down to the basement, and unlocks the cabinet described by Dmitri. The bottom drawer holds a little cardboard case, which he opens.

The first picture is of a blonde woman with garishly red lips sitting naked on a sofa with her legs apart, gripping her rather large breasts and thrusting them forward.

With an exclamation of distaste the director shuts the case. 'Take them away!' he says. 'I don't want to hear any more about this.'

There are another half-dozen pictures of the same kind, as he, Simón, discovers when he opens the case in the privacy of his room. But in addition, underneath the pictures, there is an envelope which contains a pair of women's panties, black; a single silver earring of simple design; a photograph of a young girl, recognizably Ana Magdalena, holding a cat and smiling for the camera; and finally, held together with a rubber band, letters to *Mi amor* from AM. There is no date on any of them, nor any return address, but he gathers they were posted from the seaside resort of Aguaviva. They describe various holiday activities (swimming, gathering shells, walking on the dunes) and mention Joaquín and Damian by name. 'I long to be in your arms again,' says one letter. 'I long for you passionately (*apasionadamente*),' says another.

He reads them through, slowly, from beginning to end, reads them a second time, getting used to the handwriting, which is rather childish, not what he would have expected at all, each *i* surmounted with a careful little circle, then puts them back in the envelope together with the photograph, the earring and the panties, puts the envelope back in the case, and puts the case under his bed.

His first thought is that Dmitri wanted him to read the letters – wanted him to know that he, Dmitri, was loved by a woman whom he, Simón, might have desired from afar but whom he was not man enough to possess. But the more he thinks about it, the less plausible this explanation seems. If Dmitri had in fact been having an affair with Ana Magdalena, if his talk of worshipping the ground on which she trod and her disdainful treatment of him in return had been nothing but a cover for clandestine couplings in the basement of the museum, why did he in his various confessions claim to have forced himself on her? Further, why would Dmitri want him, Simón, to learn the truth about the two of them when in all likelihood he, Simón, would promptly inform the authorities, who would just as promptly order a new trial? Is the simplest explanation not after all the best one: that Dmitri trusted him to burn the case and its contents without examining them?

But the greater puzzle remains: if Ana Magdalena was not the woman she seemed to all the world to be, and her death not the kind of death it seemed to be, why had Dmitri lied to the police and to the court? To protect her name? To save her husband from humiliation? Was Dmitri, out of nobility of spirit, taking all the guilt upon himself so that the name of the Arroyos should not be dragged through the mud?

Yet what could Ana Magdalena have said or done, on the night of the fourth of March, to get herself killed by a man whom she longed – longed *apasionadamente* – to be in the arms of?

On the other hand, what if Ana Magdalena never wrote the letters at all? What if they are forgeries, and what if he, Simón, is being used as a tool in a plot to blacken her name?

He shivers. *He is truly a madman!* he says to himself. *The judge was right after all! He belongs in a madhouse, in chains, behind a door with a sevenfold lock!*

He curses himself. He should never have involved himself in Dmitri's affairs. He should never have answered his summons, never have spoken to the museum director, never have looked inside the case. Now the genie is out of the bottle and he has no idea what to do. If he turns the letters over to the police, he becomes an accomplice in a plot whose purpose is dark to him; similarly if he hands them back to the museum director; while if he burns them or conceals them he becomes an accomplice in another plot, a plot to present Ana Magdalena as a spotless martyr.

In the middle of the night he gets up, removes the case from under his bed, wraps it in a spare counterpane, and puts it on top of the wardrobe.

Then in the morning, as he is about to set off for the depot to collect the pamphlets he will be distributing that day, Inés' car draws up and Diego gets out, the boy with him.

Diego is clearly in a bad mood. 'All day yesterday and again today this child has been nagging us,' he says. 'He has worn us down, both Inés and me. Now here we are. Tell him, David – tell Simón what you want.'

'I want to see Dmitri. I want to go to the salt mine. But Inés won't let me.'

'Of course she won't. I thought you understood. Dmitri isn't in the salt mine. He has been sent to a hospital.'

'Yes, but Dmitri doesn't want to go to a hospital, he wants to go to the salt mine!'

'I am not sure what you think goes on in a salt mine, David, but first of all the salt mine is hundreds of kilometres away and second of all a salt mine is not a holiday resort. That is why the judge sent Dmitri to a hospital: to save him from the salt mine. A salt mine is a place where you go to suffer.'

'But Dmitri doesn't want to be saved! He wants to suffer! Can we go to the hospital?'

'Certainly not. The hospital where they have sent Dmitri is not a normal hospital. It is a hospital for dangerous people. The public isn't allowed in.'

'Dmitri isn't dangerous.'

'On the contrary, Dmitri is extremely dangerous, as he has proved. Anyhow, I am not going to take you to the hospital, nor is Diego. I want nothing more to do with Dmitri.'

'Why?'

'I don't have to tell you why.'

'It's because you hate Dmitri! You hate everybody!'

'You use that word far too sweepingly. I don't hate anybody. I just want nothing more to do with Dmitri. He is not a good person.'

'He is a good person! He loves me! He recognizes me! You don't love me!'

'That is not true. I do love you. I love you a great deal more than Dmitri does. Dmitri doesn't know the meaning of love.'

'Dmitri loves lots of people. He loves them because he has a big heart. He told me. Stop laughing, Diego! Why are you laughing?'

Diego cannot stop laughing. 'Did he really say that – that if you have a big heart you can love lots of people? Maybe he meant lots of girls.'

Diego's laughter fires the boy even further. His voice rises. 'It's true! Dmitri has a big heart and Simón has a tiny heart – that's what Dmitri says. He says Simón has a tiny little heart like a bed-bug, so he can't love anybody. Simón, is it true that Dmitri did sexual intercourse to Ana Magdalena to make her die?'

'I am not going to answer that question. It's stupid. It's ridiculous. You don't know what sexual intercourse is.'

'I do! Inés told me. She has done sexual intercourse lots of times and she hates it. She says it's horrible.'

'Be that as it may, I am not going to answer any more questions about Dmitri. I don't want to hear his name again. I am finished with him.'

'But why did he do sexual intercourse to her? Why won't you tell me? Did he want to make her heart stop?'

'That's enough, David. Calm down.' And to Diego: 'You can see the child is upset. He has been having nightmares ever since ... ever since the event. You should be helping him, not laughing at him.'

'Tell me!' the boy shouts. 'Why won't you tell me? Did he want to make a baby inside her? Did he want to make her heart stop? Can she have a baby even if her heart stops?'

'No, she can't. When the mother dies the child inside her dies too. That is the rule. But Ana Magdalena wasn't going to have a baby.'

'How do you know? You don't know anything. Did Dmitri make her baby turn blue? Can we make her heart start again?'

'Ana Magdalena was not going to have a baby and no, we can't make her heart beat again because that is not the way the heart works. Once the heart stops, it stops forever.'

'But when she has a new life her heart will beat again, won't it?'

'In a sense, yes. In the life to come Ana Magdalena will have a new heart. Not only will she have a new life and a new heart, she will remember nothing of this sorry mess. She won't remember the Academy and she won't remember Dmitri, which will be a blessing. She will be able to start afresh, just as you and I did, washed clean of the past, without bad memories to weigh her down.'

'Did you forgive Dmitri, Simón?'

'I am not the one whom Dmitri injured, so it is not for me to forgive him. It is Ana Magdalena's forgiveness that he should be seeking. And señor Arroyo's.'

'I didn't forgive him. He doesn't want anyone to forgive him.'

'That is just boasting on his part, perverse boasting. He wants us to think of him as a wild person who does things that normal people are afraid to do. David, I am sick and tired of talking about that man. As far as I am concerned he is dead and buried. Now I have to go off on my rounds. Next time you have bad dreams, remember that you have only to wave your arms and they will evaporate like smoke. Wave your arms and shout *Begone!* like Don Quixote. Give me a kiss. I will see you on Friday. Goodbye, Diego.'

'I want to go to Dmitri! If Diego won't take me I'll go by myself!'

'You can go, but they won't let you in. The place where he is kept is not a normal hospital. It is a hospital for criminals, with walls around it, and guards with guard dogs.'

'I'll take Bolívar along. He will kill the guard dogs.'

Diego holds open the door of the car. The boy gets in and sits with his arms folded, a pout on his face.

'If you want my opinion,' says Diego quietly, 'he is out of control, this one. You and Inés should do something about it. Send him to school, to begin with.'

He was wrong about the hospital, as it turns out, completely wrong. The psychiatric hospital he had pictured, the hospital in the remote countryside with the high walls and the guard dogs, does not exist. All that exists is the city hospital with its rather modest psychiatric wing – the same hospital where Dmitri used to work before he joined the museum staff. Among the orderlies there are some who remember him with affection from the old days. Ignoring the fact that he is a self-confessed murderer, they pamper him, bringing him snacks from the staff kitchen, keeping him supplied with cigarettes. He has a room to himself in the part of the wing marked Restricted Access, with a shower cubicle and a desk with a lamp.

All of this – the snacks, the cigarettes, the shower cubicle – he learns about when, the day after Diego's visit, he comes home from his bicycle rounds and finds the self-confessed murderer stretched out on the bed, asleep, while the boy sits cross-legged on the floor playing a game of cards. So surprised is he that he lets out a cry, to which the boy, raising a finger to his lips, whispers '*Shh!*'

He strides over and gives Dmitri an angry shake. 'You! What are you doing here?'

Dmitri sits up. 'Calm yourself, Simón,' he says. 'I'll be gone shortly. I just want to be sure that . . . you know . . . Did you do as I told you?'

He brushes the question aside. 'David, how does this man come to be here?'

Dmitri himself responds. 'We came by bus, Simón, like normal people. Calm yourself. Young David came to visit me like the good friend he is. We had a chat. Then I put on an orderly's uniform, as in the old days, and the youngster took me by the hand and we walked out, the pair of us, just like that. *He's my son*, I said. *What a sweet boy*, they said. Of course the uniform helped. People trust a uniform – that's one of the things you learn about life. We walked out of the hospital and came straight here. And when you and I have settled our business I will catch the bus back. No one will even notice I was gone.'

'David, is it true? A hospital for the criminally insane, and they let this man walk out?'

'He wanted bread,' says the boy. 'He said there was no bread for him in the hospital.'

'That's nonsense. He gets three meals a day there, with as much bread as he wants.'

'He said there was no bread so I took him bread.'

'Sit down, Simón,' says Dmitri. 'And will you do me a favour?' He takes out a pack of cigarettes and lights one. 'Don't insult me, please, not in front of the boy. Don't call me criminally insane. Because it is not true. A criminal perhaps, but not insane, not in the slightest.

'Do you want to hear what the doctors say, the ones who were told to find out what is wrong with me? No? All right, I'll skip the doctors. Let us talk about the Arroyos instead. I hear they had to close down the Academy. That's a pity. I liked the Academy. I liked to be with the young ones, the little dancers, all so happy, so full of life. I wish I had gone to an academy like that when I was a child. Who knows, I might have turned out differently. Still, it's no use crying over spilt milk, is it? What's done is done.'

Spilt milk. The phrase outrages him. 'There have been a lot of people crying over the milk you spilled,' he bursts out. 'You have left some broken hearts behind you and a lot of anger.'

'Which I can understand,' says Dmitri, puffing leisurely on his cigarette. 'You think I am not aware of the enormity of my crime, Simón? Why else do you think I volunteered for the salt mines? The salt mines are not for crybabies. You have to be a man to cope with the salt mines. If they would only give me my marching papers from the hospital I would be off to the salt mines tomorrow. *Dmitri here*, I would say to the mine captain, *fit and well and reporting for duty!* But they won't let me out, the psychologists and the psychiatrists, the specialists in deviant this and deviant that. *Tell me about your mother*, they say. *Did your mother love you? When you were a baby did she give you her breast? What was it like, sucking on her breast?* What am I supposed to say? What do I remember of my mother and her breasts when I can barely remember yesterday? So I just say whatever comes into my head. *It was like sucking a lemon*, I say. Or *It was like pork, it was like sucking a pork rib.* Because that's how it works, psychiatry, isn't it? – you say the first thing that comes into your head and then they go away and analyse it and come up with what is wrong with you.

'They are all so interested in me, Simón! It amazes me. I'm not interested in me but they are. To me I'm just a common criminal, as common as weed. But to them I am something special. I have no conscience, or else I have too much conscience, they can't decide which. If you have too much conscience, I want to tell them, your conscience eats you up and there is nothing left of you, like a spider eating a wasp or a wasp eating a spider, I can never remember which, nothing left but the shell. What do you think, young man? Do you know what conscience is?'

The boy nods.

'Of course you do! You understand old Dmitri better than anyone – better than all the psychologists in the world. *What do you dream about?* they say. *Maybe you dream about falling down dark holes and being swallowed by dragons.* – *Yes*, I say, *yes, that's exactly it!* Whereas you never needed to ask me about my dreams. You took one look and understood me at once. *I understand you and I don't forgive you.* I'll never forget that. He is really special, Simón, this boy of yours. A special case. Wise beyond his years. You could learn from him.'

'David is not a special case. There is no such thing as a special case. He is not a special case, nor are you. No one is taken in by the show of craziness you put on, Dmitri, not for one minute. I hope you do get sent to the salt mines. That will put an end to your nonsense.'

'Well spoken, Simón, well spoken! I love you for it. I could kiss you, only you wouldn't like that, you not being a kissing man. Whereas your son here has always been ready to give old Dmitri a kiss, haven't you, my boy?'

'Dmitri, why did you make Ana Magdalena's heart stop?' asks the boy.

'Good question! That's what the doctors want to know most of all. It excites them, the thought of it – pressing a beautiful woman so tight in your arms that you stop her heart – only they are too ashamed to ask. They don't dare to ask straight out, like you, no, they have to come at it in a roundabout way, like snakes. *Did your mother love you? What did it taste like, your mother's milk?* Or that stupid judge: *Who are you? Are you yourself?*

'Why did I stop her heart? I'll tell you. We were together, she and I, when suddenly a thought came into my head – popped into my head and wouldn't leave me. I thought: *Why not put your hands around her throat while she is, you know, in the throes of it, and give her a bit of a throttle? Show her who is master. Show her what love is really like.*

'Killing the one you love: that is something that old Simón here will never understand. But you understand, don't you? You understand Dmitri. From the first moment you understood.'

'Wouldn't she marry you?'

'Marry me? No. Why would a lady like Ana Magdalena marry someone like me? I'm dirt, my boy. Old Simón is right. I'm dirt, and my dirt rubs off on everyone I touch. That's why I must go to the salt mines, where everyone is dirt, where I will be at home. No, Ana Magdalena spurned me. I loved her, I worshipped her, I would have done anything for her, but she would have nothing to do with me, you saw it, everyone could see it. So I gave her a big surprise and stopped her heart. Taught her a lesson. Gave her something to think about.'

A silence falls. Then he, Simón, speaks. 'You asked about your papers, the papers you wanted me to destroy.'

'Yes. Why else would I take the trouble to leave my hospital home and come here? To find out about the papers, of course. Go on. Tell me. I trusted you and you broke that trust. Is that what you are going to say? Say it.'

'I haven't broken any trust. But I will say this. I have seen what was in the case, including you know what. Therefore I know that the story you tell me is not true. I won't say any more. But I am not going to stand here meekly like a sheep and be lied to.'

Dmitri turns to the boy. 'Do you have anything to eat, my boy? Dmitri is feeling a bit peckish.'

The boy jumps up, rummages in the cupboard, returns with a packet of biscuits.

'Ginger snaps!' says Dmitri. 'Would you like a ginger snap, Simón? No? What about you, David?'

The boy takes a biscuit from him and bites into it.

'So it is public knowledge, is it?' says Dmitri.

'No, it is not public knowledge.'

'But you are going to use it against me.'

'Use what against you?' asks the boy.

'Never mind, my son. This is something between old Simón and me.'

'It depends on what you mean by *against*. If you keep your promise and disappear into the salt mines for the rest of your life, then what we are referring to ceases to be of consequence, one way or the other.'

'Don't play logic games with me, Simón. You know and I know what *against* means. Why didn't you do as you were told? Now look at the mess you are in.'

'I? I am not the one in a mess, you are in a mess.'

'No, Simón. Tomorrow or the next day or the one after that I will be free to go to the salt mines and pay my debt and clear my conscience, while you – *you* – will have to stay behind with this mess on your hands.'

'What mess, Dmitri?' asks the boy. 'Why won't you tell me?'

'I'll tell you what mess. *Poor Dmitri! Did we really do him justice? Shouldn't we have tried harder to save him, to turn him into a good citizen and a productive member of society? What must it be like for him, languishing in the salt mines while we live our easy lives in Estrella? Shouldn't we have shown him a modicum of mercy? Shouldn't we summon him back, saying, All is forgiven, Dmitri, you can have your old job back, and your uniform, and your pension, only you must say you are sorry, so that we can feel better inside?* That's the mess, my boy. Wallowing in excrement like a pig. Wallowing in your own shit. Why didn't you just do what I told you, Simón, instead of getting sucked into this stupid charade of saving me from myself? *Send him to the doctors, tell them to screw off the old head and screw on a new one.* And the pills they give you! It's worse than the salt mines, being in the mad ward! Just getting through twenty-four hours is like wading through mud. Tick tock tick tock. I can't wait to start living again.'

He, Simón, has reached the end of his tether. 'That's enough, Dmitri. Please leave now. Leave at once, or I will call the police.'

'Oh, so it's goodbye, is it? And what about you, David? Are you going to say goodbye to Dmitri too? *Goodbye – see you in the next life*. Is that how it is going to be? I thought we had an understanding, you and I. Has old Simón been working on you, shaking your confidence in me? *He's a bad man, how can you love such a bad man?* Who ever stopped loving a person because he was bad? I did my worst to Ana Magdalena, yet she never stopped loving me. She hated me, maybe, but that doesn't mean she didn't love me. Love and hate: you can't have the one without the other. Like salt and pepper. Like black and white. That's what people forget. She loved me and she hated me, like any normal person. Like Simón here. Do you think Simón loves you all the time? Of course he doesn't. He loves you and he hates you, it's all mixed up inside him, only he won't tell you. No, he keeps it secret, pretends it's all nice and placid inside him, no waves, no ripples. Like the way he talks, our famous man of reason. But believe me, old Simón here is as much of a mess inside as you or I. In fact, more of a mess. Because at least I don't pretend to be what I am not. *This is how I am*, I say, *and this is how I talk, all mixed up*. Are you listening, my boy? Catch my words while you can, because Simón here wants to drive me away, out of your life. Listen hard. When you listen to me, you listen to the truth, and what do we want, finally, but the truth?'

'But when you see Ana Magdalena in the next life, you won't make her heart stop again, will you?'

'I don't know, my boy. Maybe there won't be a next life – not for me, not for any of us. Maybe the sun will suddenly loom large in the sky and engulf us, and that will be the end of us all. No more Dmitri. No more David. Just a big ball of fire. That's how I see things, sometimes. That's my vision.'

'And then?'

'And then nothing. Lots of flames, then lots of silence.'

'But is it true?'

'True? Who is to say? It's all in the future, and the future is a mystery. What do you think?'

'I think it's not true. I think you are just saying so.'

'Well, if you say it's not true then it's not true, because you, young David, are Dmitri's king, and your word is Dmitri's command. But to get back to your question, no, I won't do it again. The salt mines will cure me for good of my badness, my rages and my murderousness. They will knock all such nonsense out of me. So you needn't fret, Ana Magdalena is safe.'

'But you mustn't do sexual intercourse to her again.'

'No sexual intercourse! This youngster of yours is very strict, Simón, very absolute. But he'll come round as he grows older. Sexual intercourse – it's part of human nature, my boy, there's no escaping it. Even Simón will agree. There is no escaping it, is there, Simón? No escaping the thunderbolt.'

He, Simón, is mute. When was he last hit by a thunderbolt? Not in this life.

Then suddenly Dmitri seems to lose interest in them. Restlessly his eyes flicker around the room. 'Time to go. Time to return to my lonely cell. Do you mind if I hold on to the biscuits? I like to nibble on a biscuit now and then. Come and see me again, young man. We can go for a ride on the bus, or visit the zoo. I'd enjoy that. I always enjoy chatting to you. You are the only one who really understands old Dmitri. The psychologists and the psychiatrists with their questions, they just can't work out what I am, man or beast. But you see right through me, into my heart. Now give Dmitri a hug.'

He lifts the boy off the ground in a tight embrace, whispers words in his ear that he, Simón, cannot hear. The boy nods vigorously.

'Goodbye, Simón. Don't believe everything I say. It is just air, air that blows where it listeth.'

The door closes behind him.

Chapter 15

From the roster of Spanish courses on offer at the Institute he chooses Spanish Composition (Elementary). 'Students registering for this course should have a command of spoken Spanish. We will learn to write clearly, logically, and with good style.'

He is the oldest in the class. Even the teacher is young: an attractive young woman with dark hair and dark eyes who tells them to call her simply Martina. 'We will go around the room and each of you will tell me who you are and what you hope to gain from the course,' says Martina. When his turn comes, he says: 'My name is Simón, and I am in the advertising business, though at a lowly level. I have been speaking Spanish for well over a year and have become fairly fluent. The time has come for me to learn to write clearly, logically, and with good style.'

'Thank you, Simón,' says Martina. 'Next?'

Of course he wants to write well. Who would not? But that is not why he is here, not exactly. Why he is here he will discover in the process of being here.

Martina hands out copies of the course reader. 'Please treat your reader with consideration, as you would treat a friend,' says Martina. 'At the end of the course I will ask you to hand it back, so that it can become a friend to another student.' His own copy is well thumbed, with many underlinings in ink and pencil.

They read two specimens of the business letter: a letter from Juan applying for a job as a salesman; and a letter from Luisa to her landlord terminating the lease on her apartment. They take note of the form of salutation and the form of closure. They examine the paragraphing and the form of the paragraph. 'A paragraph is a unit of thought,' says Martina. 'It lays out a thought and links it to the preceding and succeeding thoughts.'

For their first assignment they are to practise composing in paragraphs. 'Tell me something about yourselves,' says Martina. 'Not everything but something. Tell it to me in the space of three paragraphs, linked each to the next.'

He approves of Martina's philosophy of composition and does his best with his assignment. 'I arrived in this land with one over-riding purpose in mind,' he writes: 'to protect from harm a certain small boy who had fallen under my care and to conduct him to his mother. In due course I found his mother and united him with her.'

That is his first paragraph.

'However, my duties did not end there,' he writes. *However*: the linking word. 'I continued to watch over the mother and child and see to their welfare. When their welfare was threatened I brought them to Estrella, where we have been made welcome and where the boy, who goes by the name David and who lives at present with his mother Inés and his uncle Diego (Inés and I no longer share a residence), has flourished.'

End of second paragraph. Commencement of third and final paragraph, introduced by the linking word *now*.

'Now, reluctantly, I must accept that my duty is done, that the boy may have no further need of me. It is time for me to close a certain chapter of my life and open a new one. Opening that new chapter is linked to the project of learning to write – linked in a way that is not yet clear to me.'

That is enough. Those are the required three paragraphs, fittingly linked. The fourth paragraph, the paragraph that, were he to write it, would be superfluous to the assignment, would be about Dmitri. He does not have the linking word yet, the word that would make the fourth paragraph follow clearly and logically from the third; but after the linking word he would write: 'Here in Estrella I met a man named Dmitri who later gained notoriety as a rapist and murderer. Dmitri has on several occasions ridiculed the way I speak, which strikes him as overly cool and rational.' He reflects, then replaces the word *cool* with the word *cold*. 'Dmitri believes that the style reveals the man. Dmitri would not write as I write now, in paragraphs linked one to the other. Dmitri would call that passionless writing, as he would call me a passionless man. A man of passion, Dmitri would say, pours himself out without paragraphing.

'Though I have no respect for this man Dmitri,' he would continue, in what would be a fifth paragraph, 'I am troubled by his criticism. Why am I troubled? Because he says (and here I may well agree with him) that a coldly rational person is not the best guide for a boy who is impulsive and passionate by nature.

'Therefore (sixth paragraph), I want to become a different person.' That is where he comes to a halt, in mid-paragraph. It is enough, more than enough.

In the second meeting of the class Martina discusses further the genre of the business letter, in particular the letter of application. 'The letter of application can be thought of as an act of seduction,' she says. 'In it we present ourselves in the most favourable light. *This is who I am,* we say – *am I not attractive? Hire me and I will be yours.*' There is a ripple of amusement around the room. 'But of course our letter must at the same time be businesslike. There must be a balance. A certain art is thus required to compose a good letter of application: the art of self-presentation. Today we will be studying that art with a view to mastering it and making it our own.'

He is intrigued by Martina: so young yet so confident.

There is a ten-minute break halfway through the class. While the students drift out into the corridor or to the washroom, Martina reads through their assignments. When they reconvene she hands them back. On his assignment she has written: 'Good paragraphing. Unusual content.'

Their second assignment is to write a letter of application for what Martina calls 'your dream job, the job you most want to land'. 'Remember to sound attractive,' she adds. 'Make yourself wanted.'

'*Estimado señor Director,*' he writes, 'I am responding to the notice in today's *Star* inviting applications for the position of museum attendant. While I have no experience in the field, I do have several qualities which make me desirable. In the first place, I am a mature and dependable person. In the second place, I have a love or at least a respect for the arts, including the visual arts. In the third place, I have no great expectations. If I were to be appointed at the rank of Attendant, I would not expect to be promoted to Principal Attendant the next day, much less Director.'

He divides the block of prose he has written into five parts, five brief paragraphs.

'I cannot honestly claim,' he adds, 'that being a museum attendant has ever been a dream of mine. However, I have reached a point of crisis in my life. *You must change*, I say to myself. But change into what? Perhaps the advertisement on which my eye fell was a sign intended for me, a sign from the heavens. *Follow me*, said the *Star*. So I follow, and this letter constitutes my following.'

That is his sixth paragraph.

He hands in his letter to Martina, all six paragraphs. During the break he does not leave the room but remains at his desk, watching covertly as she reads, watching the quick, decisive movements of her pen. He notices when she comes to his letter: she takes longer over it, reading with a frown on her face. She glances up and sees him watching her.

At the end of the break she returns the assignments. On his she has written: *Please see me after the class.*

He waits, after the class, until the other students have left.

'Simón, I have read your assignments with interest,' she says. 'You write well. However, I wonder whether this is the best course for you. Do you not feel that you would be more at home in a course in creative writing? It is not too late to switch courses, you know.'

'If you are telling me I should withdraw from the course I will withdraw,' he replies. 'But I do not conceive of my writing as creative. To me it is the same kind of writing one does in a diary. Diarizing is not creative writing. It is a form of letter-writing. One writes letters to oneself. However, I understand what you are saying. I am out of place here. I won't waste any more of your time. Thank you.' He takes the course reader out of his bag. 'Let me return this to you.'

'Don't take offence,' she says. 'Don't go. Don't withdraw. I will go on reading your assignments. But I will read them in exactly the same way as I read the other students' work: as a teacher of writing, not as a confidante. Do you accept that?'

'I do,' he says. 'Thank you. I appreciate your kindness.'

As a third assignment they are asked to describe their previous work experience and set down a résumé of their educational qualifications.

'I used to be a manual labourer,' he writes. 'Nowadays I earn a living by putting pamphlets in letter boxes. That is because I am not as strong as I once used to be. Besides lacking physical strength I also lack passion. This, at least, is the opinion of Dmitri, the man I wrote of earlier, the man of passion. Dmitri's passion boiled over one evening to such an extent that he killed his mistress. As for me, I have no desire to kill anyone, least of all someone I might love. Dmitri laughs when I say that – when I say I would never kill someone I loved. According to Dmitri, at a buried level each of us desires to kill the one we love. Each of us desires to kill the beloved, but only a few elect souls have the courage to act on their desire.

'A child can smell a coward, says Dmitri. A child can smell a liar too, and a hypocrite. Hence, according to Dmitri, the dwindling away of David's love for me, who have proved myself to be a coward, a liar, and a hypocrite. By contrast, in David's attraction toward characters like Dmitri himself (a self-confessed murderer) and his uncle Diego (in my opinion a wastrel and a bully, but let that pass) he finds a deep wisdom. Children come into the world with an intuition of what is good and true, he says, but lose that power as they become socialized. David is, according to him, an exception. David has retained his innate faculties in their purest form. For that he respects him – in fact reveres him or, as he puts it, recognizes him. *My sovereign, my king,* he calls him, not without an element of mockery.

'*How can you recognize someone you have never seen before?* That is the question I would like to put to Dmitri.

'Meeting Dmitri (whom I dislike and indeed from a moral point of view despise) has been an educational experience, for me. I would go so far as to list it among my educational qualifications.

'I believe I am open to new ideas, including Dmitri's. I think it is highly likely that Dmitri's judgement on me is correct: that as a father or stepfather or guide to life I am not the right person for a child like David, an exceptional child, a child who never fails to remind me that I do not know him or understand him. Therefore perhaps the time has come for me to withdraw and find myself another role in life, another object or soul on which or on whom to pour whatever it is that pours out of me, sometimes as mere talk, sometimes as tears, sometimes in the form that I persist in calling loving care.

'*Loving care* is a formulation I would use without hesitation in a diary. But of course this is not a diary. So the claim to be animated by loving care is a large one.

'To be continued.

'In the form of a footnote, let me add a few words about tears.

'Certain music brings tears to my eyes. If I am without passion, where do these tears come from? I have yet to see Dmitri moved to tears by music.

'In the form of a second footnote, let me say something about Inés' dog Bolívar, that is, about the dog who came with Inés when she consented to become David's mother, but who has now become David's dog in the sense that we speak of someone who guards us as "our" guardian though we have no power over him or her or it.

'Like children, dogs are said to be able to smell out cowards and liars and so forth. Yet Bolívar has, from the first day and without reserve, accepted me into their family. To Dmitri this should surely be food for thought.'

When señora Martina – he cannot call her simply Martina, despite her youth – distributes the checked assignments to the rest of the class, she does not return his. Instead, as she passes his desk, she murmurs, 'After class, please, Simón.' Those words, and the light waft of a scent for which he has no name.

Señora Martina is young, she is pretty, she is intelligent, he admires her assurance and her competence and her dark eyes, but he is not in love with her, as he was not in love with Anna Magdalena, whom he knew better (and had seen naked) but who is dead now. It is not love that he wants from señora Martina but something else. He wants her to listen to him and tell him whether his speech – the speech he is trying his best to write down on the page – rings true or whether on the contrary it is one long lie from beginning to end. Then he wants her to tell him what to do with himself: whether to continue to set off on his bicycle rounds in the mornings and lie on his bed in the afternoons, resting and listening to the radio and (more and more often) drinking, and then afterwards fall asleep and sleep the sleep of the dead for eight or nine or even ten hours; or whether to go out into the world and do something quite different.

It is a lot to expect of a teacher of prose composition, a lot more than she is paid to do. But then, for the child who boarded the ship on the far shore, it was a lot to expect that the solitary man in the drab clothes should take him under his wing and guide his steps in a strange land.

His classmates – with whom he has yet to exchange more than a nod – file out of the room. 'Sit down, Simón,' says señora Martina. He sits down opposite her. 'This is more than I can deal with,' she says. She regards him levelly.

'It is only prose,' he says. 'Can you not deal with it as prose?'

'It is an appeal,' she says. 'You are appealing to me. I have a job in the mornings and classes to teach in the evenings plus a husband and a child and a home to take care of. It is too much.' She lifts the assignment into the air as if to assess its weight. 'Too much,' she repeats.

'We are sometimes called on when we least expect it,' he says.

'I understand what you are saying,' she says, 'but it is too much for me.'

He takes the three pages from her hand and stows them in his bag. 'Goodbye,' he says. 'Thank you again.'

There are two things that can happen now. One is that nothing will happen. The other is that señora Martina will have a change of heart and track him down to his room, where he will be lying on his bed of an afternoon listening to the radio, and say, *Very well, Simón, enlighten me: say what it is that you want from me.* He gives her three days.

Three days pass. Señora Martina does not knock at his door. Clearly it is the first thing that has happened: nothing.

His room, which was painted long ago in a depressing egg-yolk colour, has never grown to become a home to him. The aged couple from whom he rents it keep their distance, for which he is grateful, but there are nights when, through the flimsy walls, he can hear the man, who has something wrong with him, coughing and coughing.

He haunts the corridors of the Institute. He attends a short course on cooking, looking for ways to enrich his dull diet; but the dishes the instructor discusses require an oven, and he does not have an oven. He emerges with nothing to show but the little tray of spices that all the students are given: cumin, ginger, cinnamon, turmeric, red pepper, black pepper.

He drops in on a class in astrology. Discussion turns to the Spheres: whether the stars belong to the Spheres or on the contrary follow trajectories of their own; whether the Spheres are finite or infinite in number. The lecturer believes the number of Spheres is finite – finite but unknown and unknowable, as she puts it.

'If the number of Spheres is finite, then what lies beyond them?' asks a student.

'There is no beyond,' replies the lecturer. The student looks nonplussed. 'There is no beyond,' she repeats.

He is not interested in the Spheres, or even in the stars, which as far as he is concerned are lumps of insensate matter moving through empty space in obedience to laws of mysterious origin. What he wants to know is what the stars have to do with the numbers, what the numbers have to do with music, and how an intelligent person like Juan Sebastián Arroyo can talk about stars, numbers, and music in the same breath. But the lecturer shows no interest in numbers or music. Her subject is the configurations assumed by the stars, and how those configurations influence human destiny.

There is no beyond. How can the woman be so sure of herself? His own opinion is that, whether or not there is a beyond, one would drown in despair were there not an idea of a beyond to cling to.

Chapter 16

From the sisters Inés receives a summons: a matter of urgency has
arisen, will she and he, Simón, come out to the farm.

They are welcomed with tea and freshly baked chocolate cake.
At the sisters' urging, David wolfs down two large slices.

'David,' says Alma, when he has finished, 'I have something
that might interest you – a family of marionettes Roberta came
across in the attic, that we used to play with when we were young.
Do you know what a marionette is? Yes? Would you like to see
them?'

Alma conducts the boy out of the room; they can get down to
business.

'We have had a visit from señor Arroyo,' says Valentina. 'He
brought along those two nice boys of his. He wants to know
whether we would consider helping to put his Academy back on
its feet again. He has lost many students as a result of this tragic
affair, but he is hopeful that, if the Academy reopens soon, some
will come back. What is your opinion, Inés, Simón? You are the
ones with direct experience of the Academy.'

'Let me begin,' says he, Simón. 'It is all very well for señor
Arroyo to declare his Academy reopened, but who is going to
do the teaching? And who will take care of the administration?

Señora Arroyo used to carry the entire burden. Where in Estrella will he find someone to fill her place, someone who shares his outlook, his philosophy?'

'He tells us that his sister-in-law will be coming to help out,' says Valentina. 'He also speaks highly of a young man named Alyosha. He feels that Alyosha will be able to take over some of the workload. But essentially the Academy will become an academy of music rather than an academy of dance, and señor Arroyo himself will do the teaching.'

Inés now speaks, and loses no time in making her position clear. 'When we first sent David to the Arroyos, it was promised to us – promised, mind you – that besides the dancing he would be getting a normal education. We were told he would learn to read and write and handle numbers as children do in normal schools. He got none of that. Señor Arroyo is a nice man, I am sure, but he is not a proper teacher. I would be very reluctant to put David back in his care.'

'What do you mean when you say he is not a proper teacher?' asks Valentina.

'I mean his head is in the clouds. I mean he doesn't know what is going on under his nose.'

Glances pass among the sisters. He, Simón, leans over to Inés. 'Is this the best time?' he murmurs.

'Yes, this is the best time,' says Inés. 'It is always best to be frank. We are talking about a child's future, a young child whose education thus far has been a calamity, who is falling further and further behind. I am very reluctant to submit him to yet another experiment.'

'Well, that settles the matter,' says Consuelo. 'You are David's mother, you have the right to decide what is best for him. Are we to understand then that you consider the Academy to be a bad investment?'

'Yes,' says Inés.

'And you, Simón?'

'That depends.' He turns to Inés. 'If the Academy of Dance closes for good, Inés, and if there is no place for David in the Academy of Singing, which may well be the case, and if the public schools are out of bounds, what are you proposing we should do with him? Where is he to get an education?'

Before Inés can reply, Alma returns with the boy, who bears a battered-looking plywood box. 'Alma says I can have them,' he announces.

'It's the marionettes,' says Alma. 'We have no use for them, I thought David might like to take them over.'

'Of course,' says Consuelo. 'I hope you will enjoy playing with them.'

Inés is not to be diverted. 'Where is David going to get an education? I told you. We should hire a private teacher, someone who is properly qualified with a proper diploma, someone who doesn't have outlandish beliefs about where children come from or how a child's mind works, someone who will sit down with David and cover the syllabus that normal schools cover and help him to make up the ground he has lost. That is what I think we should do.'

'What do you think, David?' says he, Simón. 'Shall we get you a private teacher?'

David seats himself with the box on his lap. 'I want to be with señor Arroyo,' he says.

'You only want to go to señor Arroyo because you can twist him around your finger,' says Inés.

'If you make me go to another school I'll run away.'

'We won't make you go anywhere. We will hire a teacher who will come and teach you at home.'

'I want to go to señor Arroyo. Señor Arroyo knows who I am. You don't know who I am.'

Inés gives a snort of exasperation. Though his heart is not in it, he, Simón, takes up the baton. 'It doesn't matter how special we are, David, there are certain things we all have to sit down and learn. We have to learn to read – and I don't mean read just one book – otherwise we won't know what is going on in the world. We have to be able to do sums, otherwise we won't be able to handle money. I think Inés also has it in mind – correct me if I am wrong, Inés – that we need to learn good habits like self-discipline and respect for the opinions of others.'

'I do know what is going on in the world,' says the boy. 'You are the one who doesn't know what is going on in the world.'

'What is going on in the world, David?' says Alma. 'We feel so cut off from the world, out here on the farm. Will you tell us?'

The boy lays the box of marionettes aside, trots over to Alma, whispers at length in her ear.

'What did he say, Alma?' asks Consuelo.

'I don't feel I can tell you. Only David can do that.'

'Will you tell us, David?' asks Consuelo.

The boy shakes his head decisively from side to side.

'Then that is the end of the matter,' says Consuelo. 'Thank you, Inés, thank you, Simón, for your advice on señor Arroyo and his Academy. If you do decide to hire a tutor for your son, I am sure we will be able to assist with the fees.'

As they are leaving, Consuelo takes him to one side. 'You must get a grip on the boy, Simón,' she murmurs. 'For his own sake. Do you understand what I mean?'

'I understand. There is another side to him, believe me. He is not always so cocksure. And his heart is good.'

'I am relieved to hear that,' says Consuelo. 'Now you must go.'

It takes him a long time to gain entry to the Academy or ex-Academy. He rings the bell, waits, rings again, on and on, then begins to rap on the door, first with his knuckles, eventually with the heel of his shoe. At last he hears stirrings within. The key turns in the lock and the door is opened by Alyosha, looking dishevelled, as if he has just woken up, though it is well past noon.

'Hello, Alyosha, do you remember me? David's father. How are you? Is the maestro in?'

'Señor Arroyo is at his music. If you want to see him you will have to wait. It may be a long wait.'

The studio where Ana Magdalena used to give her classes stands empty. The cedar floor that was polished daily by young feet in dancing slippers has lost its gleam.

'I'll wait,' he says. 'My time is not important.' He follows Alyosha to the refectory and sits down at one of the long tables.

'Tea?' says Alyosha.

'That would be nice.'

Faintly he can hear the tinkle of a piano. The music breaks off, starts again, breaks off again.

'I am told that señor Arroyo would like to reopen the Academy,' he says, 'and that you may take over some of the teaching.'

'I will be teaching the recorder and leading the elementary dance class. That is the plan. If we reopen.'

'So you will persist with dance classes. I had understood that the Academy was going to become purely an academy of music. An academy of pure music.'

'Behind music there is always dance. If we listen with attention, if we give ourselves to the music, the soul will begin to dance within us. That is one of the cornerstones of señor Arroyo's philosophy.'

'And you believe in his philosophy?'

'Yes, I do.'

'David won't be coming back, unfortunately. He wants to, very much so, but his mother is set against it. I myself don't know what to think. On the one hand, I find the philosophy of the Academy, the philosophy you share, hard to take seriously. I hope you don't mind my saying so. In particular the astrological stuff. On the other hand, David is attached to the Arroyos, particularly to the memory of Ana Magdalena. Deeply attached. He clings to it. He won't let go.'

Alyosha smiles. 'Yes, I have seen that. At first he used to test her. You must have witnessed it: how he tests people, asserts his will over them. He tried giving her orders; but she didn't tolerate it, not for a moment. *While you are in my care you will do as I say*, she said to him. *And don't give me such looks. Your looks have no power over me.* After that he never tried his tricks again. He respected her. He obeyed her. With me it's different. He knows I am soft. I don't mind.'

'How about his classmates? Do they miss her too?'

'All the young ones loved Ana Magdalena,' says Alyosha. 'She was strict with them, she was demanding, but they were devoted to her. After her passing I did my best to shield them, but there were too many stories swirling around, and then of course their parents came and fetched them away. So I can't tell you for sure how they were affected. It was a tragedy. One can't expect children to come away from such a tragedy untouched.'

'No, one can't. There is also the matter of Dmitri. They must have been shaken by that. Dmitri was a great favourite among them.'

Alyosha is about to reply when the door to the refectory bursts open and Joaquín and his brother rush excitedly in, followed a moment later by a stranger, a grey-haired woman supporting herself on a cane.

'Aunt Mercedes says we can have biscuits,' says Joaquín. 'Can we?'

'Of course,' says Alyosha. Awkwardly he performs the introduction. 'Señora Mercedes, this is señor Simón, who is the father of one of the boys at the Academy. Señor Simón, this is señora Mercedes, who is visiting us from Novilla.'

Señora Mercedes, Aunt Mercedes, offers him a bony hand. In her narrow, aquiline features and sallow skin he can find no resemblance to Ana Magdalena.

'Let us not interrupt you,' she says in a voice so low that it is almost a croak. 'The boys just came for a snack.'

'You interrupt nothing,' he, Simón, replies. It is not true. He would like to hear more from Alyosha. He is impressed by the young man, by his good sense, his seriousness. 'I am just marking time, waiting to see señor Arroyo. Perhaps, Alyosha, you can remind him that I am here.'

With a sigh señora Mercedes lowers herself onto a chair. 'Your son is not with you?' she says.

'He is at home with his mother.'

'His name is David,' says Joaquín. 'He is the best in the class.' He and his brother have seated themselves at the far end of the table with the can of biscuits before them.

'I have come to discuss my son's future with señor Arroyo,' he explains to Mercedes. 'His future and the future of the Academy, after the recent tragedy. Allow me to say how stricken we all are by your sister's death. She was an exceptional teacher and an exceptional person.'

'Ana Magdalena was not my sister,' says Mercedes. 'My sister, Joaquín's and Damian's mother, passed away ten years ago. Ana Magdalena is – was – Juan Sebastián's second wife. The Arroyos are a complicated family. Thankfully I am not part of that complication.'

Of course! Twice married! What a stupid mistake on his part! 'My apologies,' he says. 'I wasn't thinking.'

'But of course I knew her, Ana Magdalena,' señora Mercedes continues, unperturbed. 'She was even, briefly, a student of mine. That was how she came to meet Juan Sebastián. That was how she entered the family.'

His stupid mistake has, it seems, opened the way for old animosities to be aired.

'You taught dance?' he says.

'I taught dance. I still do, though you would not think so, looking at me.' She raps on the floor with her cane.

'I confess I find dance somewhat of a foreign language,' he says. 'David has given up trying to explain it to me.'

'Then what are you doing, sending him to an academy of dance?'

'David is his own master. His mother and I have no control over him. He has a lovely voice but won't sing. He is a gifted dancer but won't dance for me. Refuses point-blank. Says I don't understand.'

'If your son were to explain his dance he would not be able to dance any more,' says Mercedes. 'That is the paradox within which we dancers are trapped.'

'Believe me, señora, you are not the first to tell me so. From señor Arroyo, from Ana Magdalena, from my son, I hear continually how obtuse my questioning is.'

Mercedes gives a laugh, low and hard, like a dog's bark. 'You need to learn to dance, Simón – may I call you Simón? It will cure you of your obtuseness. Or put a stop to your questioning.'

'I fear I am past cure, Mercedes. To be truthful, I don't see the question to which dance is the answer.'

'No, I can see you don't. But you must have been in love sometime. When you were in love, did you not see the question to which love was the answer, or were you an obtuse lover too?'

He is silent.

'Were you not perhaps in love with Ana Magdalena, just a little?' she persists. 'That seemed to be her effect on most men. And you, Alyosha – what about you? Were you in love with Ana Magdalena too?'

Alyosha colours but does not speak.

'I ask seriously: What was the question to which Ana Magdalena was in so many cases the answer?'

It is a real question, he can see that. Mercedes is a serious woman, a serious person. But is it one to be debated in front of children?

'I was not in love with Ana Magdalena,' he says. 'I have not been in love for as long as I can remember, not with anyone. But, in the abstract, I acknowledge the force of your question. What is it that we lack when we lack nothing, when we are sufficient unto ourselves? What is it that we miss when we are not in love?'

'Dmitri was in love with her.' It is Joaquín who interrupts, in his clear and as yet unbroken child's voice.

'Dmitri is the man who killed Ana Magdalena,' he, Simón, explains.

'I know about Dmitri. Across the country I doubt there is anyone who does not know his story. Thwarted in love, Dmitri turned on the unattainable object of his desire and killed her. Of course it was a terrible thing he did. Terrible but not hard to understand.'

'I disagree,' he says. 'From the beginning I found his actions incomprehensible. His judges found them incomprehensible too. That is why he is locked up in a psychiatric hospital. Because no sane being could have done what he did.'

Dmitri was no thwarted lover. That is what he cannot say, not openly. That is what is truly incomprehensible, more than incomprehensible. *He killed her because he felt like it. He killed her to see what it was like, strangling a woman. He killed her for no reason.*

'I don't understand Dmitri, nor do I want to,' he presses on. 'What happens to him is a matter of indifference to me. He can languish in psychiatric wards until he is old and grey, he can be sent to the salt mines to work himself to death – it is all the same.'

A glance passes between Mercedes and Alyosha. 'A sore spot, evidently,' says Mercedes. 'Forgive me for touching on it.'

'How about a walk?' says Alyosha to the boys. 'We can go to the park. Bring some bread – we can feed the goldfish.'

They leave. He and Mercedes are alone. But he is in no mood for talk; nor evidently is she. Through the open door comes the sound of Arroyo at the keyboard. He closes his eyes, tries to calm himself, to let the music find its way in. Alyosha's words come back to him: *If we listen with attention the soul will begin to dance within us.* When did his soul last dance?

From the way the music kept stopping and starting he had assumed that Arroyo was practising. But he was wrong. The pauses last too long for that, and the music itself seems sometimes to lose its way. The man is not practising but composing. He listens with a different kind of attention.

The music is too variable in its rhythm, too complicated in its logic for a ponderous being like him to follow, but it brings to mind the dance of one of those little birds that hover and dart, their wings beating too fast to see. The question is, where is the soul? When will the soul emerge from its hiding place and open its wings?

He is not on close terms with his soul. What he knows about the soul in general, what he has read, is that it flits away when confronted with a mirror and therefore cannot be seen by the one who owns it, the one whom it owns.

Unable to see his soul, he has not questioned what people tell him about it: that it is a dry soul, deficient in passion. His own, obscure intuition — that, far from lacking in passion, his soul aches with longing for it knows not what — he treats sceptically as just the kind of story that someone with a dry, rational, deficient soul will tell himself to maintain his self-respect.

So he tries not to think, to do nothing that might alarm the timid soul within. He gives himself to the music, allowing it to enter and wash through him. And the music, as if aware of what is up, loses its stop–start character, begins to flow. At the very rim of consciousness the soul, which is indeed like a little bird, emerges and shakes its wings and begins its dance.

That is how Alyosha finds him: sitting at the table with his chin propped on his hands, fast asleep. Alyosha gives him a shake. 'Señor Arroyo will see you now.'

Of the woman with the cane, the sister-in-law Mercedes, there is no sign. How long has he been absent?

He trails behind Alyosha down the corridor.

Chapter 17

The room into which he is ushered is pleasantly bright and airy, lit by glass panels in the roof through which sunlight pours. It is bare save for a table with a mess of papers on it and a grand piano. Arroyo rises to greet him.

He had expected a man in mourning, a broken man. But Arroyo, wearing a plum-coloured smoking jacket over pyjamas and slippers, seems as solid and cheerful as ever. He offers him, Simón, a cigarette, which he declines.

'A pleasure to see you again, señor Simón,' says Arroyo. 'I have not forgotten our conversation on the shores of Lake Calderón, concerning the stars. What shall we discuss today?'

After the music and then the slumber his tongue is slow, his mind befuddled. 'My son David,' he says. 'I have come to talk about him. About his future. David has been growing a little wild of late. In the absence of schooling. We have applied for him to enter the Academy of Singing, but our hopes are not high. We are worried about him, his mother particularly so. She has been thinking of hiring a private tutor. But now we hear rumours that you may be opening your doors again. We are wondering . . .'

'You are wondering, if we reopen, who will do the teaching. You are wondering who will take the place of my wife. Who indeed! Because your son was very close to her, as you know. Who can replace her in his heart?'

'You are correct. He still holds on to the memory of her. Will not let go. But there is more to it than that.' The fog begins to retreat. 'David has great respect for you, señor Arroyo. He says you know who he is. *Señor Arroyo knows who I am.* I, on the other hand – so he says – do not know and have never known. I must ask: What does he mean when he says that you know who he is?'

'You are his father yet you do not know who he is?'

'I am not his true father, nor have I ever claimed to be. I think of myself as a kind of stepfather. I met him on the ship coming here. I could see that he was lost, therefore I took charge of him, took care of him. Later I was able to unite him with his mother, Inés. That is our story, in a nutshell.'

'And now you want me to tell you who he is, this child whom you met on board ship. If I were a philosopher I would reply by saying: It depends on what you mean by *who*, it depends on what you mean by *he*, it depends on what you mean by *is*. Who is he? Who are you? Indeed, who am I? All I can tell you with certainty is that one day a being, a male child, appeared out of nowhere on the doorstep of this Academy. You know that as well as I do because you brought him. Since that day it has been my pleasure to be his musician accompanist. I have accompanied him in his dances, as I accompany all the children in my care. I have also talked with him. We have talked a lot, your David and I. It has been enlightening.'

'We agree to call him David, señor Arroyo, but his true name, if I can use that expression, if it means anything, is of course not David, as you must know if you know who he really is. David is just the name on his card, the name they gave him at the docks.

Equally well I could say that Simón is not my true name, just a name given to me at the docks. To me names are not important, not worth making a fuss about. I am aware that you take a different line, that when it comes to names and numbers you and I belong to different schools of thought. But let me say my say. In my school of thought names are simply a convenience, just as numbers are a convenience. There is nothing mysterious about them. The boy we are talking about could equally well have had the name *sixty-six* attached to him, and I the name *ninety-nine*. *Sixty-six* and *ninety-nine* would have done just as well as *David* and *Simón*, once we got used to them. I have never grasped why the boy I am now calling David finds names so significant – his name in particular. Our so-called true names, the names we had before *David* and *Simón*, are only substitutes, it seems to me, for the names we had before them, and so on backwards. It is like paging through a book, back and back, looking for page one. But there is no page one. The book has no beginning; or the beginning is lost in the mists of the general forgetting. That, at least, is how I see it. So I repeat my question: What does David mean when he says you know *who he is*?'

'And if I were a philosopher, señor Simón, I would respond by saying: It depends on what you mean by *know*. Did I meet the boy in a previous life? How can I be sure? The memory is lost, as you say, in the general forgetting. I have my intuitions, as no doubt you have your intuitions, but intuitions are not memories. You remember meeting the boy on board ship and deciding he was lost and taking charge of him. Perhaps he remembers the event differently. Perhaps you were the one who looked lost; perhaps *he* decided to take charge of *you*.'

'You misjudge me. I may have memories but I have no intuitions. Intuitions are not part of my stock-in-trade.'

'Intuitions are like shooting stars. They flash across the skies, here one moment, gone the next. If you don't see them, perhaps it is because your eyes are closed.'

'But *what* is flashing across the skies? If you know the answer, why don't you tell me?'

Señor Arroyo grinds his cigarette dead. 'It depends on what you mean by *answer*,' he says. He rises, grips him, Simón, by the shoulders, stares into his eyes. 'Courage, my friend,' he says in his smoky breath. 'Young David is an exceptional child. The word I use for him is *integral*. He is integral in a way that other children are not. Nothing can be taken away from him. Nothing can be added. Who or what you or I believe him to be is of no importance. Nonetheless, I take seriously your wish to have your question answered. The answer will come when you least expect it. Or else it will not come. That too happens.'

Irritably he shakes himself loose. 'I cannot tell you, señor Arroyo,' he says, 'how much I dislike these cheap paradoxes and mystifications. Do not misunderstand me. I respect you as I respected your late wife. You are educators, you take your profession seriously, your concern for your students is genuine – I doubt none of that. But regarding your system, *el sistema Arroyo*, I have the most profound doubts. I say so in all deference to you as a musician. Stars. Meteors. Arcane dances. Numerology. Secret names. Mystical revelations. It may impress young minds but please don't try to foist it on me.'

On his way out of the Academy, preoccupied, in a bad humour, he stumbles into Arroyo's sister-in-law, almost knocking her over.

Her stick goes clattering down the stairs. He recovers the stick for her, apologizes for his clumsiness.

'Don't apologize,' she says. 'There ought to be a light on the stairway, I don't know why the building has to be so dark and gloomy. But since I have you, give me your arm. I need cigarettes, and I don't want to send one of the boys, it sets a bad example.'

He assists her to the kiosk at the street corner. She is slow, but he is in no hurry. It is a pleasant day. He begins to relax.

'Would you like a cup of coffee?' he proposes.

They sit at a sidewalk cafe, enjoying the sun on their faces.

'I hope you weren't offended by my remarks,' she says. 'I mean my remarks about Ana Magdalena and her effect on men. Ana Magdalena was not my type, but in fact I was quite fond of her. And the death she met – no one deserves to die like that.'

He is silent.

'As I mentioned, I taught her when she was young. She showed promise, she worked hard, she was serious about her career. But the transition from girlhood to womanhood was hard for her to deal with. It is always a difficult time for a dancer, in her case especially so. She wanted to preserve the purity of her lines, the purity that comes easily to us when we are immature, but she failed, the new womanliness of her body kept coming out, kept expressing itself. So in the end she gave up, found other things to do. I lost touch with her. Then after my sister's death she suddenly re-emerged at Juan Sebastián's side. I was surprised – I had no idea they were in contact – but I said nothing.

'She was good for him, I will say that, a good wife. He would have been lost without someone like her. She took over the children – the younger one was just a baby then – and became a mother to them. She extracted Juan Sebastián from the clock-repair business, where he had no future, and got him to open his Academy. He has flourished ever since. So don't mistake me. She was an admirable person in many ways.'

He is silent.

'Juan Sebastián is a man of learning. Have you read his book? No? He has written a book on his philosophy of music. You can still find it in the bookshops. My sister helped him. My sister had a musical training. She was an excellent pianist. She and Juan Sebastián used to plays duets together. Whereas Ana Magdalena, while she is or was a perfectly intelligent young woman, was neither a musician nor what I would call a person of intellect. For intellect she substituted enthusiasm. She took over Juan Sebastián's philosophy holus-bolus and became an enthusiast for it. She applied it to her dance classes. God knows what the little ones made of it. Let me ask, Simón: What did your son make of Ana Magdalena's teaching?'

What did David make of Ana Magdalena's teaching? He is about to give his reply, his considered reply, when something comes over him. Whether it is the memory flooding back of his angry outburst to Arroyo, or whether he is simply tired, tired of being reasonable, he cannot say, but he can feel his face crumple, and the voice that issues from his throat he can barely recognise as his own, so cracked and parched is it. 'My son, Mercedes, was the one who discovered Ana Magdalena. He witnessed her on her deathbed. His memories of her are contaminated by that vision, that horror. Because she had been dead, you know, for some time. Not a sight that any child should be exposed to.

'My son, to answer your question, is trying to cling to the memory of Ana Magdalena as she was in life and to the stories he heard from her. He would like to believe in a heavenly realm where the numbers dance eternally. He would like to think that, when he dances the dances she taught him, the numbers descend and dance with him. At the end of each school day Ana Magdalena used to gather the children around her and sound what she called her arc – which I later found was just an ordinary tuning fork – and get them to close their eyes and hum together on that tone. It would settle their souls, she told them, bringing them into harmony with the tone that the stars gave out as they wheeled on their axes. Well, that is what my son would like to hold on to: the heavenly tone. By joining in the dance of the stars, he would like to believe, we participate in their heavenly being. But how can he, Mercedes, *how can he*, after what he saw?'

Mercedes reaches across the table and pats his arm. 'There, there,' she says. 'You have been through a trying time, all of you. Perhaps it would be best if your son put the Academy behind him, with its bad memories, and went to a normal school with normal teachers.'

A second great wave of exhaustion sweeps over him. What is he doing, exchanging words with this stranger who understands nothing? 'My son is not a normal child,' he says. 'I am sorry, I am not feeling well, I cannot continue.' He signals to the waiter.

'You are distressed, Simón. I will not detain you. Let me just say, I am here in Estrella not for the sake of my brother-in-law, who barely tolerates me, but for my sister's children, two lost little boys to whom no one gives a second thought. Your son will move on, but what is their future? Having lost first their mother then their stepmother, they are left behind in this hard world of men and men's ideas. I weep for them, Simón. They need softness as all children need softness, even boy children. They need to be caressed and cuddled, to inhale the soft odours of women and feel the softness of a woman's touch. Where are they going to get that? They will grow up incomplete, unable to flower.'

Softness. Mercedes hardly strikes him as soft, with her sharp beak of a nose and her bony, arthritic hands. He pays, rises. 'I must go,' he says. 'It is David's birthday tomorrow. He will be seven. There are preparations to be made.'

Chapter 18

Inés is determined that the boy's birthday will be celebrated fittingly. To the party have been invited as many of his classmates from the old Academy as she has been able to track down, as well as the boys from the apartment block with whom he plays football. From the *pastelería* she has ordered a cake shaped like a football; she has brought home a gaily painted *piñata* in the form of a donkey and from her friend Claudia borrowed the paddles with which the children will beat it to pieces; she has engaged a conjuror to put on a magic show. She has not revealed to him, Simón, what her birthday gift will be, but he knows she has spent a lot of money on it.

His first impulse is to match Inés in munificence, but he checks that impulse: as he is the minor parent, so his gift should be the minor gift. In the back room of an antiques store he finds exactly the right thing: a model ship much like the ship they came on, with a smokestack and a propeller and a captain's bridge and tiny passengers carved in wood leaning on the rails or promenading on the upper deck.

While he is exploring the shops of the old quarter of Estrella he looks out for the book Mercedes mentioned, Arroyo's book on music. He fails to find it. None of the booksellers have heard of it. 'I have been to some of his recitals,' says one of them. 'He is an amazing pianist, a true virtuoso. I had no idea he wrote books too. Are you sure of it?'

By arrangement with Inés, the boy spends the night before the party with him in his rented room so that she can ready the apartment.

'Your last night as a small boy,' he remarks to the boy. 'As of tomorrow you will be a seven-year-old, and a seven-year-old is a big boy.'

'Seven is a noble number,' says the boy. 'I know all the noble numbers. Do you want me to recite them?'

'Not tonight, thank you. What other branches of numerology have you studied besides the noble numbers? Have you studied fractions, or are fractions off limits? Don't you know the term *numerology*? Numerology is the science that señor Arroyo practises in his Academy. Numerologists are people who believe that numbers exist independently of us. They believe that even if a great flood came and drowned all living creatures, the numbers would survive.'

'If the flood was really big, up to the sky, the numbers would be drowned too. Then there would be nothing left, only the dark stars and the dark numbers.'

'The dark stars? What are they?'

'The stars between the bright stars. You can't see them because they are dark.'

'Dark stars must be one of your discoveries. There is no mention of dark stars or dark numbers in numerology as I understand it. Furthermore, according to the numerologists, numbers cannot drown, no matter how high the floodwaters rise. They cannot drown because they neither breathe nor eat nor drink. They just exist. We human beings come and we go, we voyage from this life to the next, but the numbers stay the same forever and ever. That is what people like señor Arroyo write in their books.'

'I found out a way of coming back from the new life. Shall I tell you? It's brilliant. You tie a rope to a tree, a long, long rope, then when you get to the next life you tie the other end of the rope to a tree, another tree. Then when you want to come back from the next life you just hold on to the rope. Like the man in the *larebinto*.'

'*Laberinto*. That's a very clever plan, very ingenious. Unfortunately I see a flaw in it. The flaw is that while you are swimming back to this life, holding on to the rope, the waves will reach up and wash you clean of your memories. So when you reach this side you will remember nothing of what you saw on the other side. It will be as if you had never visited the other side at all. It will be as if you had slept without dreaming.'

'Why?'

'Because, as I said, you will have been immersed in the waters of forgetting.'

'But why? Why do I have to forget?'

'Because that is the rule. You cannot come back from the next life and report what you saw there.'

'Why is it the rule?'

'A rule is just a rule. Rules don't have to justify themselves. They just are. Like numbers. There is no *why* for numbers. This universe is a universe of rules. There is no *why* for the universe.'

'Why?'

'Now you are being silly.'

Later, when David has fallen asleep on the sofa and he himself is lying in bed listening to the scurrying of mice in the ceiling, he wonders how the boy will look back on these conversations of theirs. He, Simón, thinks of himself as a sane, rational person who offers the boy a sane, rational elucidation of why things are the way they are. But are the needs of a child's soul better served by his dry little homilies than by the fantastic fare offered at the Academy? Why not let him spend these precious years dancing the numbers and communing with the stars in the company of Alyosha and señor Arroyo, and wait for sanity and reason to arrive in their own good time?

A rope from land to land: he should tell Arroyo about that, send him a note. 'My son, the one who says you know his true name, has come up with a plan for our general salvation: a rope bridge from shore to shore; souls pulling themselves hand over hand across the ocean, some toward the new life, some back toward the old one. If there were such a bridge, says my son, it would mean the end of forgetfulness. We would all know who we are, and rejoice.'

He ought really to write to Arroyo. Not just a note but something longer and fuller that would say what he might have said had he not stormed out of their meeting. If he were not so sleepy, so lethargic, he would switch on the light and do it. 'Esteemed Juan Sebastián, forgive my show of petulance this morning. I am going through a troubled time, though of course the burden under which I labour is far lighter than yours. Specifically, I find myself at sea (I use a common metaphor), drifting further and further from solid land. How so? Allow me to be candid. Despite strenuous efforts of the intellect, I cannot believe in the numbers, the higher numbers, the numbers on high, as you do and as everyone connected with your Academy seems to do, including my son David. I understand nothing about the numbers, neither a jot nor a tittle, from beginning to end. Your faith in them has helped you (I surmise) to get through these difficult times, whereas I, who do not share that faith, am touchy, irascible, prone to outbursts (you beheld one this morning) – am in fact becoming hard to bear, not only to those around me but to myself.

'*The answer will come to you when you least expect it. Or not.* I have a distaste for paradoxes, Juan Sebastián, which you seem not to share. Is that what I must do to attain peace of mind: swallow paradoxes as they arise? And while you are about it, help me to understand why a child schooled by you, when asked to explain the numbers, should reply that they cannot be explained, can only be danced. The same child, before attending your Academy, was afraid of stepping from one paving stone to the next lest he fall through the gap and disappear into nothingness. Yet now he dances across gaps without a qualm. *What magical powers does dancing have?*'

He should do it. He should write the note. But will Juan Sebastián write back? Juan Sebastián does not strike him as the kind of man who will get out of bed in the middle of the night to throw a rope to a man who, if not drowning, is at least floundering.

As he descends into sleep an image comes to him from the football games in the park: the boy, head down, fists clenched, running and running like an irresistible force. Why, why, why, when he is so full of life – of this life, this present life – is he so interested in the next one?

The first arrivals at the party are two boys from one of the apartments below, brothers, uncomfortable in their neat shirts and shorts with their wetted-down hair. They hurry to offer their colourfully wrapped present, which David deposits in a space he has cleared in a corner: 'This is my present pile,' he announces. 'I am not going to open my presents until everyone has gone.'

The present pile already contains the marionettes from the sisters on the farm and his, Simón's, gift, the ship, packed in a cardboard box and tied with a ribbon.

The doorbell rings; David rushes off to greet new guests and accept more gifts.

Since Diego has taken on the task of passing round refreshments, there is little for him to do. He suspects that most of their guests take Diego to be the boy's father and him, Simón, to be a grandfather or some even more remote relative.

The party goes well, though the handful of children from the Academy are wary of the more boisterous children from the apartments and cluster together, whispering among themselves. Inés – her hair fashionably waved, wearing a smart black-and-white frock, in every respect a mother of whom a boy can feel proud – looks pleased with the proceedings.

'That's a nice dress,' he remarks to her. 'It suits you.'

'Thank you,' she says. 'It is time for the birthday cake. Can you bring it in?'

So it is his privilege to bear to the table the giant football cake, set in its bed of green marzipan, and to smile benevolently as with a single *whoosh* David blows out all seven candles.

'Bravo!' says Inés. 'Now you have to wish.'

'I already made my wish,' says the boy. 'It's a secret. I'm not going to tell anyone.'

'Not even me?' says Diego. 'Not even in my ear?' And he inclines his head intimately.

'No,' says the boy.

There is a setback with the cutting of the cake: as the knife sinks in, the chocolate shell cracks and the cake breaks into two unequal halves, one of which rolls off the board and tumbles in fragments on the tabletop, knocking over a glass of lemonade.

With a cry of triumph David brandishes the knife over his head: 'It's an earthquake!'

Inés hastens to mop up the mess. 'Be careful with that knife,' she says. 'You could hurt someone.'

'It's my birthday, I can do what I want.'

The telephone rings. It is the conjuror. He is running late, he will be another forty-five minutes, perhaps an hour. Inés slams down the receiver in a fury. 'What way is that to run a business!' she cries.

There are too many children for the apartment. Diego has twisted a balloon into the shape of a manikin with huge ears; this becomes the object of a chase among the boys. They tear through the rooms, knocking over furniture. Bolívar rouses himself and emerges from his lair in the kitchen. The children recoil in alarm. It falls to him, Simón, to hold the dog back by the collar.

'His name is Bolívar,' announces David. 'He won't bite, he only bites bad people.'

'Can I pat him?' asks one of the girls.

'Bolívar isn't in a friendly mood right now,' replies he, Simón. 'He is used to sleeping in the afternoons. He is very much a creature of habit.' And he manhandles Bolívar back into the kitchen.

Blessedly, Diego persuades the rougher boys, David among them, to go out to the park for a game of football. He and Inés are left behind to entertain the timid ones. Then the footballers return in a rush to gobble up the last of the cake and biscuits.

There is a knock at the door. The conjuror stands there, a flustered-looking little man with rosy cheeks, wearing a top hat and tails, carrying a wicker basket. Inés does not give him a chance to speak. 'Too late!' she cries. 'What way is this to treat customers? Go! You are not getting a penny from us!'

The guests leave. Armed with a pair of scissors, David begins to open his gifts. He unwraps the gift from Inés and Diego. 'It's a guitar!' he says.

'It's a ukulele,' says Diego. 'There's a booklet too that tells you how to play it.'

The boy strums the ukulele, producing a jangled chord.

'It has first to be tuned,' says Diego. 'Let me show you how.'

'Not now,' says the boy. He opens his, Simón's, present. 'It's brilliant!' he cries out. 'Can we take it to the park and sail it?'

'It's a model,' he replies. 'I am not sure it will float without tipping. We can experiment in the bathtub.'

They fill the bathtub. The boat floats gaily on the surface, with no sign of tipping. 'It's brilliant!' repeats the boy. 'It's my best present.'

'Once you have learned to play it, the ukulele will grow to be your best present,' he says. 'The ukulele isn't just a model, it is the real thing, a real musical instrument. Have you said thank you to Inés and Diego?'

'Juan Pablo says the Academy is a sissy school. He says only sissies go to the Academy.'

He knows who Juan Pablo is: one of the boys from the apartments, older and bigger than David.

'Juan Pablo has never been through the doors of the Academy. He has no idea what goes on there. If you were a sissy, would Bolívar let you boss him around – Bolívar who in the next life will be a wolf?'

Inés catches him at the door as he is leaving, thrusts some papers into his hands. 'There's a letter here from the Academy, and yesterday's newspaper, the Tuition Offered pages. We must decide on a tutor for David. I have marked the likely ones. We can't wait any longer.'

The letter, addressed jointly to Inés and him, is not from Arroyo's Academy but from the Academy of Singing. Due to the exceptionally high standard of applications for the coming quarter, it informs them, there will regrettably be no place for David. They are thanked for their interest.

With the letter in his hand he returns the next morning to the Academy of Dance.

Grimly he seats himself in the refectory. 'Tell señor Arroyo I am here,' he instructs Alyosha. 'Say I will not leave until I have spoken to him.'

Minutes later the master himself appears. 'Señor Simón! You are back!'

'Yes, I am back. You are a busy man, señor Arroyo, so I will be brief. I mentioned last time that we had applied for David to enter the Academy of Singing. That application has now been turned down. We are left with a choice between the public schools and private tuition.

'There are certain facts I have kept from you that you ought to be aware of. When my partner Inés and I left Novilla and came to Estrella, we were fleeing the law. Not because we are bad people but because the authorities in Novilla wanted to take David away from us, on grounds which I will not go into, and place him in an institution. We resisted. We are thus, technically speaking, lawbreakers, Inés and I.

'We brought David here and found a home for him in your Academy – a temporary home, as it turned out to be. I come to the point. If we enrol David in a public school, we have every reason to expect he will be identified and sent back to Novilla. So we are avoiding the public schools. The census, which is less than a month away, is an added complication. We will have to hide all traces of him from the census-takers.'

'I will be hiding my sons too. David can join them. There are plenty of dark corners in this building.'

'Why do you need to hide your sons?'

'They were not counted in the last census, therefore they have no numbers, therefore they do not exist. They are ghosts. But go on. You were telling me you will be avoiding the public schools.'

'Yes. Inés is in favour of a private tutor for David. We tried the experiment of a tutor once before. It was not a success. The boy has a forceful personality. He is used to getting his own way. He needs to become more of a social animal. He needs to be in a class with other children, under the guiding hand of a teacher he respects.

'I am aware that your means are straitened, señor Arroyo. If you can see your way clear to reopening the Academy, and if David can come back, I offer you my assistance without remuneration. I can do janitorial work – sweeping and cleaning and carrying firewood and so forth. I can help with the boarders. I am not shy of physical labour. In Novilla I worked as a stevedore.

'I may not be David's father but I am still his guardian and protector. Unfortunately, he seems to be losing the respect for me that he used to have. That is part of the wildness of his present condition. He derides me as the old man who follows him around wagging a finger and admonishing him. But you he respects, señor Arroyo, you and your late wife.

'If you reopen your doors your old students will come back, I am convinced of that. David will be the first. I don't pretend to understand your philosophy, but being under your wing does the boy good, I can see that.

'What do you say?'

Señor Arroyo has listened to him with great earnestness, not interrupting him once. Now he speaks.

'Señor Simón, since you are frank with me I will be frank with you. You say your son derides you. That is not in fact true. He loves and admires you, even if he does not always obey you. He tells me with pride of how, when you were a stevedore, you used to carry the heaviest loads, heavier than any of your younger comrades. What he does hold against you is that, though you act as his father, you do not know who he is. You are aware of this. We discussed it before.'

'He does not merely hold it against me, señor Arroyo, he hurls it in my face.'

'He hurls it in your face and it upsets you, as it should. Let me rephrase what I said to you when last we met, and perhaps offer you some reassurance.

'We have, each of us, had the experience of arriving in a new land and being allotted a new identity. We live, each of us, under a name that is not our own. But we soon get used to it, to this new, invented life.

'Your son is an exception. He feels with unusual intensity the falsity of his new life. He has not yielded to the pressure to forget. What he remembers I cannot say, but it includes what he believes to be his true name. What is that name? Again I cannot say. He refuses to reveal it or is unable to reveal it, I do not know which. Perhaps it is best, on the whole, that his secret be kept secret. What difference does it make, as you said the other day, whether he is known to us as David or Tomás, as sixty-six or ninety-nine, as Alpha or Omega? Would the earth tremble under our feet were his true name to be revealed, would the stars fall from the skies? Of course not.

'So be consoled. You are not the first father to be denied, nor will you be the last.

'Now to the other matter. You volunteer your services to the Academy. Thank you. My inclination is to accept, with gratitude. My late wife's sister has also kindly offered to help. She is – I don't know whether she told you – a distinguished teacher, though of another school. And my desire to reopen the Academy has received support in further quarters too. All of which encourages me to believe we may overcome our present difficulties. However, give me a little more time to come to a decision.'

The discussion ends there. He takes his leave. *Our present difficulties*: the phrase leaves a bad taste behind. Does Arroyo have any idea of what his difficulties are? How much longer can he be shielded from the truth about Ana Magdalena? The longer Dmitri stays on at the hospital, killing time, the likelier it is he will start boasting to his friends about the maestro's icy wife who could not keep her hands off him. The story will spread like wildfire. People will snigger behind Arroyo's back; from being a figure of tragedy he will become a figure of fun. He, Simón, ought by now to have found a way of warning him, so that, when the whispering begins, he will be prepared for it.

And the letters, the incriminating letters! He should have burnt them long ago. *Te quiero apasionadamente.* For the thousandth time he curses himself for getting involved in Dmitri's affairs.

Chapter 19

It is in this vexed state of mind that he arrives home and finds, sprawled outside his door, none other than Dmitri, dressed in the uniform of a hospital orderly, sopping wet – it has been raining again – yet smiling broadly.

'Hello, Simón. Terrible weather, isn't it? Will you let me in?'

'No, I will not. How did you get here? Is David with you?'

'David knows nothing about this. I came unaided: caught a bus, then walked. No one gave me a second glance. *Brr!* It's cold. What wouldn't I give for a hot cup of tea!'

'Why are you here, Dmitri?'

Dmitri chuckles. 'Quite a surprise, isn't it? You should see your face. *Aiding and abetting*: I can see the words passing through your mind. Aiding and abetting a criminal. Don't worry. I'll be off soon. You won't see me again, not in this life. So come on, let me in.'

He unlocks the door. Dmitri enters, sweeps the cover off the bed, wraps himself in it. 'That's better!' he says. 'You want to know why I am here? I will tell you, so listen carefully. When dawn comes, a few brief hours from now, I will be taking the road to the north, to the salt mines. That is my decision, my final decision. I will consign myself to the salt mines, and who knows what will become of me there. People have always said, "Dmitri, you are like a bear, nothing can kill you." Well, maybe that was once true, but not any more. The whiplash, the chains, the bread and water – who knows how long I will be able to endure before I fall to my knees and say, "Enough! Dispose of me! Give me the *coup de grâce*!"

'There are only two men of intellect in this benighted town, Simón, you and señor Arroyo; and Arroyo is out of the question, it would not be seemly, me being the murderer of his wife and so on. So that leaves you. You I can still talk to. You think I talk too much, I know that, and you are right, in a way, I can be a bit of a bore. But look at it from my point of view. If I don't talk, if I don't explain myself, who am I? An ox. A nobody. Maybe a psychopath. Maybe. But certainly a nothing, a zero, with no place in the world. You don't understand that, do you? Parsimonious with words, that's you. Each word checked and weighed before you send it out. Well, it takes all kinds.

'I loved that woman, Simón. The moment I laid eyes on her I knew she was my star, my destiny. A hole opened up in my existence, a hole that she and she alone could ever fill. If the truth be told, I am in love with her still, Ana Magdalena, though she is buried in the ground or else burnt to ash, no one will tell me which. *So what?* you say – *people fall in love every day*. But not as I was in love. I was unworthy of her, that is the plain truth. Do you understand? Can you understand what it was like to be with a woman, to be with her in the fullest of senses, I put it delicately, when you forget where you are and time is suspended, that sort of being-with, the rapturous sort, when you are in her and she is in you – to be with her like that and yet be aware in a corner of your mind that there is something wrong about all of it, not morally wrong, I have never had much truck with morality, have always been the independent type, morally independent, but wrong in a cosmological sense, as if the planets in the heavens above our heads were misaligned, were saying to us *No, no, no*? Do you understand? No, of course you don't, and who can blame you. I'm explaining myself badly.

'As I said, I was unworthy of her, of Ana Magdalena. That's what it comes down to in the end. I should not have been there, sharing her bed. It was wrong. It was an offence — against the stars, against something or other, I don't know what. That was the feeling I had, the obscure feeling, the feeling that wouldn't go away. Can you understand? Do you have any glimmering?'

'I am completely incurious about your feelings, Dmitri, past and present. You don't have to tell me any of this. I am not encouraging you.'

'Of course you are not encouraging me! No one could be more respectful of my right to privacy. You are a decent fellow, Simón, one of the rare breed of truly decent men. But I don't want to be private! I want to be human, and to be human is to be a speaking animal. That is why I am telling you these things: so that I can be human again, hear a human voice issuing again from this breast of mine, Dmitri's breast! And if I can't tell them to you, who can I tell them to? Who is left? So let me tell you: we used to do it, make love, she and I, whenever we could, whenever there was an hour to spare, or even a minute or two or three. I can be frank about these things, can't I? Because I have no secrets from you, Simón — not since you read those letters you were not supposed to read.

'Ana Magdalena. You saw her, Simón, you must agree, she was a beauty, a true beauty, the real thing, flawless from top to toe.

I should have been proud to have a beauty like that in my arms, but I wasn't. No, I was ashamed. Because she deserved better, better than an ugly, hairy, ignorant nobody like me. I think of those cool arms of hers, cool as marble, clasped around me, drawing me into her – *me! me!* – and I shake my head. Something wrong there, Simón, something deeply wrong. Beauty and the beast. That is why I used the word *cosmological*. Some mistake among the stars or the planets, some mix-up.

'You don't want to encourage me, and I appreciate that, I really do. It's respectful on your part. Still, you must be wondering about Ana Magdalena's side of the question. Because if I was indeed unworthy of her, as I am sure I was, what was she doing in bed with me? The answer, Simón, is: *I truly don't know.* What did she see in me when she had a husband a thousand times worthier of her, a husband who loved her and proved his love for her, or so she said anyhow?

'No doubt the word *appetite* occurs to you: Ana Magdalena must have had an appetite for whatever it was I offered. But it wasn't so! The appetite was all on my side. On her side, nothing but grace and sweetness, as if a goddess were stepping down to grace a mortal man with a taste of immortal being. I should have worshipped her, and I did, I truly did, until the fateful day when it all went bad. That's why I am off to the salt mines, Simón: because of my ingratitude. It's a terrible sin, ingratitude, perhaps the worst of the lot. Where did it come from, that ingratitude of mine? Who knows. The heart of man is a dark forest, as they say. I was grateful to Ana Magdalena until one day – *boom!* – I turned ungrateful, just like that.

'And why? Why did I do the last thing to her – the ultimate thing? I beat my head – *why, you dolt, why, why?* – but I get no answer. Because I regret it, there's no doubt about that. If I could bring her back from wherever she is, from her hole in the ground or scattered like dust on the waves, I would do so in a flash. I would grovel before her, *A thousand regrets, my angel*, I would say (that's what I used to call her sometimes, *my angel*), *I won't do it again*. But regret doesn't work, does it – regret, contrition. Time's arrow: you can't reverse it. No going back.

'They don't understand these things in the hospital. Beauty, grace, gratitude – it's all a closed book to them. They peer into my head with their lamps and their microscopes and their telescopes, searching for the crossed wire or the switch that is on when it is supposed to be off. *The fault is not in my head, it's in my soul!* I tell them, but of course they ignore me. Or they give me pills. *Swallow this*, they say, *see if it puts you right. – Pills don't work on me*, I tell them, *only the lash will work! Give me the lash!*

'Only the lash will work on me, Simón, the lash and the salt mines. End of story. Thank you for hearing me out. From now on, I promise, my lips will be sealed. Never again will the sacred name of Ana Magdalena cross them. Year after year I will labour in silence, digging up salt for the good folk of the land, until one day I can no more. My heart, my faithful old bear's heart, will give in. And as I breathe my last, the blessed Ana Magdalena will descend, cool and lovely as ever, and put a finger to my lips. *Come, Dmitri*, she will say, *join me in the next life, where the past is forgiven and forgotten*. That's how I imagine it.'

As he speaks the words *forgiven and forgotten,* Dmitri's voice chokes. His eyes glisten with tears. Despite himself he, Simón, is moved. Then Dmitri recovers himself. 'I come to the point,' he says. 'Can I stay the night? Can I sleep here and gather my forces? Because tomorrow will be a long, hard day.'

'If you promise to be gone in the morning, and if you swear that I will never see you again, never never, yes, you can sleep here.'

'I swear! Never again! On the head of my mother I swear! Thank you, Simón. You are a real sport. Who would have guessed that you, the most correct, most upright man in town, would end up aiding and abetting a criminal. Another favour. Can you lend me some clothes? I would offer to buy them, but I don't have any money, they took it away from me in the hospital.'

'I will give you clothes, I will give you money, I will give whatever it takes to be rid of you.'

'Your generosity puts me to shame. Truly. I have done you a wrong, Simón. I used to make jokes about you behind your back. You didn't know that, did you?'

'Lots of people make jokes about me. I am used to it. They slide off me.'

'You know what Ana Magdalena said about you? She said you pretend to be an estimable citizen and a man of reason, but really you are just a lost child. Those were her words: a child who doesn't know where he lives or what he wants. An insightful woman, don't you think? Whereas you, she said, meaning me, Dmitri – at least you know what you want, at least one can say that about you. And it's true! I always knew what I wanted, and she loved me for it. Women love a man who knows what he wants, who doesn't beat about the bush.

'One last thing, Simón. How about something to eat, to fortify me for the journey ahead?'

'Take whatever there is in the cupboard. I am going for a walk. I need fresh air. I will be away for quite a while.'

When he returns an hour later, Dmitri is asleep in his bed. During the night he is woken by the man's snoring. He gets up from the sofa and gives him a shake. 'You are snoring,' he says. With a great heave Dmitri turns over. A minute later the snoring resumes.

The next thing he knows the birds in the trees have begun to cheep. It is bitterly cold. Dmitri is padding restlessly about the room. 'I need to be off,' he whispers. 'You said something about money and clothes.'

He gets up, switches on the light, finds a shirt and trousers for Dmitri. They are of the same height, but Dmitri has broader shoulders, a bigger chest, a thicker waist: the shirt will barely button closed. He gives Dmitri a hundred *reales* out of his wallet. 'Take my coat,' he says. 'It is behind the door.'

'I am eternally grateful,' says Dmitri. 'And now I must sally forth to meet my fate. Say goodbye to the youngster for me. If anyone comes nosing around, tell them I caught the train to Novilla.' He pauses. 'Simón, I told you I left the hospital by myself. That is not strictly true. In fact it was a downright fib. Your boy helped me. How? I gave him a call. *Dmitri cries out for freedom*, I said. *Can you help?* An hour later he was there, and walked me out, just like the first time. Clean as a whistle. No one noticed us. Uncanny. As if we were invisible. That's all. I thought I would tell you, so that the slate can be clean between us.'

Chapter 20

Claudia and Inés are planning an event at Modas Modernas: a show to promote the new spring fashions. Modas Modernas has never hosted a show before: while the two women are occupied with overseeing seamstresses and hiring models and commissioning advertisements, Diego is charged with taking care of the boy. But Diego is not up to it. He has made new friends in Estrella; he is out with them most of the time. Sometimes he stays out all night, returns at first light, sleeps until noon. Inés berates him but he pays no heed. 'I'm not a nursemaid,' he says. 'If you want a nursemaid, hire one.'

All of this David reports to him, Simón. Bored with being alone in the apartment, the boy has joined him on his bicycle rounds. They work well together. The boy's energy seems boundless. He races from house to house, stuffing into the letter boxes pamphlets that open up a new world of wonders: not only of the key ring that glows in the dark and the Wonderbelt that melts fat away while you sleep and the Electrodog that barks whenever the doorbell rings, but also of señora Victrix, astral consultations, by appointment only; of Brandy, lingerie model, also by appointment only; and of Ferdi the Clown, guaranteed to bring your next party to life; to say nothing of cooking classes, meditation classes, classes in anger management, and two pizzas for the price of one.

'What does this mean, Simón?' asks the boy, holding out a flyer printed on cheap brown paper.

Man the Measurer of All Things, reads the pamphlet. *A lecture by the eminent scholar Dr Javier Moreno. Institute of Further Studies, Thursday series, 8 p.m. Entrance free, donations welcome.*

'I'm not sure. I expect it is about land surveying. A land surveyor is someone who divides land into parcels so that it can be bought and sold. You won't find it interesting.'

'And this?' says the boy.

'*Walkie-talkie.* That is a nonsense name for a telephone without wires. You carry it around with you and talk to friends at a distance.'

'Can I get one?'

'They come in pairs, one for you and one for your friend. Nineteen *reales* ninety-five. That's a lot of money for a toy.'

'It says Rush Rush Rush While Stocks Last.'

'You can ignore that. The world is not going to run out of walkie-talkies, I assure you.'

The boy is full of questions about Dmitri. 'Do you think he is at the salt mines yet? Are they really going to whip him? When can we go and visit him?'

He responds as truthfully as he can, given that he knows nothing whatever about salt mines. 'I am sure the prisoners don't spend every day mining salt,' he says. 'They will have recreation periods when they can play football or read books. Dmitri will write to us once he has settled down, telling us about his new life. We just have to be patient.'

More difficult to answer are questions about the crime for which Dmitri has gone to the salt mines, questions that come back again and again: 'When he made Ana Magdalena's heart stop, was it sore? Why did she turn blue? Am I going to turn blue when I die?' Most difficult of all is the question, 'Why did he kill her? Why, Simón?'

He does not want to evade the boy's questions. Unanswered, they may well fester. So he makes up the easiest, most bearable story he can. 'For the space of a few minutes Dmitri went crazy,' he says. 'It happens to certain people. Something snaps inside their head. Dmitri went crazy in his head, and in his craziness he killed the person he most loved. Soon afterwards he came to himself. The craziness went away and he was full of regret. He tried desperately to bring Ana Magdalena back to life but did not know how. So he decided to do the honourable thing. He confessed to his crime and asked to be punished. Now he has gone to the salt mines to work off his debt – the debt he owes to Ana Magdalena and señor Arroyo and all the boys and girls of the Academy who lost the teacher they loved so much. Every time we sprinkle salt on our food we can remind ourselves that we are helping Dmitri to work off his debt. And one day in the future, when his debt is fully paid, he can come back from the salt mines and we can all be reunited.'

'But not Ana Magdalena.'

'No, not Ana Magdalena. To see her we will have to wait for the next life.'

'The doctors wanted to give Dmitri a new head, one that wouldn't go crazy.'

'That is correct. They wanted to make sure he never went crazy again. Unfortunately it takes time to replace a person's head, and Dmitri was in a hurry. He left the hospital before the doctors had a chance to cure his old head or give him a new one. He was in a hurry to pay his debt. He felt that paying his debt was more important than having his head cured.'

'But he can go crazy again, can't he, if he still has his old head.'

'It was love that drove Dmitri crazy. In the salt mines there will be no women to fall in love with. So the chance that Dmitri will go crazy again is very slight.'

'You won't go crazy, will you, Simón.'

'No, I won't. I don't have that kind of head, the kind that goes crazy. Nor do you. Which is fortunate for us.'

'But Don Quixote did. He had the kind of head that goes crazy.'

'That is true. But Don Quixote and Dmitri are very different kinds of people. Don Quixote was a good person, so his craziness led him to do good deeds like saving maidens from dragons. Don Quixote is a good model to follow in your life. But not Dmitri. From Dmitri there is nothing good to be learned.'

'Why?'

'Because, quite aside from the craziness in his head, Dmitri is not a good person with a good heart. At first he seems friendly and generous, but that is just an outward appearance meant to deceive you. You heard him say that the urge to kill Ana Magdalena came out of nowhere. That is not true. It did not come from nowhere. It came from his heart, where it had been lurking for a long time, waiting to strike like a snake.

'There is nothing you or I can do to help Dmitri, David. As long as he refuses to look into his heart and confront what he sees there, he will not change. He says he wants to be saved, but the only way to be saved is to save oneself, and Dmitri is too lazy, too satisfied with the way he is, to do that. Do you understand?'

'And ants?' says the boy. 'Do ants have bad hearts too?'

'Ants are insects. They don't have blood, therefore they don't have hearts.'

'And bears?'

'Bears are animals, so their hearts are neither good nor bad, they are just hearts. Why do you ask about ants and bears?'

'Maybe the doctors should take a bear's heart and put it in Dmitri.'

'That's an interesting idea. Unfortunately doctors have not yet worked out a way of putting a bear's heart in a human being. Until that can be done, Dmitri will have to take responsibility for his actions.'

The boy gives him a look that he finds hard to interpret: merriment? derision?

'Why are you looking at me like that?' he says.

'Because,' says the boy.

The day comes to an end. He returns the boy to Inés and makes his way back to his room, where the dreaded fog soon settles over him. He pours himself a glass of wine, then a second glass. *The only way to be saved is to save oneself.* The child turns to him for guidance, and what does he offer but glib, pernicious nonsense. Self-reliance. If he, Simón, had to rely on himself, what hope would he have of salvation? Salvation from what? From idleness, from aimlessness, from a bullet in the head.

From the wardrobe he takes down the little case, opens the envelope, stares at the girl with the cat in her arms, the girl who two decades later would choose this image of herself to give to her lover. He rereads her letters, from beginning to end.

Joaquín and Damian have made friends with two girls from the boarding house. We invited them along to the beach today. The water was icy cold, but they all dived in and didn't seem to mind. We were a happy family among lots of other happy families, but in truth I wasn't really there. I was absent. I was with you, as I am with you in my heart every minute of every day. Juan Sebastián senses it. I do all I can to make him feel loved, but he is aware that something has altered between us. My Dmitri, how I long for you, how I shiver when I think of you! Ten whole days! Will the time ever pass? . . .

I lie awake at night thinking of you, impatient for the time to pass, longing to be naked in your arms again . . .

Do you believe in telepathy? I stood on the cliffs, looking out over the sea, concentrating all my energies on you, and a moment came when I can swear I heard your voice. You spoke my name, and I spoke back. This happened yesterday, Tuesday; it must have been ten o'clock in the morning. Was it so for you too? Did you hear me? Can we speak to each other across space? Tell me it is true! . . .

I yearn for you, my darling, yearn apasionadamente! *Only two more days!*

He folds the letters, puts them back in their envelope. He would like to believe they are forgeries penned by Dmitri himself, but that is not true. They are what they say they are: the words of a woman in love. He keeps warning the child against Dmitri. If you want a model in life, look to me, he says: look to Simón, the exemplary stepfather, the man of reason, the dullard; or, if not me, then to that harmless old madman Don Quixote. But if the child really wants an education, who better is there to study than the man who could inspire such an unsuitable, such an incomprehensible love?

Chapter 21

From her handbag Inés produces a crumpled letter. 'I meant to show this to you but I forgot,' she says.

Addressed jointly to señor Simón and señora Inés, written on Academy of Dance notepaper on which the Academy's crest has been scored through with a stroke of the pen, signed by Juan Sebastián Arroyo, the letter invites them to a reception in honour of the distinguished philosopher Javier Moreno Gutiérrez, to be held on the premises of the Museum of Fine Arts. 'Follow signs to entrance on Calle Hugo, ascend to second floor.' Light refreshments will be served.

'It's this evening,' says Inés. 'I can't go, I'm too busy. And on top of that there is the census business. When we scheduled the show we forgot completely about it, and by the time we remembered it was too late, the notices had already gone out. The show starts at three tomorrow afternoon, and by six o'clock all commercial premises have to be closed and employees sent home. I don't know how we are going to manage. You go to the reception. Take David with you.'

'What is a reception? What is the census business?' demands the boy.

'A census is a count,' he, Simón, explains. 'Tomorrow night they are going to count all the people in Estrella and make a list of their names. Inés and I have decided to keep you hidden from the census officers. You won't be alone. Señor Arroyo will be hiding his sons too.'

'Why?'

'Why? For various reasons. Señor Arroyo believes that attaching numbers to people turns them into ants. We want to keep you off the official lists. As for the reception, a reception is a party for grown-ups. You can come along. There will be stuff to eat. If you find it too boring you can go and visit Alyosha's animal menagerie. You haven't visited them in a long while.'

'If they count me in the census will they recognize me?'

'Maybe. Maybe not. We don't want to take the risk.'

'But are you going to hide me forever?'

'Of course not – just during the census. We don't want to give them a reason to pack you off to that dreary school of theirs at Punta Arenas. Once you are past school age you can relax and be your own master.'

'And I can have a beard too, can't I?'

'You can wear a beard, you can change your name, you can do all kinds of things to avoid being recognized.'

'But I want to be recognized!'

'No, you don't want to be recognized, not yet, you don't want to take that risk. David, I don't think you understand what it means to recognize or be recognized. But let us not argue about it. When you are grown up you can be whoever you wish, do whatever you like. Until then, Inés and I would like you to do as you are told.'

He and the boy arrive late at the reception. He is surprised at how many guests there are. The distinguished philosopher and guest of honour must have quite a following.

They greet the three sisters.

'We heard maestro Moreno speak during his last visit,' says Consuelo. 'When was that, Valentina?'

'Two years ago,' says Valentina.

'Two years ago,' says Consuelo. 'Such an interesting man. Good evening, David, don't we get a kiss?'

Dutifully the boy kisses each of the sisters on the cheek.

Arroyo joins them, accompanied by his sister-in-law Mercedes, who wears a grey silk dress with a striking scarlet mantilla, and by maestro Moreno himself, a short, squat little man with flowing locks, pockmarked skin, and wide, thin lips like a frog's.

'Javier, you know señora Consuelo and her sisters, but let me introduce you to señor Simón. Señor Simón is a philosopher in his own right. He is also the father of this excellent young man, whose name is David.'

'David is not my real name,' says the boy.

'David is not his real name, I should have mentioned that,' says señor Arroyo, 'but it is the name under which he passes while he is in our midst. Simón, I believe you have already met my sister-in-law Mercedes, who is visiting from Novilla.'

He bows to Mercedes, who gives him a smile in return. Her aspect has softened since they last spoke. A handsome woman, in her rather fierce way. He wonders what the other sister was like, the dead one.

'And what brings you to Estrella, señor Moreno?' he asks, making conversation.

'I do a lot of travelling, señor. My profession makes of me an itinerant, a peripatetic. I give talks all over the country, at the various Institutes. But, to tell the truth, I am in Estrella to see my old friend Juan Sebastián. He and I share a long history. In the old days we ran a clock-repair business together. We also played in a quartet.'

'Javier is a first-rate violinist,' says Arroyo. 'First-rate.'

Moreno shrugs. 'Perhaps, but an amateur nevertheless. As I said, the two of us ran a business, but then Juan Sebastián began to have doubts about it, so, to cut a long story short, we closed down. He created his Academy of Dance while I went my own way. But we remain in contact. We have our disagreements, but broadly speaking we see the world in the same way. If we didn't, how would we have been able to work together all those years?'

It comes back to him. 'Ah, you must be the señor Moreno who gave the lecture on land surveying! We saw the advertisement, David and I.'

'Land surveying?' says Moreno.

'Topographical measurement.'

'*Man the Measure of All Things*,' says Moreno. 'That is the title of the talk I will be giving tonight. It will not be about land sur- veying at all. It will be about Metros and his intellectual legacy. I thought that was clear.'

'My apologies. The confusion is mine. We are looking forward to hearing you. But *Man the Measurer* was definitely the title under which the lecture was advertised – I know because I distributed the leaflets myself, that is my business. Who is Metros?'

Moreno is about to reply, but a couple who have impatiently been waiting their turn break in. 'Maestro, we are so excited that you are back! In Estrella we feel so cut off from the true life of the mind! Will this be your only appearance?'

He drifts away.

'Why did señor Arroyo call you a philosopher?' asks the boy.

'It was a joke. Surely you know señor Arroyo's manner by now. It is because I am not a philosopher that he calls me a philosopher. Have something to eat. It is going to be a long evening. After the reception there is still señor Moreno's lecture. You will enjoy it. It will be like a story-reading. Señor Moreno will stand on a platform and tell us about a man named Metros, whom I have never heard of but who is evidently important.'

The refreshments promised in the invitation turn out to be a big pot of tea, warm rather than hot, and some plates of hard little biscuits. The boy bites into one of them, pulls a face, spits it up. 'It's horrible!' he says. He, Simón, quietly cleans up the mess.

'There is too much ginger in the biscuits.' It is Mercedes, who has appeared noiselessly at their side. Of the cane there is no sign; she seems to move quite easily. 'But don't tell Alyosha. You don't want to hurt him. He and the boys were baking all afternoon. So you are the famous David! The boys tell me you are a good dancer.'

'I can dance all the numbers.'

'So I hear. Is there any other kind of dancing you do besides number-dancing? Can you do human dancing?'

'What is human dancing?'

'You are a human being, aren't you? Can you do any of the dances that human beings do, such as dancing for joy or dancing breast to breast with someone you are fond of?'

'Ana Magdalena didn't teach us that.'

'Would you like me to teach you?'

'No.'

'Well, until you learn to do what human beings do you can't be a full human being. What else don't you do? Do you have friends you play with?'

'I play football.'

'You play sports, but do you ever just play? Joaquín says you never talk to the other children at school, you just give orders and tell them what to do. Is that true?'

The boy is silent.

'Well, it is certainly not easy conducting a human conversation with you, young David. I think I will look for someone else to talk to.' Teacup in hand, she drifts off.

'Why don't you go and say hello to the animals?' he suggests to David. 'Take Alyosha's biscuits along. Maybe the rabbits will eat them.'

He makes his way back to the circle around Moreno.

'About Metros the man we know nothing,' Moreno is saying, 'and not much more about his philosophy, since he left no written record. Nevertheless, he looms large over the modern world. That, at least, is my opinion.

'According to one strand of legend, Metros said there is nothing in the universe that cannot be measured. According to another strand, he said that there can be no absolute measurement – that measurement is always relative to the measurer. Philosophers are still arguing about whether the two claims are compatible.'

'And which do you believe?' asks Valentina.

'I straddle the gap, as I will try to explain in tonight's talk. After which my friend Juan Sebastián will have a chance to respond. We have set up the evening as a debate – we thought that would make it more lively. Juan Sebastián has in the past been critical of my interest in Metros. He is critical of metra in general, of the idea that everything in the universe can be measured.'

'That everything in the universe should be measured,' says Arroyo. 'There is a difference.'

'That everything in the universe should be measured – thank you for correcting me. That is why my friend decided to quit clock-making. What is a clock, after all, but a mechanism for imposing a metron on the flux of time?'

'A metron?' says Valentina. 'What is that?'

'The metron is named after Metros. Any unit of measurement qualifies as a metron: a gram, for example, or a metre, or a minute. Without metra the natural sciences would not be possible. Take the case of astronomy. We say that astronomy concerns itself with the stars, but that is not strictly true. In fact it concerns itself with the metra of the stars: their mass, their distance from each other, and so forth. We can't put the stars themselves into mathematical equations, but we can perform mathematical operations on their metra and thereby uncover the laws of the universe.'

David has reappeared at his side, tugging at his arm. 'Come and see, Simón!' he whispers.

'The mathematical laws of the universe,' says Arroyo.

'The mathematical laws,' says Moreno.

For a man so unappealing in his exterior, Moreno speaks with remarkable self-assurance.

'How fascinating,' says Valentina.

'Come and see, Simón!' the boy whispers again.

'In a minute,' he whispers back.

'Fascinating indeed,' echoes Consuelo. 'But it is getting late. We should be making our way to the Institute. A quick question, señor Arroyo: When will you be reopening the Academy?'

'The date is not yet settled,' says Arroyo. 'What I can tell you is that, until we find a teacher of dance, the Academy will be solely an academy of music.'

'I thought señora Mercedes was going to be the new dance teacher.'

'Alas, no, Mercedes has duties in Novilla that she cannot escape. She visited Estrella to see her nephews, my sons, not to do any teaching. We have yet to appoint a teacher of dance.'

'You have yet to appoint a teacher of dance,' says Consuelo. 'I know nothing about this Dmitri person beyond what I read in the newspaper, but – excuse me for saying so – I hope that in future you will be more careful about the staff you appoint.'

'Dmitri was not employed by the Academy,' says he, Simón. 'He worked as an attendant in the museum downstairs. It is the museum that should be more careful about the staff it appoints.'

'A homicidal maniac in this very building,' says Consuelo. 'The thought makes me shiver.'

'He was indeed a homicidal maniac. He was also personable. The children of the Academy loved him.' He is standing up not for Dmitri but for Arroyo, the man who was so wrapped up in his music that he allowed his wife to drift into a fatal entanglement with an underling. 'Children are innocent. Being innocent means taking things at face value. It means opening your heart to someone who smiles at you and calls you his fine little man and dishes out sweets.'

David speaks. 'Dmitri says he couldn't help himself. He says passion made him kill Ana Magdalena.'

There is a moment of frozen silence. With a frown Moreno examines the strange boy.

'Passion is no defence,' says Consuelo. 'We all feel passion at one time or another, but we don't go killing people because of it.'

'Dmitri has gone away to the salt mines,' says David. 'He is going to dig up lots of salt to make up for killing Ana Magdalena.'

'Well, we will make sure we don't use any of Dmitri's salt on the farm, won't we?' She glances sternly at her two sisters. 'How much salt is a human life worth? Perhaps you could ask that of your Metra man.'

'Metros,' says Moreno.

'I beg your pardon: *Metros*. Simón, can we give you a lift?'

'Thank you, but no – I have my bicycle here.'

As the gathering disperses, David takes him by the hand and leads him down a dark stairway to the little enclosed garden behind the museum. A light rain is falling. By moonlight the boy unlatches a gate and on hands and knees crawls into a hutch. There is an explosion of squawking among the hens. He emerges with a struggling creature in his arms: a lamb.

'Look, it's Jeremiah! He used to be so big that I couldn't lift him, but Alyosha forgot to give him milk to drink and now he has grown small!'

He strokes the lamb. It tries to suck his finger. 'No one in this world grows small, David. If he has turned small, it is not because Alyosha hasn't been feeding him, it is because he is not the real Jeremiah. He is a new Jeremiah who has taken the place of the old Jeremiah because the old Jeremiah has grown up and turned into a sheep. People find young Jeremiahs endearing, but not old Jeremiahs. No one wants to cuddle old Jeremiahs. That is their misfortune.'

'Where is the old Jeremiah? Can I see him?'

'The old Jeremiah is back in the meadows with the other sheep. One day when we have time we can go and search for him. But right now we have a lecture to attend.'

Out on Calle Hugo it has begun to rain more heavily. As he and the boy hesitate in the doorway there is a hoarse whisper: 'Simón!' A figure wrapped in a cloak or blanket looms before them, a hand beckons. Dmitri! The boy dashes forward and clasps him around the thighs.

'What on earth are you doing here, Dmitri?' he, Simón, demands.

'*Shh*!' says Dmitri; and, in an exaggerated whisper: 'Is there somewhere we can go?'

'We are not going anywhere,' he says, not lowering his voice. 'What are you doing here?'

Without replying Dmitri grasps his arm and propels him across the empty street – he is astonished at the man's strength – into the doorway of the tobacconist's.

'Did you escape, Dmitri?' says the boy. He is excited; his eyes sparkle in the moonlight.

'Yes, I escaped,' says Dmitri. 'I had unfinished business, I had to escape, I had no choice.'

'And are they searching for you with bloodhounds?'

'This weather is no good for bloodhounds,' says Dmitri. 'Too wet for their noses. The bloodhounds are back in their kennels, waiting for the rain to stop.'

'That's nonsense,' says he, Simón. 'What do you want with us?'

'We need to talk, Simón. You were always a decent fellow, I always felt I could talk to you. Can we go to your place? You have no idea what it is like, having no home, nowhere to lay one's head. Do you recognize the coat? It's the one you gave me. It made quite an impression on me, the gift of your coat. When I was universally excoriated, for what I did, you gave me a coat and a bed to sleep in. That's something only a genuinely decent fellow would do.'

'I gave it to you to be rid of you. Now let go of us. We are in a hurry.'

'No!' says the boy. 'Tell us about the salt mines, Dmitri. Do they really whip you in the salt mines?'

'There is a lot I could say about the salt mines,' says Dmitri, 'but it will have to wait. There is something more pressing on my mind, namely repentance. I need your help, Simón. I never repented, you know. Now I want to repent.'

'I thought that was why we have salt mines: as a place of penitence. What are you doing here when you should be there?'

'It's not as simple as that, Simón. I can explain it all, but it will take time. Do we have to huddle here in the cold and the wet?'

'I could not care less if you are cold and wet. David and I have an appointment to keep. The last time I saw you you said you were off to the salt mines to surrender yourself for punishment. Did you ever go to the salt mines, or was that another lie?'

'When I left you, Simón, I fully intended to go to the salt mines. That was what my heart told me. *Accept your punishment like a man*, said my heart. But other factors supervened. *Supervened*: nice word. Other factors made themselves felt. Therefore no. I have not actually been to the salt mines, not yet. I'm sorry, David. I let you down. I told you I was going but I didn't go.

'The truth is, I've been brooding, Simón. This has been a dark time for me, brooding on my fate. It was quite a shock to discover that I didn't have it in me after all to accept what was due to me, namely a spell in the salt mines. Quite a shock. My manhood was involved. If I had been a man, a real man, I would have gone, no doubt about that. But I wasn't a man, I discovered. I was less than a man. I was a coward. That was the fact I had to face. A murderer and on top of that a coward. Can you blame me for feeling upset?'

He, Simón, has had enough. 'Come, David,' he says. And to Dmitri: 'Be warned, I am going to telephone the police.'

He half expects the boy to protest. But no: with a backward glance at Dmitri the boy follows him.

'The pot calling the kettle black,' Dmitri calls out after them. 'I saw the way you looked at Ana Magdalena, Simón! You lusted after her too, only you were not man enough for her!'

In the middle of the rain-beaten street, exhausted, he turns to face Dmitri's tirade.

'Go on! Call your precious police! And you, David: I expected better of you, I really did. I thought you were a stout little soldier. But no, it turns out you are under their thumb – that cold bitch Inés and this man of paper. They have mothered you and fathered you until there is nothing left of you but a shadow. Go! Do your worst!'

As if gathering strength from their silence, Dmitri emerges from the shelter of the doorway and, holding the coat on high above his head like a sail, strides across the street back to the Academy.

'What is he going to do, Simón?' whispers the boy. 'Is he going to kill señor Arroyo?'

'I have no idea. The man is mad. Fortunately there is no one at home, they have all gone to the Institute.'

Chapter 22

Though he pedals as hard as he can, they arrive late for the lecture. Making as little noise as possible, he and the boy sit down in their wet clothes in the back row.

'A shadowy figure, Metros,' Moreno is saying. 'And like his comrade Prometheus, bringer of fire, perhaps only a figure of legend. Nevertheless, the arrival of Metros marks a turning point in human history: the moment when we collectively gave up the old way of apprehending the world, the unthinking, animal way, when we abandoned as futile the quest to know things in themselves, and began instead to see the world through its metra. By concentrating our gaze upon fluctuations in the metra we enabled ourselves to discover new laws, laws that even the heavenly bodies have to obey.

'Similarly on earth, where in the spirit of the new metric science we measured mankind and, finding that all men are equal, concluded that men should fall equally under the law. No more slaves, no more kings, no more exceptions.

'Was Metros the measurer a bad man? Were he and his heirs guilty of abolishing reality and putting a simulacrum in its place, as some critics claim? Would we be better off if Metros had never been born? As we look around us at this splendid Institute, designed by architects and built by engineers schooled in the metra of statics and dynamics, that position seems hard to maintain.

'Thank you for your attention.'

The applause from the audience, which nearly fills the theatre, is long and loud. Moreno shuffles his notes together and descends the dais. Arroyo takes the microphone. 'Thank you, Javier, for that fascinating and masterly overview of Metros and his legacy, an overview which you offer to us, appropriately, on the eve of the census, that orgy of measurement.

'With your consent, I will briefly respond. After my response, the floor will be open to debate.'

He gives a signal. The two Arroyo boys rise from their seats in the front row, strip off their outer clothes, and, wearing singlets and shorts and golden slippers, join their father on the stage.

'The city of Estrella knows me as a musician and as director of the Academy of Dance, an academy where no distinction is made between dance and music. Why not? Because, we believe, music and dance together, music-dance, is its own way of apprehending the universe, the human way but also the animal way, the way that prevailed before the coming of Metros.

'As we in the Academy do not distinguish between music and dance, so we do not distinguish between mind and body. The teachings of Metros constituted a new, mental science, and the knowledge they brought into being was a new, mental knowledge. The older mode of apprehension comes from body and mind moving together, body-mind, to the rhythm of music-dance. In that dance old memories come to the surface, archaic memories, knowledge we lost when we voyaged here across the oceans.

'We may title ourselves an Academy, but we are not an academy of greybeards. Instead our members are children, in whom those archaic memories, memories of a prior existence, are far from extinguished. That is why I have asked these two young men, my sons Joaquín and Damian, students of the Academy, to join me on the stage.

'The teachings of Metros are based on number, but Metros did not invent number. The numbers existed before Metros was born, before humankind came into being. Metros merely used them, subjecting them to his system. My late wife used to call numbers in the hands of Metros ant numbers, copulating endlessly, dividing and multiplying endlessly. Through dance she returned her students to the true numbers, which are eternal and indivisible and uncountable.

'I am a musician, ill at ease with argumentation, as perhaps you can hear. To allow you to see how the world was before the arrival of Metros I will fall silent while Joaquín and Damian perform a pair of dances for us: the dance of Two and the dance of Three. Thereafter they will perform the more difficult dance of Five.'

He gives a signal. Simultaneously, in counterpoint, one on either side of the stage, the boys commence the dances of Two and Three. As they dance, the agitation stirred up in his, Simón's, breast by the confrontation with Dmitri dies down; he is able to relax and take pleasure in their easy, fluent movements. Though Arroyo's philosophy of dance is as obscure to him as ever, he begins to see, in the dimmest of ways, why the one dance is appropriate to Two and the other to Three, and so to glimpse, in the dimmest of ways, what Arroyo means by dancing the numbers, calling the numbers down.

The dancers conclude at the same moment, on the same beat, in mid-stage. For a moment they pause; then, taking their cue from their father, who now accompanies them on the flute, they embark together on the dance of Five.

He can see at once why Arroyo called Five difficult: difficult for the dancers, but difficult too for the spectators. With Two and Three he could feel some force within his body – the tide of his blood or whatever he wants to call it – move in accord with the boys' limbs. With Five there is no such feeling. There is some pattern to the dance – that he can faintly apprehend – but his body is too stupid, too stolid to find it and follow it.

He glances at David beside him. David is frowning; his lips move wordlessly.

'Is something wrong?' he whispers. 'Are they not doing it right?'

The boy tosses his head impatiently.

The dance of Five comes to an end. Side by side, the Arroyo boys face the audience. There is a polite if mystified ripple of applause. At this moment David leaps from his seat and runs down the aisle. Startled, he, Simón, gets to his feet and follows, but is too late to prevent him from clambering onto the stage.

'What is it, young man?' asks Arroyo with a frown.

'It is my turn,' says the boy. 'I want to dance Seven.'

'Not now. Not here. This is not a concert. Go and sit down.'

Amid murmuring from the audience he, Simón, mounts the stage. 'Come, David, you are upsetting everyone.'

Peremptorily the boy shakes him off. 'It is my turn!'

'Very well,' says Arroyo. 'Dance Seven. When you have finished I expect you to go and sit quietly again. Do you agree?'

Without a word the boy slips off his shoes. Joaquín and Damian make way; in silence he begins his dance. Arroyo watches, eyes narrowed in concentration, then raises the flute to his lips. The melody he plays is right and just and true; yet even he, Simón, can hear that it is the dancer who leads and the master who follows. From some buried memory the words *pillar of grace* emerge, surprising him, for the image he holds to, from the football field, is of the boy as a compact bundle of energy. But now, on the stage of the Institute, Ana Magdalena's legacy reveals itself. As if the earth has lost its downward power, the boy seems to shed all bodily weight, to become pure light. The logic of the dance eludes him entirely, yet he knows that what is unfolding before him is extraordinary; and from the hush that falls in the auditorium he guesses that the people of Estrella find it extraordinary too.

The numbers are integral and sexless, said Ana Magdalena; their ways of loving and conjugating are beyond our comprehension. Because of that, they can be called down only by sexless beings. Well, the being who dances before them is neither child nor man, boy nor girl; he would even say neither body nor spirit. Eyes shut, mouth open, rapt, David floats through the steps with such fluid grace that time stands still. Too caught up even to breathe, he, Simón, whispers to himself: *Remember this! If ever in the future you are tempted to doubt him, remember this!*

The dance of Seven ends as abruptly as it began. The flute falls silent. With chest heaving slightly, the boy faces Arroyo. 'Do you want me to dance Eleven?'

'Not now,' says Arroyo abstractedly.

From the back of the hall a call reverberates through the auditorium. The call itself is indistinct – *Bravo? Slavo?* – but the voice is familiar: Dmitri's. His heart sinks. Will the man never cease to haunt him?

Arroyo bestirs himself. 'It is time to return to the subject of our lecture, Metros and his legacy,' he announces. 'Are there questions you would like to address to señor Moreno?'

An elderly gentleman stands up. 'If the antics of the children are over, maestro, I have two questions. First, señor Moreno, you said that, as heirs of Metros, we have measured ourselves and found we are all equal. Being equal, you say, it follows that we should be equal in the eyes of the law. No longer should anyone be above the law. No more kings, no more super-men, no more exceptional beings. But – I come to my first question – is it really a good thing that the rule of law should allow no exceptions? If the law is applied without exception, what place is left for mercy?'

Moreno steps forward and mounts the dais. 'An excellent question, a profound question,' he replies. 'Should there not be room for mercy under the law? The answer our lawgivers have given is, yes, there should indeed be room for mercy, or – to speak in more concrete terms – for remission of sentence, *but only when such is merited*. The offender owes a debt to society. Forgiveness of his debt must be earned by a labour of contrition. Thus the sovereignty of measure is preserved: the substance of the offender's contrition shall, so to speak, be weighed, and an equivalent weight be deducted from his sentence. You had a second question.'

The speaker glances around. 'I will be brief. You have said nothing about money. Yet as a universal measure of value, money is surely the principal legacy of Metros. Where would we be without money?'

Before Moreno can reply, Dmitri, bareheaded, wearing his, Simón's, coat, plunges down the aisle and in a single movement mounts the stage, bellowing all the time, 'That's enough, that's enough, that's enough!

'Juan Sebastián,' he shouts – he needs no microphone – 'I am here to beg your forgiveness.' He turns to the audience. 'Yes, I beg this man's forgiveness. I know you are occupied with other matters, important matters, but I am Dmitri, Dmitri the outcast, and Dmitri has no shame, he is beyond shame as he is beyond many other things.' He turns back to Arroyo. 'I must tell you, Juan Sebastián,' he continues without pause, as if his speech has been long rehearsed, 'I have been through dark times of late. I have even thought of doing away with myself. Why? Because I have grown to realize – and it has been a bitter realization – that never will I be free until the burden of guilt is lifted from my shoulders.'

If Arroyo is disconcerted, he gives no sign of it. With shoulders squared he confronts Dmitri.

'Where shall I turn for relief?' demands Dmitri. 'To the law? You heard what the man said about the law. The law takes no reckoning of the state of a man's soul. All it does is make up an equation, fit a sentence to a crime. Take the case of Ana Magdalena, your wife, whose life was cut off just like that. What gives some stranger, some man who never laid eyes on her, the right to put on a scarlet robe and say, *A lifetime in the lock-up, that's what her life is worth*? Or *Twenty-five years in the salt mines*? It makes no sense! Some crimes are not measurable! They are off the scale!

'And what would it achieve anyway, twenty-five years in the salt mines? An outward torment, that's all. Does the outward torment cancel the inner torment, like a plus and a minus? No. The inner torment rages on.'

Without warning he sinks to his knees before Arroyo.

'I am guilty, Juan Sebastián. You know it and I know it. I have never pretended otherwise. I am guilty and in great need of your forgiveness. Only when I have your forgiveness will I be healed. Lay your hand on my head. Say, *Dmitri, you did me a terrible wrong, but I forgive you*. Say it.'

Arroyo is silent, his features frozen in disgust.

'What I did was bad, Juan Sebastián. I don't deny it and don't want it to be forgotten. Let it always be remembered that Dmitri did a bad thing, a terrible thing. But surely that doesn't mean I should be damned and cast into the outer darkness. Surely I can have a little grace extended to me. Surely someone can say, *Dmitri? I remember Dmitri. He did a bad thing but at heart he wasn't a bad fellow, old Dmitri.* That will be enough for me – that one drop of saving water. Not to absolve me, just to recognize me as man, to say, *He is still ours, he is still one of us.*'

There is a minor commotion at the back of the auditorium. Two uniformed police officers march purposefully down the aisle toward the stage.

With his arms above his head Dmitri rises to his feet. 'So this is how you answer me,' he cries out. '*Take him away and lock him up, this troublesome spirit.* Who is responsible for this? Who called the police? Where are you skulking, Simón? Show your face! After all I have been through, do you think a prison cell frightens me? There is nothing you can do that is equal to what I do to myself. Do I look to you like a happy man? No, I don't. I look like a man sunk in the depths of misery, because that is where I am, night and day. It is only you, Juan Sebastián, who can draw me up from the deep well of my misery, because you are the one I wronged.'

The police officers have halted at the foot of the stage. They are young, mere boys, and in the glare of the lights suddenly unsure of themselves.

'I wronged you, Juan Sebastián, I wronged you profoundly. Why did I do it? I have no idea. Not only do I have no idea why I did it, I cannot believe I did it. That is the truth, the naked truth. I swear to it. It's incomprehensible – incomprehensible from the outside and incomprehensible from the inside too. If the facts were not staring me in the face, I would be tempted to agree with the judge – you remember the judge at the trial? – of course not, you weren't there – I would be tempted to say, *It wasn't I who did it, it was someone else*. But of course that isn't true. It is not as if I am a schizophrenic or a hebephrenic or any of the other things they say I could be. I am not divorced from reality. My feet are on the ground and have always been. No: it was me. It was me. A mystery yet not a mystery. A mystery that it is not a mystery. How did it come to be *I* who did the deed – *I* of all people? Can you help me answer that question, Juan Sebastián? Can anyone help me?'

Of course the man is a fake through and through. Of course his remorse is confected, part of a scheme to save himself from the salt mines. Nevertheless, when he, Simón, tries to imagine how this man, who every day visited the kiosk on the square to fill his pockets with lollipops for the children, could have closed his hands around Ana Magdalena's alabaster throat and crushed the life out of her, his imagination fails him. It fails or it quails. What the man did may not be a true mystery but it is a mystery nonetheless.

From the back of the stage the boy's voice rings out. 'Why don't you ask me? You ask everyone else but you never ask me!'

'Quite right,' says Dmitri. 'My fault, I should have asked you too. Tell me, my pretty young dancer, what shall I do with myself?'

Gathering their resolve, the two young police officers make to ascend the stage. Brusquely Arroyo waves them back.

'No!' the boy shouts. 'You have got to *really* ask me!'

'All right,' says Dmitri, 'I'll really ask you.' He kneels down again, clasps his hands, composes his face. 'David, please tell me – no, it's no good, I can't do it. You are too young, my boy. You have to be a grown-up to understand love and death and things like that.'

'You are always saying it, Simón is always saying it – *You don't understand, you are too young.* I *can* understand! Ask me, Dmitri! *Ask me!*'

Dmitri repeats the rigmarole of unfolding and folding his hands, closing his eyes, letting his face go blank.

'*Dmitri, ask me!*' Now the boy is positively screaming.

There is a stir among the audience. People are getting up and leaving. He catches the eye of Mercedes sitting in the front row. She raises a hand in a gesture he cannot read. The three sisters, beside her, are stony-faced.

He, Simón, signals to the police officers. 'That's enough, Dmitri, enough of a show. Time for you to go.'

While one officer holds Dmitri still, the other handcuffs him.

'So,' says Dmitri in his normal voice. 'Back to the madhouse. Back to my lonely cell. Why don't you tell your youngster, Simón, what is going on at the back of your mind? Your father or uncle or whatever he calls himself is too delicate to tell you, young David, but in secret he hopes I am going to cut my throat, let my blood flow down the drains. Then they can hold an inquest and conclude that the tragedy occurred while the balance of the deceased's mind was disturbed and that will be the end of Dmitri. Shut the file on him. Well, let me tell you, I am not going to do away with myself. I am going to go on living, and I am going to go on plaguing you, Juan Sebastián, until you relent.' Laboriously he tries to prostrate himself again, holding his handcuffed hands above his head. 'Forgive me, Juan Sebastián, forgive me!'

'Take him away,' says he, Simón.

'No!' cries the boy. His face is flushed, he is breathing fast. He raises a hand, points dramatically. 'You must bring her back, Dmitri! *Bring her back!*'

Dmitri struggles into a sitting position, rubs his bristly chin. 'Bring whom back, young David?'

'You know! You must bring Ana Magdalena back!'

Dmitri sighs. 'I wish I could, young fellow, I wish I could. Believe me, if Ana Magdalena were suddenly to appear before us I would bow down and wash her feet with tears of joy. But she won't come back. She is gone. She belongs to the past, and the past is forever behind us. That's a law of nature. Even the stars can't swim against the flow of time.'

Through all of Dmitri's speech the boy has continued to hold his hand on high, as if only thus can the force of his command be sustained; but it is clear to him, Simón, and perhaps to Dmitri too, that he is wavering. Tears are brimming in his eyes.

'Time to go,' says Dmitri. He allows the police officers to help him to his feet. 'Back to the doctors. *Why did you do it, Dmitri? Why? Why? Why?* But maybe there is no why. Maybe it's like asking why is a chicken a chicken, or why is there a universe instead of a great big hole in the sky. Things are as they are. Don't cry, my boy. Be patient, wait for the next life, and you will see Ana Magdalena again. Hold on to that thought.'

'I'm not crying,' says the boy.

'Yes, you are. There is nothing wrong with a good cry. It clears out the system.'

Chapter 23

The day of the census has dawned, the day too of the show at Modas Modernas. The boy wakes up listless, surly, without appetite. Might he be ill? He, Simón, feels his brow, but it is cool.

'Did you see Seven last night?' the boy demands.

'Of course. I couldn't keep my eyes off you. You danced beautifully. Everyone thought so.'

'But did you see Seven?'

'Do you mean the number seven? No. I don't see numbers. It's a failing on my part. I see only what is before my eyes. You know that.'

'What are we going to do today?'

'After all the excitement last night, I think we should have a quiet day. I would suggest we take a peek at Inés' fashion show, but I don't think gentlemen will be welcome. We can go and fetch Bolívar, if you like, and take him for a walk, as long as we are off the streets by six. Because of the curfew.'

He expects a string of *Why?* questions, but the boy shows no interest in the census or the curfew. *Where is Dmitri now?*: another question that does not come. Have they seen the last of Dmitri? Can the forgetting of Dmitri commence? He prays that it is so.

As it turns out, it is near midnight when the census officers come knocking at the door. He picks up the boy, half asleep, whimpering, wrapped in a blanket, and stows him bodily in the cupboard. 'Not a sound,' he whispers. 'It is important. Not a sound.'

The census-takers, a young couple, apologize for their lateness. 'This is not a part of the city we are familiar with,' says the woman. 'Such a maze of crooked streets and alleys!' He offers them tea, but they are in a hurry. 'We still have a long list of addresses to cover,' she says. 'We will be up all night.'

The census business takes no time at all. He has already filled out the form. *Number of persons in family*: 'ONE,' he has written. *Marital status*: 'SINGLE.'

When they are gone he liberates the boy from confinement and returns him to bed, fast asleep.

In the morning they stroll over to see Inés. She and Diego are sitting down to breakfast; she is as bright and cheerful as he has ever seen her, prattling on and on about the show, which – everyone agrees – was a great success. The ladies of Estrella flocked to see the new spring fashions. The low necklines, the high waists, the simple reliance on black and white, have won general approval. Pre-sales have exceeded all expectations.

The boy listens with glazed eyes.

'Drink your milk,' Inés tells him. 'Milk gives you strong bones.'

'Simón locked me in the wardrobe,' he says. 'I couldn't breathe.'

'It was only while the census-takers were there,' he says. 'A nice young couple, very polite. David was as quiet as a mouse. All they saw was a lonely old bachelor roused from his slumbers. It was over in five minutes. No one dies of asphyxiation in five minutes.'

'It was the same here,' says Inés. 'In and out in five minutes. No questions.'

'So David remains invisible,' says he, Simón. 'Congratulations, David. You have escaped again.'

'Until the next census,' says Diego.

'Until the next census,' he, Simón, agrees.

'With so many millions of souls to count,' says Diego, 'what does it matter if they miss one?'

'What does it matter indeed,' echoes he, Simón.

'Am I really invisible?' asks the boy.

'You don't have a name, you don't have a number. That is enough to make you invisible. But don't worry, we can see you. Any ordinary person with eyes in his head can see you.'

'I'm not worried,' says the boy.

The doorbell rings: a young man bearing a letter, hot and flushed after his long ride. Inés invites him in, offers him a glass of water.

The letter, addressed to Inés and Simón jointly, is from Alma, the third sister. Inés reads it aloud.

'After we came home from the Institute my sisters and I talked late into the night. Of course no one could have foreseen that Dmitri would burst in like that. Nevertheless, we were dismayed at the way the proceedings were conducted. Señor Arroyo was much to blame, we felt, for inviting children onto the stage. It did not speak well for his judgement.

'While my sisters and I retain the greatest respect for señor Arroyo as a musician, we feel that the time has come for us to distance ourselves from the Academy and the coterie he has gathered around himself there. I am therefore writing to inform you that if David should return to the Academy we will no longer be paying his fees.'

Inés breaks off reading. 'What is this about?' she says. 'What happened at the Institute?'

'It's a long story. Señor Moreno, the visitor for whom the reception was held, gave a lecture at the Institute which David and I attended. After the lecture Arroyo called his sons onto the stage to perform one of their dances. It was meant as a sort of artistic response to the lecture, but he lost control and everything slid into chaos. I'll give you the details some other time.'

'Dmitri came,' says the boy. 'He shouted at Simón. He shouted at everyone.'

'Dmitri again!' says Inés. 'Will we never be rid of the man?' She turns back to the letter.

'As childless spinsters,' writes Alma, 'my sisters and I are hardly qualified to offer advice on the rearing of children. Nonetheless, David seems to us excessively indulged. It would do him good, we believe, if his natural high spirits were sometimes reined in.

'Allow me to add a word of my own. David is a rare child. I will remember him with affection, even if I do not see him again. Greet him from me. Tell him I enjoyed his dancing.

'Yours, Alma.'

Inés folds the letter and pushes it under the jam pot.

'What does it mean, I am excessively indulged?' demands the boy.

'Never you mind,' says Inés.

'Are they going to take the marionettes back?'

'Of course not. They are yours to keep.'

There is a long silence.

'What now?' says he, Simón.

'We look for a tutor,' says Inés. 'As I said from the beginning. Someone with experience. Someone who will not put up with any nonsense.'

The door to the Academy is opened not by Alyosha but by Mercedes, who has resumed her cane.

'Good day,' he says. 'Would you be so good as to inform the maestro that the new help is reporting for duty.'

'Come in,' says Mercedes, 'The maestro is shut away, as usual. What duty are you reporting for?'

'Cleaning. Carrying. Whatever needs to be done. I am, as of today, handyman to the Academy: factotum, dogsbody.'

'If you mean what you say, the kitchen floor can do with a scrub. The bathrooms too. Why are you offering yourself? There is no money to pay you.'

'We have come to an arrangement, Juan Sebastián and I. It does not involve money.'

'For a mań who does not dance, you seem uncommonly devoted to Juan Sebastián and his Academy. Does this mean that your son will be returning?'

'No. His mother is opposed to it. His mother thinks he has run wild under Juan Sebastián.'

'Which is not untrue.'

'Which is not untrue. His mother thinks it is high time he commences a normal education.'

'And you? What do you think?'

'I do not think, Mercedes. In our family I am the stupid one, the blind one, the danceless one. Inés leads. David leads. The dog leads. I stumble along behind, hoping for the day to come when my eyes will be opened and I will behold the world as it really is, including the numbers in all their glory, Two and Three and the rest of them. You offered me lessons in the dance, which I declined. Can I change my mind now?'

'It is too late. I leave today. I catch the train to Novilla. You should have grasped the nettle while you had the chance. If you want lessons, why not ask your son?'

'David thinks I am unteachable, past redemption. Is there not time for a single lesson? A quick introduction to the mysteries of the dance?'

'I will see what I can do. Come back after lunch. I will speak to Alyosha, ask him to play for us. In the meantime, do something about your footwear. You can't dance in boots. I make no promises, Simón. I am not Ana Magdalena, not a devotee of *el sistema Arroyo*. You won't see visions while you are with me.'

'That's all right. Visions will come when they come. Or they will not.'

He finds the shoe shop without difficulty. The same salesman serves him as before, the tall, sad-faced man with the little moustache. 'Dancing slippers for yourself, señor?' He shakes his head. 'We don't have them – not in your size. I don't know how to advise you. If we don't carry them, no other shop in Estrella will.'

'Show me the biggest size you have.'

'The largest size we have is a thirty-six, and that is a lady's size.'

'Show it to me. In gold.'

'Unfortunately we have thirty-six only in silver.'

'In silver then.'

Of course his foot does not fit into size thirty-six.

'I'll take them,' he says, and hands over fifty-nine *reales*.

Back in his room he slits open the toe-ends of the slippers with a razor blade, forces his feet in, laces them up. His toes project obscenely. Good enough, he says to himself.

When she sees the slippers Mercedes laughs out loud. 'Where did you get the clown shoes? Take them off. It will be better if you dance barefoot.'

'No. I paid for the clown shoes, I am going to wear them.'

'Juan Sebastián!' Mercedes calls. 'Come and look!'

Arroyo wanders into the studio and nods to him. If he notices the shoes, if he finds them funny, he gives no sign of it. He sits down at the piano.

'I thought Alyosha would be playing for us,' says he, Simón.

'Alyosha is not to be found,' says Mercedes. 'Don't worry, it is not beneath Juan Sebastián to play for you, he plays for children every day.' She sets her cane aside, takes up position behind him, grips his upper arms. 'Close your eyes. You are going to rock from side to side, your weight first on your left foot, then on your right, back and forth, back and forth. Imagine, if it helps, that behind you, moving in time with you, is some unattainably beautiful young goddess, not ugly old Mercedes.'

He obeys. Arroyo begins to play: a simple tune, a child's tune. He, Simón, is not as steady on his feet as he thought he would be, perhaps because he hasn't eaten. Nevertheless, he rocks back and forth in time to the music.

'Good. Now bring the right foot forward, a short step, and back; then the left foot forward and back. Good. Repeat the movement, right forward and back, left forward and back, until I tell you to stop.'

He obeys, stumbling now and then in the slippers with their strange soft soles. Arroyo inverts the tune, varies it, elaborates:

while the pulse remains steady, the little aria begins to reveal a new structure, point by point, like a crystal growing in the air. Bliss washes over him; he wishes he could sit down and listen properly.

'Now I am going to let go of you, Simón. You are going to raise your arms to balance yourself, and you are going to continue with right-and-back, left-and-back, but with each step you are going to turn to your left in a quarter circle.'

He does as she says. 'How long must I go on?' he says. 'I am feeling dizzy.'

'Go on. You will get over the dizziness.'

He obeys. It is cool in the studio; he is conscious of the high space above his head. Mercedes recedes; there is only the music. Arms extended, eyes closed, he shuffles in a slow circle. Over the horizon the first star begins to rise.

penguin.co.uk/vintage